CHASING AFTER DESTINY

The Destiny Series Book 4

EMMA EASTER

Chasing After Destiny
by Emma Easter

Paperback Edition

CKN Christian Publishing
An Imprint of Wolfpack Publishing

6032 Wheat Penny Avenue
Las Vegas, NV 89122

This book is a work of fiction. Any references to historical events, real people or real places are used fictitiously. Other names, characters, places and events are products of the author's imagination, and any resemblance to actual events, places or persons, living or dead, is entirely coincidental.

Paperback ISBN: 978-1-64734-707-9
Ebook ISBN: 978-1-64734-706-2

CHASING AFTER DESTINY

ONE

Sofia Ross finished cooking dinner for her and George and hurriedly went to set it on the dining table. She smiled as she inhaled the delicious aroma of the spaghetti carbonara, and then went back into the kitchen to get the Caesar salad she had made earlier in the day that she'd kept in the refrigerator. She took it to the dining room and placed it beside the spaghetti.

Lighting a few scented candles, she turned off the lights in the dining and living rooms and stepped back to inspect how everything looked. She smiled at the romantic ambience of the place. She never cooked, but she'd decided to cook today because she wanted to pamper George. She hadn't seen him in what seemed like forever. She missed him so much and couldn't wait to see him again after his three-week business trip to Southeast Asia. Excitement ran through her as she glanced at the clock on the wall. Soon, George would be here.

She walked out of the dining room to the bedroom, and for the hundredth time, she straightened the sheets and rearranged the rose petals she had scattered across the bed. Her body tingled with anticipation as she thought about spending the night with George. It had been such a long time since they were together. She smiled as she imagined waking up next to him. She had Skyped a couple of times with him, but she was eagerly looking forward to finally having him physically present with her.

She went to stand in front of the full-length mirror near the bedroom door and gazed at herself. She ran her hand through her bangs and fluffed her dark hair for the umpteenth time. Fingering her pink lingerie and the matching silk robe she wore over it, the one George had bought her on their last trip together to Italy, she couldn't help smiling. Once again, waves of excitement and anticipation ran through her as she remembered his phone call earlier that day. He had told her he was back in town and wanted to see her immediately because he had something important to tell her. She could already guess what it was. She'd been telling herself to calm down since he called. But it had been hard to hold down her excitement until he arrived at her apartment. She hadn't stopped smiling since then as she imagined him proposing to her. She would finally be able to marry the man she loved so much after years of being the other woman and having to hide their relationship because of his wife.

For a long moment, she frowned at the thought of George's wife. Anger and bitterness raced through her as she recalled how much of a thorn in her flesh the woman had been over the years. She had used threats and tears to get George to stay with her, even after she found out about their affair. What sort of woman did that? She had held on tightly to George and threatened to leave him, taking their children with her. George worked as the CEO of her father's company, and she had also threatened to have George fired if he did not break off the affair. At the time, George had promised his wife that he would end their affair, but of course he had done no such thing. They both loved each other very much, which was something his wife didn't understand.

Sofia sighed and went to sit on the bed. For a few years after they started dating, she had refused to admit that she loved George because she wanted to maintain some level of emotional freedom, and she was afraid of having her heart broken. She'd wanted to protect herself, especially because she had struggled with depression for as long as she could remember. Most people didn't know that about her because she was outwardly a very jovial person. But from time to time, when something unexpected happened and life seemed too hard to bear, she'd gone to a very dark place and become suicidal. Thankfully, she'd never physically hurt herself, though she'd done so emotionally.

She sighed again. She'd finally opened her heart about two years ago and decided to admit to herself that she loved George. Finally, she could now rest in the knowledge that she would never lose him, that they would be together forever. He had probably found a way to escape the clutches of that woman. He was talented and a hard worker. He would find some other job easily. He didn't have to work for his wife's — hopefully soon ex-wife's — father.

Her mind went to George's three children, and a thread of guilt went through her. What would they think about their father divorcing their mom? And what would they think about her, the other woman who had "stolen" their father's heart?

She pressed her lips tightly together and shut her eyes, unable to shake the guilt that had gripped her. His youngest child was just seven. Would the fact that his parents were soon going to be separated affect him? It was one of the things she worried about whenever she thought of one day being able to finally marry George. She bit her lips, exhaled, and then forced the guilt out of her mind. George was a good father. He did not have to be married to his children's mother in order to be actively involved in their lives.

A smile tugged at her lips, and she gave in to it. She had every right to be pleased that she and George would finally be able to take the next step in their relationship. She went to stand in front of the mirror again and gazed at herself. She checked her hair again, and then applied a fresh layer of lip gloss.

Being away from George for so long had made her realize not just how much she loved him, but that she could not live without him. Once he was divorced, they would not have to keep enduring the pain and frustration they felt whenever he had to stay away from her for a while because his wife was getting suspicious about their affair. Now, they could both openly let everyone know that they were together, that they would be together forever.

Happiness flooded her. She could not wait to be his wife, and she was itching to tell someone about what she suspected — that he was going to ask her to marry him today. If only Lily were here so she could share her good news once George proposed. But Lily was away on her honeymoon and would not be back anytime soon. She had been slightly envious of Lily when Lily told her about her wedding and subsequent honeymoon, but not anymore. Soon, it would be her turn.

She smiled in self-mockery as she thought about Lily's reaction to her good news. Lily would not particularly think it was 'good news.' Lily was a goody-two-shoes and extremely religious. She had never been a fan of her relationship with George because George was married. Maybe it was for the best that Lily wasn't here.

Sofia exhaled. She was still dying to share her news with someone, but she had no one else who she truly yearned to share it with. She had a lot of acquaintances and friends, but none were as trustworthy and as caring as Lily was. The only other person she could think to call once George proposed was Edith, her college friend. But Edith was unpredictable and sometimes abrasive. Sofia could never be sure of her reaction. She could be happy for her or she could tell her that George was a jerk and that marrying him would be a mistake. Yes, Lily also didn't approve of her relationship with George, but at least she spoke out her disapproval with less vehemence. Edith, on the other hand, was nice and complimentary to George one day, and the next she was calling him names.

Sofia left the bedroom again and went to the dining room. She sat at the table and looked at the food she had set for her and George. She hoped he would like her cooking and that she could persuade him to spend the night with her. He had rented this apartment for her a few years ago, gotten her the job she now had in a sister company to the one where he worked, and taken her on multiple trips abroad. In general, he treated her like a princess. Virtually all she had now had been bought by him. He was such a generous man.

Her mind went back to when they first met about five years ago. She'd been twenty-one then, while he'd been about to turn forty. She had met him at an acquaintance's housewarming party. He'd walked over to her and, without mincing words, had asked her out. She had refused immediately, but she had not been able to get rid of him. She'd met him again on two other occasions. Whether it was coincidental or he had planned it all because of her, she still didn't know. As much as she tried to put him at arm's length because she was afraid he was too old for her, his wooing had been constant and persistent.

She was not very pleased when he appeared at her door some days later, but for some reason, she let him into the tiny apartment she shared with another girl. He was such a perfect gentleman that when he came back days later, she let him come in again.

After that he became a regular at her apartment and showered her with gifts regularly. And then he got her a job, for which she was forever grateful to him. He was so charming, even though he was much older than her, that she had been unable to resist his wooing for long. They soon began dating and gradually became inseparable.

She'd found out he was married a month after, but by then she'd been too into him to really care. However, she soon began to care a year or so later, when she'd started to vie for more and more of his time with his wife.

She sighed. At least all that would be over soon. Once his divorce was through, she would not have to compete with his wife for his attention anymore. Soon she would be his wife, and they would be able to take their trips abroad without being afraid that someone who knew him would spot them together and report back.

She frowned as she glanced at the clock on the wall. It was already eight-thirty. George had told her he would he here by eight o'clock.

Where are you, George?

She sighed again. Hopefully his wife was not the cause of his delay. That woman had no shame. He had probably told her that he wanted a divorce, and she was most likely pleading with him, trying to get him to stay with her, or threatening to tell her father and get him fired from his job and then leave with their kids. It was exactly what she had told him when she'd found out about the affair.

Sofia pursed her lips. George had told her that his wife had cried and threatened him until he was forced to let her have her way. But he had told her that it would never happen again. He'd told her that he would leave his wife in a month, once he was able to put his finances and some other stuff he was working on together. It was more than a month now. Sofia was confident that he was finally ready to make her his wife as soon as possible, and that meant filing for a divorce.

Once again she glanced at the clock on the wall, and then began to grow worried. Why was it taking so long? It wasn't typical of him. He was a man who liked to keep time. She placed her hand on her forehead as troubling thoughts ran through her mind. What if George had given in to his wife's threats again?

No, that was impossible. George had given her his word that he would let his wife know that he wanted a divorce as soon as possible and that he wanted to marry her. He would not give in to his wife's manipulation. He wouldn't do that again. And he loved her dearly and couldn't wait to spend the rest of his life with her.

She glanced at the clock again and fear gripped her. Why wasn't George here? Where was he?

Where are you, my love? She was itching to have him here in her apartment. She wanted to be in his arms now. She looked at the food on the table. Their dinner was getting cold. She sat waiting for another minute, and then she stood up and went to pick up her phone from the coffee table in the living room. She started to dial George number and then turned toward the door when the doorbell rang. Relief flooded her heart, and she dropped the phone on the sofa and rushed to answer it. She flung the door wide open and cried out, "George, I have missed you so...!"

And then she gasped and her mouth fell open as she stared in bewilderment. George's wife stood beside him.

TWO

Sofia turned to George and frowned, puzzled as to why his wife was here with him. Her heart raced as a disturbing thought crept into her mind. What if George's wife had convinced him to break up with her and was here to make sure he did it?

No, it cannot be. She bit her lip and then finally found her voice. "George? Why is she here?"

George was still in his business suit, which meant he'd not had any time to change before he came here. But that did not explain why he was here with his wife. The look on his face caused her to tremble and filled her with fear. He looked ashamed and scared. Sofia turned to his wife and stared at her in horror. *Please, let this not be what I am thinking.*

George's wife was in her early forties. Sofia had seen her only once in person. She had gone to visit George in his office one day, and just before she'd entered the office, a tall, slender woman with a pixie cut, a haughty demeanor, and a pretty face, walked out. She had turned to look at Sofia, frowned slightly, and then walked away. When Sofia entered George's office, his mouth had dropped open, and then he had closed the door quickly. He'd grabbed her hand and pulled her into the restroom.

"Sofia, what are you doing here?" he had asked in a hushed voice, as though there were other people to hear them.

She told him she had come to see him because she missed him and he had sighed heavily. "Thank God you didn't come in when my wife was here. Did she say anything to you?"

Sofia had blinked, surprised. At that time, she had never seen a picture of George's wife because he had never shown her one and she hadn't wanted to see his wife's picture either. "That was your wife? The woman who just came out of your office?"

"Yes, that was my wife, Elena," he had told her.

Sofia stared at the woman before her now. She still had the same haughty look and the same pixie cut. She wore bright red lipstick, almost the same shade as the one Sofia liked to wear, and the expression on her face was one of a woman who had come ready to do battle. Sofia blinked rapidly as she stared tongue-tied at Elena.

George shifted his feet, clearly also unable to speak.

"Aren't you going to introduce us, George?" his wife said. She walked into Sofia's apartment without invitation, and Sofia glared at her.

George shrugged and walked in, but he still did not look at Sofia.

Sofia turned to face him fully and asked again, "George, what is your wife doing here... in my apartment?"

Elena said, "Technically, it's not really your apartment. I am here to reclaim this place."

"What?" Sofia gritted her teeth, her blood boiling with fury. She glared at Elena. "What place? This is my apartment." She turned to George again and eyed him. His silence angered her. "What on earth is she talking about, George?"

George finally looked at her. "I'm so sorry, Sofia."

Elena looked around Sofia's apartment, a smug smile on her face. "So this is where George has been spending his days when he's not home. He's been lying to me for years. He tells me he has to go on these important business trips, or that he has to work late, when in fact what he's been doing is coming here." She faced Sofia fully, her smug smile still in place. "To be with you."

She looked Sofia over, her eyes settling on the see-through robe Sofia was wearing. Her smile melted away. "I'm not even going to ask how you can live with yourself when you are sleeping with a married man. I'm going to step back and let George tell you why we came here together." Her heels clapped on the tiled floor as she walked to the sofa and sat down. She looked up at George, and then at Sofia and said, "Well George, tell her why we are here."

Sofia felt like she was in a dream. Her heart thudded as she turned to George, hoping against hope that he was going to stand up to his wife and tell her that he wanted a divorce and wanted to marry her instead. She pleaded with her eyes. *Please George, do the right thing now. Tell her we love each other and want to get married. Tell her you want a divorce.*

George turned his gaze fully to her, and the expression on his face still held shame and embarrassment. "I'm really sorry, Sofia. I could not do it. I cannot leave my wife." He looked at his wife, and then squared his shoulders. The shame melted off his face, right before Sofia's eyes. He gave her a hard stare and said, "My family and my job are the two most important things to me. I cannot afford to lose either."

Sofia felt like he'd just stabbed her with a knife. "What are you saying, George?" she shrieked.

"I am saying that I cannot continue to see you… and I mean it this time."

Sofia's heart sank down to her feet, and she leaned against the couch so she would not sink down to the floor.

George said, "There's more Sofia." That look of shame appeared on his face again. "My wife wants me to fire you from your job and take this apartment back because" — he glanced at his wife again and looked at Sofia — "because this apartment building partly belongs to her father, and therefore to her."

Sofia could not believe her ears. She felt like she was in the middle of a nightmare. "George, please tell me you're joking," she said.

"I'm sorry," he whispered. "My wife said she would leave with our children, get her father to fire me, and make sure that I never work in this city again. I have no choice."

She yelled, "Yes, you do, George! You have a choice! We can still be together even if we have nothing. We can go through anything as long as we are together."

He glanced at his wife, who was still sitting on

the sofa with her legs crossed and watching them with a curious expression on her face. "It's so easy for you to say, Sofia." He turned back to her. "You have nothing to lose, but I have everything. My children, the job I have worked so hard for, everything." Once again, he looked at his wife before facing her. "I'm sorry. I truly am." He looked weary as he gazed at her, and then he turned away and went to stand next to his wife.

Elena looked up at Sofia and shook her head. "You should have left George alone the first time I found out you two were having an affair. But you chose not to. At that time, I didn't even know he got this apartment for you. An apartment built with my father's money, and that he had been paying the rent — with money he earned in my father's company. And to cap it all, he got a job for you in one of my father's companies." She chuckled as though she had said the funniest thing ever. "Now, you're going to lose it all." She stood up, took George's hand and walked to Sofia. "George told me the rent will expire in a couple of days. I have spoken to my father already. You have two days to get your things out of this apartment. I need it for something else."

Sofia stared at her in disbelief. She looked at George and faced Elena again. "You cannot take my apartment!" she yelled.

"It's not your apartment, and it has already been taken from you," Elena said coolly. "You know what will happen if you're not out by the time I come back here. You don't want to fight me for this apartment, I promise you. So move your things out by the time I come back." She looked around the apartment again. "What am I saying? All the furniture was bought by my husband, wasn't it? Nothing in this apartment really belongs to you. So you will move out with nothing but your trashy clothes."

"Elena!" George pleaded. "Please, give Sofia a bit more time. It's not her fault that…"

"Hush, George!" his wife said. "Don't say anything right now." She turned to Sofia again. "I know what you're thinking. You think I'm the meanest and most vindictive person you have ever met. But have you ever thought about how wicked you've been through all of this? You try to take a woman's husband away from her. To take him away from his children and…"

"That's a lie!" Sofia cut in. "I have never tried to take him away from his children. There's no way I would ever ask George not to be a part of his children's lives. It's just you who…"

"Shut up! Do you think that breaking up a marriage so the kids don't have both their parents in the same home is not the same thing? If he ever files for a divorce, I will make sure I fight for sole custody. He will not be able to see them half as much as he does now. So tell me, is that being in his children's lives? Do you even have a conscience?"

"Elena, please!" George said

George's wife glowered at Sofia. "Be out of here in two days, or…" She left her sentence unfinished, but Sofia already knew what Elena had left unsaid. She knew what to expect if she was not out of this apartment in two days.

She could not breathe or think properly as Elena linked her arms with George's. She shot Sofia one more angry look and then turned around and began to march to the door with him. George turned around to look at Sofia and mouthed, "I am sorry. Forgive me." He turned around again.

Sofia wanted to scream at him; to scratch out his wife's eyes; to slap George and tell him to snap out of it and free himself of his wife's clutches, or whatever spell she had cast over him. But she knew it would do no good, and his wife had cast no spell over him. He was a coward, and she had been stupid to believe he loved her more than his high-paying job; more than the jealous woman who stood at her door with him now. He did not love her at all. He loved his money and reputation more than he did her. He was unwilling to fight for her. She was nothing more to him than a plaything to be used and dumped. A small-town girl who had come to the city empty-handed and was now living off his goodwill. She'd given him her body in exchange for material things. Shame washed over her. She'd been such a fool.

The door banged shut as George and his wife walked out of the apartment, and Sofia sank to the floor and covered her face with her hands. She wept bitterly and then rose to her feet. She had loved George so much, and yet she was now finding out that he had not loved her at all. He had only used her.

But did you not also use him?

She sighed. Maybe a year or so after they'd met, she had used him to get her bills paid. But later on she had grown to love him. Apparently the feeling was not mutual.

She began to rail against George and against his wife. Finally, when she was spent, she sat on the sofa and began to cry again. Her life was over. She was going to lose everything that was dear to her — George, her job, this apartment — everything. Where would she go when she moved out of the apartment?

For a brief moment, she thought about her hometown, the tiny town she had left as a teenager. No one cared about her there. The man who was her father by birth probably still lived there, but he had never really cared about her. She had lost her mom when she was only eight. Being an only child, her father had apparently thought that he had no more responsibilities when her mom died and that she could take care of herself even though she was just a kid. She'd left that small town as quickly as she could, and she would never go back there again. But even here, where she knew a bunch of people, she really had no one she could confide in; no one who she could trust to help her.

She cried harder. She felt like her heart had broken in two. Even though she had railed against George and cursed him just moments ago, she missed him terribly. The thought of never seeing him again caused her heart to physically ache.

She should have listened to Lily and to the voice of reason inside her head warning her not to get close to George; to let him go because he did not belong to her. But she had gone on believing that one day he would truly belong to her; that he would leave his wife for her. She should have seen this coming, but she'd chosen not to.

She dashed angrily at the tears streaming down her face and picked up her phone from the sofa. She felt numb with sorrow. What was the point of living when she had lost everything? Overwhelming despair took hold of her, threatening to suffocate her. She shut her eyes. She would give anything to escape the way she felt now. An idea came into her heart — a way to end her sorrow — and she gave in to it. She'd found a way to escape it all.

She began to stand but sat down again, trying to hold on to the sliver of hope in her. She had to talk to someone first, someone who truly cared about her. She had to talk to Lily. But she had not been able to get through to her for almost a month now. Lily had told her that she and her new husband were going on a trip around the world for their honeymoon. Who knew where they both were now?

She dialed Lily's number, hoping against hope that Lily would answer the phone, but once again there was no dial tone. She threw her phone across the room, slid from the sofa to the floor, and cried until she could cry no more. She ran her fingers through her hair and bit her lips. *What am I doing sitting down here?*

The bathroom, specifically the top shelf where she kept her medicine, called to her. She stood up stiffly and left the living room. Slowly, she walked to the bathroom, opened the top cabinet, put her hand behind the rows of medicine bottles and brought out a bottle of pain meds. A few times, on days she'd been depressed, she'd considered swallowing some of the pills and ending it all, but she'd pulled herself back. But today, she was going to. She had never felt this hopeless in all her life. She would take as much as possible and end the pain she felt forever. She had nothing to live for anymore.

She poured the whole bottle into her hand and swallowed everything. She soon began to feel drowsy and sat down on the bathroom floor. She lay on the cold tiles as her head and ears began to ring, and then she felt herself gradually begin to fade away.

For a brief moment she thought about George, and then about Lily. Sadness flooded her heart. Lily would be sad when she found out she'd passed away, but she wasn't sure how George would feel. Tears fell down her cheeks as her vision began to blur. And then darkness swallowed her.

THREE

Jude lifted another bottle of beer to his mouth and downed it all. He dropped the empty bottle on the floor and picked up another beer bottle from the table. He laughed as the other guys around him clapped and cheered him on. Taking a swig, he shook his head as the alcohol went down his throat to his belly, filling him with a slightly burning, pleasant sensation.

He knew he needed to stop, as he'd had more than a couple of bottles already, but instead, he lifted his hand in triumph and finished the one in his other hand. He threw a challenging glare at Samuel, his friend and drinking buddy, who was sitting beside him. The other students who had come to the party at the off-campus apartment Jude shared with Samuel turned to look at Samuel. "Your turn, Sammie," Jude said, grinning.

Samuel's eyes fluttered open. He looked almost out of it, drunk out of his mind. He nodded and slowly lifted a bottle of beer to his lips and downed it. Shaking his head, he said in a slurry voice, "No more, Jude. You win." He stood up, swayed on his feet, and then collapsed again on the chair.

The others laughed.

"Finally, you yield," Jude said.

Samuel shut his eyes and leaned back.

Jude patted his shoulder and smiled. After several drinks, Samuel was wiped out, while his own vision was still clear, his mind still alert. He had won the drinking game as always. The others slapped his back and cheered him as the winner. This was what he was known for — the guy who could drink anyone on campus under the table. He laughed again as Samuel began to snore, passed out in the chair. Ben, a friend of theirs with a complexion as dark as Jude's, rushed into the living room and hurried toward him, a worried look on his face.

"Jude, I need to speak to you," Ben said when he got to him. Jude frowned as Ben grabbed his hand, pulled him up from the sofa, and began to pull him out of the living room. The other boys tried to hold on, but Ben tugged harder and finally managed to pull him out of their grasp. Jude let Ben pull him out of the room and then out onto the porch, curious and eager to know why his friend looked so agitated.

As they stood outside, Jude studied Ben. The night air blew on his face and that, combined with Ben's troubled look, helped to wash away the slight woozy effect from the large amount of alcohol he'd just consumed. He looked up at the darkening sky and then faced Ben again.

Ben leaned on the balustrade that encircled the porch and heaved a loud sigh. "There's trouble,

Jude." He rubbed his bald head. "I should have done something a long time ago, bro. I don't want you to be next."

"What are you talking about, Ben? You're scaring me, man. What is wrong?"

"It's Paul. He's been deported."

Jude grabbed the railing to steady himself. He wasn't sure if it was the bad news that made him feel suddenly dizzy or the effects of the alcohol, but this was bad. This was really bad.

"How did it happen... and when?" he asked Ben.

"A few days ago," Ben answered. "ICE came and grabbed him." Ben snapped his fingers. "Just like that! I am afraid that you are going to be next, Jude."

Jude shuddered. He shut his eyes and put his hand on his forehead. His head ached. Even though this news was sudden and had taken him by surprise, he really should not have been shocked. An acquaintance of his had been removed from the country about a year and a half ago. At that time, though, his situation had been different from what it was now. Still, when a lot of things began to change for him, he had chosen to ignore everything, even though he knew he was at risk of being deported himself. He opened his eyes and said to Ben, "What am I going to do?"

"I don't know," Ben answered.

He chided himself for not taking his immigration status seriously. A year ago, he would not have cared about any of this. In fact, he would have left America by now. He had planned to go back to his country, Bakali, as soon as he'd graduated his Master's program at the University of Arizona, but a lot had happened over the past year that made it impossible for him to do so. His dad, who had been his all and had sponsored his education to the United States, had suddenly died last year. Thankfully, his father had already paid his tuition fees. He had made enough money from his part-time job to take care of his basic needs. With no close family in his country and friends who were no more, there was nothing and no one to go back to. If he was removed from America...

He groaned and tried not to think of the implications. And yet he had to, because he was as good as deported now. His F1 visa had expired a few weeks ago.

Ben said, "Thank God I didn't listen to you when you insisted that we apply for CPT last year. At least under the optional training, I still have time to try to adjust my immigration status." He sighed. "We need to come up with a plan for you as soon as possible."

Jude put his hand on his forehead. The loud partying from inside the house, coupled with the intense fear of his inevitable deportation, had given him a migraine that he was sure would stay with him until he was removed from this country. If only Dad had not died. If only Keziah had not broken up with him...

"Jude!" Ben stared thoughtfully at him. "Maybe you could seek for asylum."

In spite of himself, Jude chuckled. "Or maybe I should move to Mexico before ICE can get a hold of me."

"I am serious, Jude," Ben said. "After all, your country is embroiled in violence now. You could say you are a refugee..."

"I doubt that will fly, especially as I am not. I have to be a true refugee or be in real danger from the government of my country to seek asylum here, and even then, the chances of being successful are slim."

Ben stared at him, and Jude shrugged. "I came across an article about asylum seekers one day and casually scanned it. I had not overstayed my visa at the time and wasn't even planning to remain in this country after my post-graduate studies."

"Well, don't say I didn't try to help you." Ben chuckled even though he still looked worried.

Jude said, "You know, you are lucky, Ben. Even if you end up not adjusting your status, you could go back to your country and live comfortably there. Your parents are well-off and will be glad to have you back. Once you go back, you will probably get a good job through their connections. But I have nothing and no one in my country to go back to anymore. Plus the violence going on there is escalating daily. I am afraid that war might break out soon." He sighed wearily. "I don't want to leave America. I have started to build a life for myself here."

Ben pursed his lips and nodded. "I guess you're right," he said. I'll probably leave the United States soon." He put his hand on Jude's shoulder, and then he gasped loudly.

"What is it?" Jude asked.

"I might have a solution for you, but it's a very unconventional one."

Jude stared curiously at him. "What solution, Ben?"

"I might know someone who can help you." Ben

smiled, and turned his face away from Jude.

"Ben, out with it! Tell me what solution you have for me."

"You know my friend, Shaffar?"

Jude frowned. "Yes… your scrawny friend with shifty eyes. That guy is a criminal, isn't he? I am surprised he hasn't been locked up yet."

Ben laughed. "He's not a criminal. Anyway, he works with a small agency that helps migrants."

Jude narrowed his eyes and asked with suspicion, "An agency that 'helps' migrants? Helps them in what way?"

"Well, they can connect you with a girl who is willing to marry you so you can get your Green card. In exchange for cash, of course."

Jude laughed harshly. "Ben! And you said your friend isn't a criminal."

Ben said, "Emphasis on the word 'willing,' Jude. The American girls they find don't mind marrying an immigrant and filing for an adjustment of status for them. They are paid in installments, with the final payment after you have gotten your Green card. I think the girl keeps most of the money, but the agency takes a percentage. Once you have the Green card, you get a quick divorce, and that is that. I think parting with some cash to get your permanent residency is not a bad deal."

Jude shook his head slowly. "What you are talking about is fraud, my friend. I won't do it! But I am not surprised that your friend, Shaffar, is a fraudster. I am just surprised that you think there is nothing wrong with what he does."

"Jude! It is really not fraud. It's simply exchanging one service for another. You have a need, and someone else has your solution. You help someone get what they want — in this case, money — in exchange for the service the person provides you."

"And that can include any illegal exchange from drug trafficking to marrying a US citizen to get a Green card."

Ben held up his hands. "Fine! If you don't want to do it, you don't have to. But do you really have a choice? This isn't the time to start moralizing."

Jude thought about what Ben had said. He was right. He had to do something right now, and he had no real options. He sighed wearily. What had he been reduced to? Not only did he spend his days partying and drinking, he was considering committing fraud. He should be sending Ben on his way, but he was actually beginning to buy into what Ben had said, even knowing it was wrong. But just like Ben said, he had no choice.

He shuddered. What would his late father the pastor have said if he were alive and knew what he was planning to do?

"What if we are caught by the authorities?" Jude asked.

Ben touched his arm and said, "Don't worry about it. Shaffar will handle it all, and it will go well. He knows exactly what to do. He's been doing this for some time now."

Jude rolled his eyes. "I'm sure he has." He exhaled. "So I am about to commit fraud."

"Don't look at it that way, Jude. If you get to know the girl well enough before you get married, it might not be fraud. Who knows? You might even fall in love with her."

Jude narrowed his eyes, and Ben held his hand

out. "Okay, I was just joking! But seriously, the quicker you get to know everything about the girl Shaffar introduces to you and vice versa, the better your chances are that you will successfully scale through your immigration interview. Once you get married and get your Green card, you won't have this threat of deportation hanging over you anymore. I can call Shaffar now if you like." Before Jude could say anything more, Ben brought his phone out of his pocket and began to dial a number.

Jude leaned his back against the balustrade and folded his arms across his chest. So he was really going to do this. But it was the only thing that might give him a chance to stay in America. Hopefully, it would all work out. He would have to leave his partying behind and concentrate on trying to build a good life for himself in this country.

"Hey, Shaffar!" Ben held his phone to his ear. "I have a business deal for you." He began to talk, and Jude listened anxiously as Ben told Shaffar about his immigration problems. Ben stopped speaking for a full minute, and then he shook his head and said, "Ten thousand dollars, Shaffar! That is a lot of money." He glanced at Jude and added, "I doubt my friend has that kind of cash."

Jude's mouth went dry, and his heart began to race. He definitely didn't have that kind of money. In fact, he didn't have anything close to it. Since he was not allowed to work, he only had about a thousand dollars to his name, and that was money he had saved while he did his CPT and the little left from what his father had sent before he died. Hopefully, Ben would be able to convince Shaffar to reduce the amount from ten thousand dollars to something he could afford. He waited impatiently for Ben to finish his conversation, all his hopes hanging on the outcome of Ben's discussion with Shaffar.

"Okay, Shaffar," Ben nodded. "I will let him know what you said and then get back to you." He lowered his phone from his ear and tucked it into his pocket. He faced Jude. "I have good news and bad news. Should I tell you the good news first?"

Jude sighed. "I guess. I already know what the bad news is. Shaffar wants me to pay ten thousand dollars, doesn't he?"

"Umm... a little over that, Jude. He wants fifteen."

"What? I don't have that kind of money. You know that."

"He said you will have to pay five thousand before the girl is introduced to you, another five thousand before you get married, and another five thousand before you get your Green card."

Jude rubbed his temples. "Where am I going to get that kind of money?"

"I can plead with him again on your behalf... ask him to reduce the amount. Maybe the girl they find for you will agree to take something less. Which brings me to my good news." Ben smiled. "Shaffar said he already has someone he can introduce to you. He said her name is Maya."

Jude felt a tug on his conscience at what he was about to do, but he pushed the guilt away and focused on Ben. He exhaled as a sliver of hope ran through him. Maybe, just maybe, this might work out for him. However, he had very little money. He said to Ben, "You know I'm not allowed to work right now. Even if Shaffar reduces the amount to half, I still don't have anywhere near that much money."

"Just as I said earlier, you don't have to pay the money all at once." He tilted his head, and his eyes studied Jude's. "So, how much do you have?"

Jude sighed. "I have about a thousand dollars left over from the money I earned during my CPT. It was a good thing that paid well, but if I had opted for the OPT, I might still be working now and have a chance to extend my visa, and then this deportation thing would not be hanging over my head."

"This is not the time to dwell on regrets, Jude. We have to act now. Shaffar owes me one. I will talk to him and see if he can accept your one thousand dollars as payment for the first installment. You have to get more money soon, though."

"But how am I going to get more money if I am not allowed to work?"

"I know you are not allowed to work, but there are ways around that..."

Jude arched his brows and glared at Ben. "You mean work illegally?"

"You heard what I said. Shaffar already has a girl willing to marry you, my man. And you need to start the process right now. I don't want you to get deported, Jude, but it's your choice."

A group of guys stumbled out of the apartment, clearly drunk. They whistled and sang as they held each other for support. One of them fell, and the others laughed. Jude watched them as they staggered away. He could go on partying and drinking, pretending that he had no problems, and then suddenly be deported back to Bakali, or he could take what was being offered to him.

"Okay, then," he said to Ben. "But do you also have some illegal work waiting for me?"

"I know you can handle that on your own, Jude. I will call Shaffar later on to let him know you're interested in proceeding with the deal. I will also try to get him to decrease the amount of money you have to pay."

Jude didn't know whether to thank Ben or scold him for pulling him into this sordid arrangement. He finally thanked his friend. At least Ben was providing a way for him to stay in this country and build a future for himself.

Ben patted his back and they exchanged their usual handshake.

"I have to go now, my man," Ben said. "I'll see you later."

"Yeah! Thanks again, Ben. Please call me as soon as you speak with Shaffar and let me know if he agrees to take one thousand dollars. I'm sure I won't be able to sleep tonight until I know that what we've talked about will work out for me."

"I'll let you know as soon as possible," Ben said. "If Shaffar agrees, he will expect you to come up with the rest of the money soon. Okay?"

Jude nodded. "Okay."

After Ben left, Jude looked up at the sky. It was a starless night, and apart from an occasional breeze, the weather was hot. It reminded him a little of his country, how hot it always was. He missed it, but he could not go back. Not when he had no more close family members there and with the madness going on right now.

He shut his eyes for a brief moment as pain tore through him. He pictured his parents in his mind smiling at him as a child; the proud look on his father's face the day he left the country to come here for his post-graduate studies. He opened his eyes again. His parents were no more. There were many times in recent days when he regretted applying to the University of Arizona. Maybe if he had not come here, his father would not have died.

Stop, Jude. Stop blaming yourself. His absence was hardly the cause of his father's heart attack. His mother had died years ago, when he was only nine. He had been really close to his father, except when it came to religious matters. They'd had many arguments about that. If only he had not argued so much with his dad.

He groaned and chided himself again. *Stop thinking about what you cannot control.* But his mind refused to shift to happier thoughts. He began to think about Keziah, and then groaned once more. Keziah, the first girl he'd ever loved, and the last. Maybe they would still be together if he'd known that she wasn't happy with him. But she'd never shown any signs that she wasn't. He had thought she was truly happy, but she had broken up with him two weeks prior to their wedding. He'd been heartbroken and tried to figure out what exactly he'd done to cause her to break their engagement. But he'd not seen it coming. He didn't know what he could have done to prevent her from leaving him.

He looked up at the sky again. He had always thought Keziah would be the only girl who he would marry and spend the rest of his life with. Now, he was thinking about marrying someone else. If things worked out, he would be married to another girl soon, even if it was only for a short time and only to get a Green card.

Guilt tore at his heart as he thought about the plans he was making to marry a US citizen just so he could stay here. He was about to involve himself in illegal activities. His father would have been so disappointed if he were alive. He knew exactly what his dad would say — that he was sinning against God.

He felt anger rising up in him. God. The same God who his father had served for years but who hadn't deemed it fit to keep him from dying. The God who hadn't helped him much during his stay in the United States. A grim determination entered his heart. He would do what he had to do even if it was illegal, and then he would live with the consequences, no matter what they were.

He entered the house again, ignored the guys who were still drinking themselves to oblivion, and went straight to the small room he slept in. It had been a box-room where Samuel stored his suitcases before he moved in. He and Samuel had met at a friend's party months after he came to America, and even though Samuel was younger than him and still doing a bachelor's degree, they had hit it off. He'd had accommodation problems then, and Samuel had asked him to move into his off-campus apartment for free. The tiny box-room had been converted to a bedroom for him. After he finished his Masters and had nowhere to go, he had remained in the apartment, as Samuel didn't mind.

He sat on his small bed and leaned back against the headboard. He had to clean up his act as best as he could if the marriage thing was going to work out. He had to at least make a good impression on the girl Shaffar had found for him. He would not be able to do that if he kept drinking his life away. The last thing he needed was to get stupidly drunk when he was with the girl, the way he did many nights now, and have her change her mind about helping him get his residence card.

He brought out his phone from his pocket and stared at it. He chuckled with self-mockery. This was probably what he would spend the rest of the night doing until he heard back from Ben. He thought about praying that this whole arrangement — the marriage, the money he needed to pay — would work out for him, but he immediately brushed the thought away.

Ben, dude, come on! Call.

Once more, the urge to pray swept over him, and he stifled it again. He was not going to ask God for any favors. God had never really listened to him, and He certainly wasn't going to start now, especially with the way he'd chosen to live his life recently. God would probably give him some illness or trouble if he prayed for help for this illegal deal he was about to enter. Guilt rose up in him, but he instantly squashed it. *No more. No more guilt.*

The jubilant voices of the remaining partiers in the living room floated to him, and for a minute he struggled with himself, yearning to join them. He had not yet met the girl Shaffar had found for him. He could drink some more tonight just to calm his nerves. Tomorrow he would clean up his act. He began to get up from the bed, and then he gritted his teeth and sat back down. No, if he began to drink tonight, he would not stop. He needed his wits about him. Before the end of tomorrow, he would find out what his fate would be — whether he would be able to afford the solution that would make him a permanent resident of this country, or be deported back to his own.

FOUR

The almighty Green card. It was all Jude thought about now. It was the first thing on his mind when he woke up in the morning and the last thing when he went to bed. It haunted his dreams and made him extremely nervous every single day.

Jude shut his eyes briefly and shut out the noise in the student cafeteria. He opened his eyes again and took a sip of his Coke as he waited for Ben to come. For a short moment, he glanced around. The cafeteria was bustling with college kids. Some were walking to empty tables with trays of food, some were seated, chatting while they ate, a few rifled through textbooks or typed away on their laptops.

The sounds of students chattering around him faded again, and his thoughts became consumed once more with his present dilemma. An intense fear had taken residence in his heart ever since Ben had told him about their mutual friend who had been deported.

Shaffar had agreed to accept the one thousand dollars Jude had on the condition that he paid the rest before he and the girl he was to marry wedded. He hadn't met her yet, but Shaffar had said they would be able to meet today and start getting to know each other. There was nothing he wanted more than to get married now so he could be on his way to getting a Green card. The problem was that he had been working two jobs for the past month trying to raise the amount he needed, but he'd only been able to raise an additional two thousand dollars, and that was spending because he spent as little as possible on himself. He was still two thousand dollars short. If he did not come up with the rest soon, there would be no marriage. It would not be long before his luck ran out and he got deported like Paul.

He took another sip of his Coke, but he couldn't even taste it as his stomach roiled with worry. If he did not get enough money to pay Shaffar, he would be deported. If he didn't get along with Maya, the girl he was to marry, she might refuse to marry him, and he would be deported. If someone found out he had overstayed his visa and was working illegally, he would be deported. If he crossed the wrong person for whatever reason and they reported him, he would be deported. If he …

Stop, Jude! He was freaking himself out. He gritted his teeth as he remembered what his father had told him before he left his country. He had told him that God would take care of him when he went to America and would bring him back safely to Bakali. But he had apparently not been at the top of God's list of people to take care of. His dad's God had forsaken him. His only hope now was in an unscrupulous fellow called Shaffar and in a girl he had never met before.

The thought of going back to Bakali and facing the fact that his father was dead and that everything he'd owned had been seized by the government, felt too much to bear. His father had acted as a pastor to several leaders in the government until he was captured by the faction that opposed the current president. He'd been accused of treason and killed like many others. Jude had been bitter at God and everyone involved in his father's killing ever since.

His cellphone rang, pulling him out of his reverie. He picked it up from the table and looked at the screen.

"Shaffar!" he said, answering the call. "What's up?"

"I have bad news, man," Shaffar said in his gravelly voice.

Jude's pulse spiked as fear gripped him. "What is it now?"

"Maya has pulled out of the deal, Jude. She decided she didn't want to go ahead with it anymore."

Jude felt as though someone had poured ice cold water over him. For a few seconds, he could not speak. All he could think about was that his life was over. He would be deported back to Bakali and, just like his father, he would be shot.

"Jude! Are you still there?" Shaffar asked.

"Yes." Jude sighed. "What am I supposed to do now? Is there any way we can convince her to change her mind?"

"I've tried everything," Shaffar said. "There's no way she is going to do it. She wants nothing to do with us."

Jude closed his eyes as fear and desperation raced

through him. This was another blow, another sign that God had not only turned his back on him but was actually punishing him by thwarting his plans.

"Jude?"

Jude opened his eyes. "What now? What are we going to do? Can you find another girl quickly enough?"

"It's never easy to find a girl, especially these days. You were lucky we found Maya before you came to us, but now that she isn't interested anymore, finding someone else will be hard. It will take a bit of time."

"But I need to get married as soon as possible," Jude said.

"I know that, but you'll have to wait for us to find someone. You have no choice. I'll ask around and see if there's another willing candidate." Shaffar chuckled. "But it means that you might have to be open to marrying a very ugly wife."

Jude shrugged. "That doesn't matter to me. It's not like we will be getting married for love. As long as she is an American citizen and can get me a Green card, she can look like an ogre for all I care."

"Yes, I know you will not be marrying for love and all, but you want to be able to look at her face. Now, if she's nasty looking...."

"Shaffar!" Jude exclaimed. "Just find someone. Okay?"

"Fine!" Shaffar laughed. "But as I said, it will take some time to find another girl."

When the call ended, Jude sighed with frustration and groaned. *This is great! This is just great!* Right on the day he was supposed to meet the girl he was to marry, she decided to pull out. He had been hoping and praying he would make a good impression on her and that they would be able to get married as soon as possible so they could start the process of filing for his permanent residence. Now there was no girl. Hopefully, Shaffar would find another willing girl soon, but if he didn't...

Jude sighed again. He had to be positive and hope for the best.

But he could not quiet the negative voice in his mind. *With the way my luck has gone these past few months, I will probably be deported before Shaffar can find someone.*

He looked up when someone approached his table.

"Hey Jude!" Ben smiled.

Jude could not muster up a smile for his friend. When Ben sat down across from him, Jude put his hand on his forehead and sighed. "Man, I'm in trouble," he said.

"What is it?" Ben asked.

"That girl, Maya — the one Shaffar arranged for me to marry?"

"Yes, what about her?"

"She pulled out of the deal, Ben. After everything, getting two jobs and working illegally to raise the money I need, after placing my hopes in the fact that I will be able to stay in this country once I get married and have my Green card. Now nothing. I'm going to be deported, Ben. I am going to be thrown out of the United States. I'll have to go back to a country where I don't even have a home or parents anymore and will be reminded about that every day."

"I am sorry, Jude," Ben said.

"Shaffar said he will try to find someone else, but who knows how long it will take to find someone willing to marry me under the circumstances and as soon as possible."

"You've raised about three thousand dollars already. There has to be someone who needs that money."

Jude shook his head. "You know a large part of that will go to Shaffar."

Ben said again, "I'm really sorry, Jude. You have been working so hard. We will just have to pray Shaffar finds someone else very soon."

Pray. Jude ran his hand across the table. Prayer would not help him. It never had. He said, "I need all the luck I can possibly get."

Two girls passed by their table, smiling at him. One of them was voluptuous with smooth dark skin and full curly hair. She was the type of girl he was usually attracted to. Under normal circumstances, he would be on his feet now, walking up to her to get her number, especially as she seemed equally interested. But now was not the time for any of that.

He thought about the possibility that a relationship might actually be the solution he was looking for now, and then immediately discarded the idea. Even if he started a relationship right now, most girls would want some time to decide if they liked him enough to stay with him, let alone marry him. And there was a very high possibility that it would not happen. Plus there was no time for all of that.

Besides, he certainly didn't want a serious relationship now, and he definitely didn't want to be married to anyone. Not a real marriage at least, with the huge amount of commitment it required and all the challenges that came with it. And the idea of starting a relationship just to get a Green card, especially when the girl he would be dating wouldn't even know that was all he wanted, did not sit well with him. The marriage he was after would simply be a business deal with both parties understanding their commitments. A Green card for cash.

He watched the pretty girl until she disappeared from sight, and for a brief moment he wondered what the girl Shaffar might find for him would look like. Would she look like that pretty girl, someone who was close to his type, or would she be completely different?

And then he dismissed the thoughts. It did not matter what the girl looked like. All that mattered was that Shaffar found someone who was willing to marry him now and who fully understood what their arrangement entailed. He turned and focused on Ben again.

Ben was grinning at him. "I see someone just caught your eye. The Jude I know would have gone after her." He chuckled. "I am sure she hasn't gone far. You can still catch up with her."

Jude shook his head. "I am in trouble, Ben. I don't have time for all that."

"Stop worrying, boy!" Ben said, patting his shoulder. "I am sure Shaffar will soon find someone for you."

Jude grunted.

Ben said, "So what if Shaffar finds someone for you today? What happens then?"

Jude rapped his knuckles on the table and tried

to press down the anxiety rising up in him. "We have to get to know each other as much as we can," he answered. "The girl and I. After we get married and she files a petition for my 'adjustment of status,' we will be invited for a USCIS interview and asked very personal questions to make sure nothing is amiss. If they get suspicious, I will definitely be deported, and she might be charged for fraud."

"Wow!" Ben leaned back in his seat. "I didn't know all that." He rubbed his chin, a thoughtful look on his face. "It sounds pretty risky. No wonder that Maya girl pulled out."

Jude quickly smothered the guilt that was rising up in him. "Yes," he said. "That is why whatever girl Shaffar finds for me has to be open to knowing everything about me in as little time as possible, and I have to do the same. We cannot leave any stone unturned. Once I get the Green card, we can get a divorce immediately." He groaned. "Why did this happen, Ben? Just when I was beginning to have such hope, Maya pulls out."

Ben leaned forward. "What about Zoe? Did you ask her? She might be willing to help you. You both know each other well enough… since you dated and all."

Jude laughed harshly. "First, we only dated for two months and I cannot say we know each other well. But I did indirectly ask her, as we are still kinda friends. She gave me the evil eye and told me I was crazy. But I deserved that. I should not have even asked such a thing of her. I tried to call to apologize, but she didn't pick up. I guess it's all for the best, anyway."

"Well, that's harsh," Ben said with a laugh.

"It's not funny, Ben," Jude said. But he smiled in spite of himself. "I don't blame her for being mad at me."

"So, what are you going to do, Jude?"

"What can I do but hope and bide my time? I have to keep believing that Shaffar will find someone soon while I continue to try to raise the rest of the money."

"I wish there was another way," Ben said.

There probably was, if there were time. But time was a luxury he didn't have. Every day he stayed in this country as an illegal immigrant meant that he could be found out and apprehended by ICE. Having to work illegally only made matters worse.

Once again, his heart began to beat really fast. This arrangement with Shaffar had to work out, or he would soon be back in his country in the midst of all that was going on there. For the third time in a week, he felt like praying and asking God for help. But as always, he brushed aside the urge to pray. He knew it would do no good. The only thing he needed now was patience... and luck. Lots of it.

FIVE

Sofia stood in front of the kitchen sink in Edith's house, washing the dishes. The kitchen, like the rest of the two-bedroom single-story house, was tiny. She dried a plate and put it in the drying rack, and then looked out the window. All she could see outside were plain single-stories as tiny as this one. Edith's house was very plainly furnished, functional and cramped; completely different from the plush apartment she had lived in for the past few years. Which she had now been forced to move out of.

Thinking about the apartment brought tears to her eyes again. Every time she thought about it, she could not help thinking about George and how much time they had spent together in that apartment. She hated herself for allowing him to use her the way he'd done, for allowing herself to fall in love with him and believing that he would leave his wife for her. She should have known better. And maybe she had, but she just hadn't wanted to face the truth even though all the signs were there.

She sighed heavily and went back to washing the dishes. Tears streamed down her face and dropped into the sink, mixing in with the soapy water. She began to think about Lily and all that Lily had told her. Her friend had warned her about dating George because he was a married man, but she had told Lily to mind her own business, believing somehow that she and George would be together forever. Now she felt like a fool. Why on earth had she believed that anyway?

Once again, she felt an overwhelming loneliness and helplessness and sighed. *Why am I still alive, anyway? What's the point of going on if I will continue to live like this?*

Her mind traveled to the day George broke up with her and her subsequent botched suicide attempt. A part of her was glad to be alive, but another just wanted to be done with life. To lie down and die. Unfortunately… or was it fortunately, her friend Edith had not let that happen.

She finished washing the dishes and dried her hands. She began to clean the kitchen floor as she thought about that day. After she'd returned from the hospital, Edith had told her that she had called her number a couple of times to ask if she was home because she wanted to come over. "When you did not answer, I decided to postpone my visit to the next day," Edith said. "But because I had to run some errands, I decided to take the opportunity to go to your apartment and see if you were home."

Edith had a frightened look on her face as she continued talking. "I got to your apartment and found your door open, so I entered. When I called your name, you didn't answer and I went looking for you around your apartment. You can imagine how horrified I was when I found you lifeless on the bathroom floor. I called for help immediately, and you were rushed to the hospital."

She narrowed her eyes in anger, having made an educated guess of what had really happened, probably from the lit candles and the dishes on the dining table, as well as the lingerie Sofia had been wearing. "Why would you do that to yourself, Sofia? No one is worth dying for."

Sofia had said nothing about that. Instead, even though she'd felt empty and regretful that she was still alive, she'd given Edith a grateful smile. At least she had someone else apart from Lily who still cared about her. She had been staying at Edith's for about a month now, but the despair she felt that day remained with her.

She finished cleaning the kitchen at last, washed and dried her hands, and then went to the tiny spare bedroom, the room she'd slept in since she'd come to live at Edith's. She stopped in front of the dresser mirror and gazed at her face. Her eyes looked sunken and miserable, her hair in disarray. She'd stopped caring about her appearance. It was completely unlike her to let herself go. She looked frightful... but she did not care.

She wiped the tears from her eyes with the back of her hand and went to sit on the narrow bed. She still hadn't stopped thinking about George and the day he'd came to the apartment with his wife to announce that he was breaking up with her. Since she'd been fired from her job, she'd hardly left this house. George had let his wife take everything from her: her job, her car, the apartment he had gotten for her, which had been her home for the past few years.

How could he do that to her? What hurt the most was that she'd allowed herself to love him only to have him throw that love in her face. She had stupidly believed that he was coming to her apartment to propose to her when in actual fact he'd come to break up with her.

She lay on the bed and covered herself with the blanket. If only she had died that day. A cloud of despair and horror came over her as she wondered what would have become of her if she'd died. She had never thought much about the afterlife, but it suddenly dawned on her that everything Lily had said about God had somehow managed to make its way into her heart even though she had tried to ignore her friend's words. She shuddered as she thought about the possibility that there might be a heaven and hell; places she had previously not believed existed. Would she have gone to heaven or hell if she'd died?

She pressed her lips together. She was certain that since she had ignored God for most of her life, he wouldn't have opened the doors of his home wide for her and let her in. For a moment, an intense fear seized her, and then she pressed the dreary thoughts out of her mind.

She groaned when the bedroom door opened and Edith came into the room. Edith had been away at work, but before she'd left in the morning, she had told Sofia that she had something important to talk to her about. Sofia did not want to discuss anything important with Edith. She did not want to discuss anything important with anyone. The last time someone had told her they had something important to discuss with her, it had ended in misery and an attempted suicide.

She covered her face with the blanket, but Edith came and snatched it off her face. "Sofia, I saw you wide awake just now." She put her hand on Sofia's shoulder and added, "You look awful."

Sofia sighed but said nothing. There was no point trying to explain to Edith why she'd been crying.

Edith kept staring intently at her, and Sofia frowned. "What?" She tried to snatch the blanket away again so she could cover her face, but Edith held it away so she could not reach it.

"What is wrong, Sofia? You look a mess."

"Well thank you," Sofia said.

"I used to envy you," Edith said. "You're beautiful and you found yourself a rich boyfriend who pampered you like a queen, bought expensive stuff for you, paid the rent for your luxury apartment, gave you a good job and took you on trips around the world."

Sofia's frown deepened. "What is this about, Edith?"

Edith continued as though she'd not heard Sofia speak.

She gave her a sympathetic look. "He gave you everything, but..."

"Edith!" Sofia stared angrily at her. "Where are you going with all of this? I do not want to talk about George right now. Can you please stop talking about him?"

Edith's sympathetic look melted away, replaced by a sneer. "How the mighty have fallen," she said, shaking her head.

"Wow, Edith! I'm glad you saved my life and all, but why are you gloating now? What have I ever done to you?"

Edith sighed and said, "I'm sorry, Sofia. We've known each other since college, and you can understand how I felt when right after we graduated, you got everything a girl could possibly dream of while I struggled."

"What are you saying, Edith? At least you still have a job, your own apartment, and you and Flynn are still together. You haven't lost everything you have. I wish I had known sooner that none of it would last."

Edith looked sympathetic again, and Sofia pressed her lips together. This was the reason she disliked Edith sometimes. She could be the nicest person in the world in one minute, and the next she was trying to make other people look really small in order to feel good about herself. And the worst thing was that Sofia felt like she had to indulge her, or Edith, in her usual unpredictable way, might decide to send her packing. And even though she was trying to be careful with Edith all the time, it would not be long before Edith complained of the inconvenience of sharing a tiny house with her and asked her to leave. Where would she go then?

Once again, she felt an overwhelming urge to speak to Lily. Lily might not have agreed with her relationship with George, but unlike Edith, she knew what to say to make her feel better.

Edith folded her arms across her chest. "We need to talk, Sofia."

Sofia stifled a groan.

"I'm really sorry for everything that has befallen

you," Edith said. "But the thing is... you know how small this house is. It's not possible for you to continue to stay here."

Sofia's heart sank. She hated to beg anyone for anything, but right now she felt vulnerable and alone. And she had nowhere to go. She would get on her knees now and plead with Edith if that would change her mind. She threaded her fingers together and gazed into her friend's eyes. "You know I have nowhere to go. Please let me stay here for a little longer. Just until I figure out what to do."

Edith shook her head. "I'm sorry, Sofia. I just can't let you stay here." She sighed again. "Flynn and I want to take the next step in our relationship. He's moving in with me tomorrow. When he does, there will be no space for you."

"But can't I just stay in this small room? I won't trouble you or Flynn."

"No, Flynn said he wants to use this room for something."

Sofia shut her eyes for a brief moment as the reality and seriousness of her situation crashed down on her. She had no job, and she didn't know when she would find one or what kind of job it would be. And then she would have to wait to be paid and try to save enough to get a decent apartment. That would take time and, from the stern look on Edith's face, time was not something she was willing to give.

Sofia pleaded again. "Can I sleep on the sofa in the living room? I won't get in the way, I promise. Once I find a job and save money to rent an apartment, I'll move out."

"But when will that be?" Edith asked. "You

haven't even started looking for a job. You have been sitting in this room moping every day."

"I will start first thing tomorrow. I promise."

"No. Flynn will be here soon and you know he doesn't like you very much. He's not going to want to share the house with you."

"And I don't like him either," Sofia murmured.

"What?"

"Nothing. Where will I go to if I move out?" Sofia asked.

"I don't know… You can move into a cheap motel, get a job flipping burgers or something, and then try to save up enough to rent an apartment."

Sofia stared at Edith, astonished by her friend's insensitive words.

"Stop looking at me like that, Sofia. You know I like to say things as they are. Don't expect to get the kind of cushy job George got you." Edith shook her head. "You had that job for quite a while, but you have nothing saved up. You spent it all while living off of your rich ex-boyfriend."

Sofia looked away in shame. Maybe Edith was right to sneer at her. She had nothing to show for her old job. She hadn't even tried to pay off her college loan. She'd been living lavishly, believing George would always be there to take care of her. How foolish she'd been. "You know I can't flip burgers," she said.

"I didn't say you should do that forever. You have a college degree. You will find a better job eventually."

"But it will take time to find a suitable job."

Edith stared at her for a long moment, and then finally said "I might have something that will pay well now, but I'm not sure you will want to do it."

Sofia sat up and stared curiously at Edith. "What is it? Tell me."

"I'm not sure that..."

"Edith! Just tell me."

"Well, Flynn knows someone who works for an agency that helps immigrants looking to settle permanently in the United States. They are looking for a girl who can work with one of their clients."

Sofia blinked. *An agency that helps immigrants?* Her heart soared with hope. Maybe she could work for this agency working to help immigrants settle in America. But she had no experience in that area. "Do I need any experience, Edith?" she asked.

"No, you don't need any experience for this particular job." Edith chuckled. "You just need to be willing."

Sofia frowned and looked at Edith with suspicion. "What kind of job is it exactly? I have never heard of that kind of job before."

Edith put her hand on Sofia's arm. "I'm not going to beat around the bush. This agency helps people who have overstayed their visa or want to expedite the process of getting their permanent resident card in the United States... and other things like that. They pair them with a citizen. Flynn's friend mostly handles that. Since you have no money, it might be a good way to make some."

Sofia was almost afraid to ask, but she did anyway. "What does this job entail exactly? Why does this agency need to pair immigrants up with citizens?" She narrowed her eyes as she stared at Edith. Considering Edith had said she was not going to beat around the bush, she was doing exactly that now.

"Umm… they pair them up to get married. You marry an immigrant who pays you in installments, and in return you help him get his Green card. Once that is done, you get your full payment and then you get a divorce and go your separate ways."

Sofia leaned back against the headboard. She felt sick to her stomach. "You're saying I should marry someone I don't know for money so that person can get a Green card in order to remain the United States?

"It's not as bad as it sounds, Sofia. You will get to know the guy as much as possible so you can both be convincing when you attend the immigration interview."

"But isn't that illegal?" Sofia asked. "What if I am caught… and where on earth did Flynn even meet these kinds of people?"

Edith waved her question away. "Don't worry your pretty head about that. If you and the guy they pair you up with do your homework properly, you should be able to convince the immigration officers that your relationship is real. You'll have to spend quite some time with him, but I believe you don't have to be married to him for long."

"How long do I have to be married?"

"Just long enough for him to get his Green card, and then you can get a divorce."

Sofia felt like throwing up. She shook her head vigorously. "I can't do it." She turned away from Edith. "Please don't ever ask me to do something like that again."

"Well then, you will have to leave the house as soon as possible."

"Edith…"

"Flynn might consider letting you stay here if you decide to accept this offer. He told his friend he might have someone who is willing to take it. But if not, then you will have to leave, Sofia. Tomorrow at the latest."

Sofia felt like weeping, but she held herself together. "What's in it for Flynn, anyway?" Sofia asked, and then laughed harshly. "Don't tell me. I know. He gets a cut from whatever the immigrant guy pays, doesn't he?"

She shook her head in disgust. She had always known there was something crooked about Edith's boyfriend. Unfortunately, he had roped Edith into his twisted ways. Now they were threatening to rope her in as well. Actually, they were not threatening. They had already tightened the noose around her. She pleaded with Edith again. "Please I do not want to do what you are suggesting. I will get out of your hair as soon as I can save enough for my own apartment."

She winced when the bedroom door opened again and Flynn walked into the room. He looked at Edith. "Babe, have you told her?"

Edith sighed. "She says she doesn't want to do it."

Flynn narrowed his eyes as he looked at Sofia, his face a mask of rage. "Well then, Sofia, I guess you will have to move out tomorrow."

Sofia glared at Flynn. There was no point pleading with him. He did not like her, and the feeling was mutual. Edith had said once that he thought she was a spoiled little gold digger who thought she owned the whole world because she had a wealthy boyfriend. But considering he'd never been able to hold down a job and was living off Edith, she found that laughable. Without a doubt, he would throw her out when he moved in the next day.

She ran Edith's request through her mind again. The more she thought about it, the more repulsed she felt. The whole thing was so wrong. And yet a part of her was prodding her to take the job, or at least consider taking it. Edith had said she would be paid well, and right now she needed the money. And she certainly didn't want to be thrown out onto the streets, nor did she want to go through this difficult time alone. Even though Edith was caustic at times, she was still the only person Sofia had to talk to. She didn't really have a choice.

She swallowed and then, against her better judgment, said in a shaky voice, "How much would I get paid to do this, exactly?" She settled her gaze on Flynn.

Flynn smiled widely, but she continued to scowl at him. Just a moment ago, he was glowering at her and threatening to throw her out onto the streets. "The client is supposed to pay fifteen thousand dollars in all. You will get about ten thousand dollars. Three thousand now, and the remaining after you get married and he gets his Green card."

"Three thousand dollars now," she said slowly. That was a lot of money. But when she was with George, she would have spent that amount shopping in one afternoon. Flynn was probably right. She was spoiled. She had let George spoil her and had forgotten how to fend for herself. George wasn't here anymore. She was on her own, and she had to learn to provide for herself.

She swallowed the sob that was rising in her

throat along with her revulsion and nodded. "I will do it."

"Good girl." Flynn grinned. "I haven't met the guy you're supposed to marry, but Shaffar tells me he's good looking." He gave her a wicked smile. "It will not be too hard for you to marry him." He turned to Edith, held out his hand to her, and said, "Come on, babe. Let's give Sofia her space for now."

Edith took Flynn's hand, and they left the bedroom together.

For a long moment after they left, Sofia sat on the bed, gazing at the wall in front of her. Her mind roiled with guilt and shame. She finally lay down on the bed. Closing her eyes, she prayed that sleep would take her so she could escape the disgust she felt at herself.

SIX

As Jude approached the house where the girl he was hoping to marry lived, he grew more and more nervous. Shaffar walked beside him with quick, confident strides. They got to the single-story building, and he studied the area. The house was tiny and in a low-income part of town. He looked around. He hadn't known what to expect, but where did he think someone who married immigrants for money would live? Surely not in a mansion.

He immediately chided himself for thinking that way. Was he not a part of this strange arrangement? Wasn't he about to meet a woman he had never seen before with the hope that she would help him remain in this country by marrying him? He slowed down as Shaffar climbed the front steps. He felt wretched, having descended to this place where he was planning to marry a citizen just so he could get a Green card and then later get divorced.

"Jude!" Shaffar turned back and stared at him. The scrawny guy was already standing on the porch, about to knock on the door. "What are you doing there? Come on."

Jude reluctantly climbed the steps and stood on the front porch with Shaffar. Anxious, he held his hand behind his back and then placed them at his sides before folding them across his chest. He was never able to stand still when he was nervous, and he could not remember the last time he was this nervous.

Shaffar knocked on the door, and Jude winced. The knock sounded as loud as a clap of thunder. Everything in him screamed for him to walk away, to not go on with this foolish plan. But he knew that would be even more foolish. He had to do this. He had no choice.

Shaffar knocked again, and Jude looked away. He did not even know what this girl who they had set him up with looked like. He had never seen a picture of her and only knew her name was Sofia. Yet, if everything went well, they would be married in less than a month. After their visit today, he would give Shaffar the money for the first installment. Hopefully, by the time he had to pay the second installment, he would have the money he needed.

Shaffar knocked on the door once more and then looked back at Jude with a frown on his face. "Where on earth are they?" he asked angrily.

Jude took deep breath and let it out slowly, trying to calm his nerves. Hopefully, in an hour or so, the meeting with Sofia would be over, at least for now, and he could breathe easily again.

The door suddenly opened, and Jude's heart skipped a beat. *Here goes nothing.* A man who looked to be in his late twenties opened the door wide and grinned at Shaffar. "You're here," he said and then nodded at Jude.

"I've been knocking for a while now, Flynn," Shaffar said, scowling.

"I'm sorry. My girlfriend and I were speaking to Sofia, trying to prepare her for your meeting." He looked at Jude again and then turned back to Shaffar. "I didn't hear you knock until now. Come in, both of you" He stepped aside so they could enter the house.

Shaffar entered, but Jude's feet felt like clay. He stood unmoving at the door, a part of him still screaming for him to walk away. The man Shaffar had called Flynn stared curiously at him, and Jude sighed and forced himself to move forward. He entered the house, and the man shut the door behind him.

He looked around the small living room. Everything was neat and tidy, though the furniture was old and nondescript. On the other side of the living room, a blonde with a short bob sat on the sofa looking at him and Shaffar. Jude felt his anxiety spike slightly, and then he pushed it down and exhaled.

The girl stood up. She looked like she was in her mid-twenties. She was not pretty, though not unattractive either. He let out a long breath. In a strange way, he felt relieved that he was not attracted to her. At least he would not have to battle any attraction for her in the process of getting his Green card or develop any kinds of feelings for her. That way there would be no complications or strings attached when it was time for them to go their separate ways.

Flynn walked up to the girl and took her hand. He turned to Shaffar and Jude and said, "This is my girlfriend, Edith."

For a brief moment, Jude was confused. Shaffar had told him the girl's name was Sofia. But this girl's name was Edith. Had Shaffar found another girl for him, and was Flynn giving up his girlfriend to marry someone else just for money? He frowned deeply and then remembered that Flynn had said he and his girlfriend had been trying to get the girl he was supposed to marry prepared for their meeting.

Edith smiled widely as her eyes studied Jude. "Well, he is very good looking," she said. "That is a plus. At least he will not repulse Sofia."

Flynn grinned. "Sofia, repulsed? Wasn't she dating that old guy before he broke up with her? She should be happy."

Edith shook her head. "Stop it, Flynn! George is not really old. He's in his forties."

Jude's frowned deepened as he watched them. They were both talking as though he was not here.

Shaffar snapped his fingers. "So, guys, let's get down to it. Where is Sofia?"

"Where is she, babe?" Flynn looked at his girlfriend. "I thought we agreed she would come out here five minutes after we did."

"I am sure she is still in her room and still as nervous as ever," Edith said.

"She is still nervous?" Flynn shook his head. "Who would have thought your friend was capable of being nervous. She walks around like a peacock every time I see her."

"She hasn't really been herself since she broke

up with George." Edith glanced at Jude and then pressed her lips tightly together as a slightly worried look crept into her face.

Jude found himself thinking about this George and why he and Sofia had broken up. He felt slightly worried. Hopefully, this guy would not suddenly appear before the deal went through to insist that he wanted Sofia back.

Flynn looked at Jude and then at Shaffar. He pointed at the couch. "Please sit down."

Jude sat on the couch, but Shaffar, who was usually unable to sit still for too long, sat on the edge. He looked up at Flynn. "Dude, are we going to start this meeting or not?"

"Edith, please go get your friend," Flynn said.

She nodded and left the living room.

Jude threaded his fingers together and thought about what Edith had said about Sofia being nervous. Surely she could not be more nervous than he was. Not only was this arrangement strange and so wrong, he felt a huge amount of pressure to try to impress this girl who he'd already pegged all his future hopes on, even though he'd never seen or spoken to her.

Shaffar nodded at Flynn. "Can we step outside for a while? Let's leave Jude to get to know Sofia when she comes in. And we have to discuss what day we should expect her to be ready to marry my man Jude."

Flynn looked at Jude and then turned to Shaffar again. "We have a lot more than that to discuss, like how much each person gets." He grinned.

Jude watched them curiously as they opened the door and stepped out together. Their conversation was a little cryptic, and they seemed to have much more to discuss than what they had revealed just now. For a minute, he wondered what else they wanted to talk about, and then he sighed and brushed aside his curiosity. It didn't really matter anyway. They handled the business part of this arrangement. He had to focus on making a good impression on the girl he was hopefully going to marry soon.

He looked around the tiny living room again, and then his mind traveled to his late parents. He missed them so much, but he was glad they were not here to see him now. What would they think if they knew what he was about to do? A vivid memory of his mother appeared in his mind. She was sitting on the couch in their living room, and he came and climbed into her lap. He had to have been about five or six. He remembered he did that regularly. He would make himself comfortable on her lap while she told him interesting Bible stories. She told him different stories everyday, and he loved the times he spent listening to her.

He remembered a particular day when she said she was going to tell him a very special story about Jesus and what he had done for him on the cross. He was eight then. She told him in a way that was easy for him to understand about how Jesus had taken away his sins when he died and then was resurrected again. After that, she had asked him if he wanted to receive Jesus into his heart.

He remembered saying that he did, and then she had prayed for him. He had felt brand new that day, but his mother had died months later. She was killed in a car crash on the way back from the market one day. He had mourned her every day for months, and the prayer about Jesus coming into his heart had been forgotten. He had been angry with God for years and then had put God completely out of his mind.

When his father died about a year ago, he had not even thought about God, not even to be angry with Him, having decided that God was not in any way involved with the lives of people on earth. But, for some reason, this threat of deportation and his desperation to remain in America, plus the consequent decision he'd made to marry a stranger, had brought God to the forefront of his mind again. Why that was, he did not know.

"Hold on to Jesus," his father had said before Jude had come to America for his studies. But he had done no such thing. Maybe that was why he had started to think about God now. He had not followed the wish of his father. Or of his mother, who, if she were still alive, would tell him the same thing his father had. He had completely forgotten about Jesus, and his childhood faith was a distant memory. However, he still had his own set of values and a moral compass, even though he had not held on to his childhood faith. What he was about to do was wrong, but he could not back away as he had no choice. Not if he wanted to remain in this country.

He held his breath as footsteps began to approach. Edith walked into the living room, followed by a tall brunette. They walked toward him, and he stood up. He studied the brunette as she came closer. She had long wavy hair and bangs that swept over her eyebrows. Her skin looked so smooth and shiny it reminded him of polished glass. She wore a long, elegant dress, an expensive-looking gold watch, and several gold bracelets on her wrist. She looked expensive… and delicate. He watched her as she came to stand before him, surprised by the way she looked. She did not fit the mold he'd been expecting. It wasn't like he'd expected someone poor, but he definitely had not expected someone who looked as rich and self-possessed as she did. She leveled a cool gaze at him, and her eyes studied him, just like he was studying her.

He did not avert his gaze. Even though he could not deny she was pretty and many men would probably consider her beautiful, she was not his type, which was a relief. She was tall, very slim, and white. She looked like one of those runway models he sometimes saw on television. She was the very opposite of what he was usually attracted to.

His mind immediately went to Keziah. She had been exactly his type and he'd been smitten the very first time he saw her. A sliver of sadness went through him, as it always did whenever he thought about her, and he instantly pressed her out of his mind. He smiled politely at Sofia, but she did not smile back.

"Let me leave you two so you can get acquainted," Edith said, smiling. She left the living room, and Sofia sat down on the sofa. She crossed her legs and looked up at him again. He sat on the couch and faced her. Not knowing what to say, he tapped his fingers on his knees, hoping she would speak first. But she did not.

The silence stretched between them, and he searched his mind for something to say. But for some reason he could not come up with anything.

He shuffled his feet, hating the awkward silence, and then glanced at her. She did not seem in the least bit uncomfortable, but she also didn't seem like she was about to start a conversation any time soon. He had to start one before she started to believe he was a boring, empty-headed person. If he did not find something to say, she might decide she did not want to go ahead and marry him. Even though he had paid the first installment so that he didn't have to worry about whether she found him boring or not, she did not look like someone who needed the money. Who knew why she was doing this. Maybe it was because she was bored with her life. The worst thing that could happen then was he bored her further. He blinked in surprise when she spoke.

"So… Jude — that's your name, isn't it?"

"Yes." He nodded. "And you are Sofia?"

For the first time since she'd come into the living room, she gave him a small smile. "Yes. This is awkward, isn't it?"

He exhaled. "Yes. It's more than awkward. It is kinda excruciating."

Her smile widened, and then it melted away. She glanced at her long, manicured nails and pursed her lips.

He scolded himself for not being able to come up with something interesting to say. He wouldn't exactly call himself the friendliest person, and quite a few people thought he was stand-offish. But they were people who didn't know him well. He could be the life of the party when he was in the mood, but he was definitely the friendliest when he was with people he knew well. He was just meeting her for the first time, and the awkwardness of their situation made it even harder not to be anxious. But he had to get out of his head so she could get to know the real him, and he, her.

She looked up at him and said, "They want us to get to know each other so the marriage can seem real, but we both know this is nothing but a business arrangement. The earlier we get married and get this over with, the earlier we can both get what we want and get a divorce." She narrowed her eyes as she stared at him. "I hope we are on the same page."

He frowned. "What do you mean?"

"I mean that I hope you understand that this is strictly a business arrangement and nothing more. We're not friends or even acquaintances, so we don't have to pretend we are when we're in private. We will do whatever we have to in order to convince the immigration officers that the marriage is real, but I don't want either of us to forget that it isn't."

Jude bristled. Why was she speaking as if he had told her he wanted anything more than exactly what she'd stated? He said coldly, "Yes, I know this is a business arrangement. How could I forget? It has already cost me a couple thousand dollars."

She shrugged, and he glared at her. She did not seem to even want to get acquainted with him, let alone get to know him enough to make the relationship believable. He was now certain that she did not care about the money and, therefore the success of this business arrangement. Why on earth she was doing this, then? If she did not care, why would she decide to go through the process?

But even if she didn't care, he did. It was therefore

left to him to try to make this work. He had a lot to lose even though she clearly did not. He injected a smile into his voice and said, "What's your last name, Sofia? And where did you grow up?"

She pressed her lips tightly together and did not answer.

He sighed loudly. So, she was the kind of girl who treated people condescendingly. It was almost as though she didn't want this to work out. He sighed again. Well, he did. And he would try his best to make it work. He had a lot to lose if he didn't. He tried again, but this time he decided to remind her that she had a part to play in their arrangement. "Sofia, you know we need to get to know each other better in order to make this relationship believable to the immigration agents."

She lifted her brows, shrugged, and still said nothing.

He groaned inwardly. This was a waste of time. He would have to tell Shaffar to find someone else; someone who cared enough about the money to try to make this work. Someone who did not look like they spent their days shopping and lounging around. But he knew it would not be a good idea. It had not been easy to find another girl who would agree to marry him in such a short notice after Maya had pulled out. They had found her by luck. If this did not work out, especially as time was not on his side, he would be in big trouble. He had to try to win her over no matter how offensive her attitude was. This had to work.

He looked at her again. She still looked disinterested. He desperately searched his mind for something to say that would capture her interest, but as hard as he tried, he could not come up with anything. He didn't even know what would interest her.

The front door opened, and he groaned loudly. Shaffar and Flynn walked into the living room still talking in hushed tones and sat on the couch across from them. Any minute now, Shaffar would say it was time to leave, and he still hadn't made any connection with Sofia.

What's wrong with you today, Jude? Why couldn't he come up with anything interesting to say?

Shaffar looked at him. "I hope you two have gotten to know each other some," he said. "It's time for us to leave, Jude." He whispered in Jude's ear, "It is all in your hands now. After today, you are on your own. You will have to sweep Sofia off her feet… or at least make her willing and ready to marry you in less than a month." He grinned. "But I'm sure you will manage just fine."

Jude said nothing, but his heart continued to race. This first meeting with Sofia had been a disaster.

Shaffar stood up and turned to Flynn. "We'll talk later, my man."

His heart beat with desperation as he looked at Sofia. *Say something to her Jude. Anything.* He opened his mouth and said the first thing he could think of. "Will you go on a date with me this Friday, Sofia?" He groaned inwardly after he'd spoken. With how disinterested she had looked throughout their meeting, she probably had no interest continuing with this arrangement, let alone go on a date with him. She would probably say no.

She looked away briefly and then turned to him again. He was surprised when he saw tears in her eyes. He blinked, even more surprised when she said angrily, "Fine! I will go on a date with you."

He stared at her for a brief moment. He did not know whether to be relieved or offended that she had so reluctantly agreed to go out with him. He finally smiled in relief. At least she did not totally loathe him. She had agreed to see him again. They could get to know each other better then, but he had to be better prepared. He could not act the same way he'd done today, not being able to think of anything interesting to say to her. Everything had to go right next time. He could not afford to mess it up.

He left the house with Shaffar, his mind focused on his future date with Sofia. It was in only two days. He already had an idea of where to take her. Somewhere he was sure she had not been in a long time. Somewhere he hoped she would enjoy and open up to him. But he could be wrong and she would hate his idea. If that happened, his journey to the altar might end as quickly as it had begun.

SEVEN

Sofia brought out a plain black dress from Edith's closet and tossed it on the bed. It was the outfit she was going to wear for her date with Jude. She sighed as Edith walked into the room, her eyes fixed on the dress, a frown on her face.

"Is that what you're going to wear for your date?" Edith asked.

Sofia glared at her. "Yes! This is what I'm going to wear. What is wrong with it?"

"You need to put in some effort, Sofia," Edith said.

"Why?" Sofia turned away from her. "What's the point of putting in any effort? It's not as if it's a real date. It's all a sham." She sat down on the bed and closed her eyes. This was what she had been reduced to. She was about to go on a date with some guy that she had to marry just so she could feed and house herself. She opened her eyes and glowered at Edith, who was staring at her as though she were a clueless child. She had no choice but to go on this date, but she did not have to like it.

Edith grabbed the black dress from the bed and shoved it back into the closet. Sofia protested, but Edith turned away from her and rifled through the closest, going through the clothes Sofia had. Most of her outfits were not in the closet as she could not fit them all into the tiny space. She still had another suitcase full of clothes, which was on the other side of the room. She had not unpacked the clothes in the suitcase as she'd needed none of them. She had not gone out since she'd moved in with Edith. She'd felt too mentally tired to venture out of the house. This date would be the first time she would actually do so.

Edith tossed a bright yellow fitted dress to her and grinned. "Wear this."

"Nope!" Sofia tossed the dress aside. "I'm not wearing it. I don't want to give that guy any ideas… like that I particularly care about the date. The earlier we both establish that this really is nothing more than a business deal, the better it will be for us. Besides, the dress reminds me way too much of George. I bought it when we were in Italy. As much as the date with Jude will not be real, I don't want to be thinking about another man. We have to get to know each other sufficiently, so that won't do."

"Well, at least you're getting your head in the game, Sofia. You need to get to know Jude well enough to recite the details of his life in your sleep if need be. You will need to know everything about him in preparation for your immigration interview. The earlier you start getting to know each other, the better."

Sofia groaned. "Please Edith, I don't want to be reminded that I am soon going to get married to a guy I don't know, and then go through all that trouble of trying to get him a Green card, just so I can have some money to live on."

Edith laughed. "You don't want to be reminded about it, and yet you're about to go on a date with Jude." She sat down on the bed next to Sofia. "At least he is not an ogre. You have to admit that he's very handsome."

Sofia snorted. "Yes, he is handsome, but what does that matter? It would not make a difference to me if he was an ogre."

"Ah ha! So you're admitting that he is handsome." Edith grinned. "Flynn did right by you."

"Anyone with eyes can see that he is handsome. But it means nothing to me." She stood up and grabbed the sundress from the bed. Shoving it back into the closet, she brought out the black dress again. "This is what I am wearing, Edith. And don't try to talk me out of it."

Edith huffed. "I'm just trying to help. This will be much easier if both of you found each other attractive." She gave Sofia a mischievous wink. "Wait, you already find him attractive."

"Did I say that?" Sofia glowered at Edith.

"You said he was handsome."

"Because he is. But as you know, he is not my type at all. I like more seasoned men."

"By seasoned, you mean older, married men." Edith shook her head.

Sofia winced as her mind went to George. "Thank you for bringing George into this conversation!"

Edith frowned. "Well, you were the one who actually brought him into the conversation first." She looked into Sofia's eyes. "Don't blow this, Sofia.

For your sake and for Jude's as well. You both have a lot to lose if you do."

"You are talking as though I'm going to get a million dollars from this deal rather than just ten thousand dollars."

"Ten thousand dollars is nothing to cough at. And at this particular point in time, it might as well be a million dollars." She put her hand on Sofia's shoulder and said softly, "There is a lot on the line. You remember that, don't you?"

"Anytime I try to forget, you're always here to remind me," Sofia snorted.

Edith smiled. "I don't want to quarrel with you, Sofia. Not now. I need for you to be in a good mood so this deal will work out."

Sofia folded her arms across her chest and stared at her. "Talking about this deal, how much is Flynn getting from it?"

"Don't worry about that, Sofia. He'll get some money, but the most important thing is that he's making connections that will bring in even more in the future."

Sofia shook her head and sighed wearily. What had she gotten herself into? She was now aligned with criminals. When she'd met Edith in college, she would never have guessed that they would one day be here talking about her marrying some immigrant so he could get his Green card in exchange for cash. She stifled the intense worry that rose up in her heart and began to undress quickly. She slipped into the knee-length black dress and turned her back to Edith so her friend could help her with the zipper.

Edith finished, and Sofia turned to look at her.

"Is this okay?" she asked Edith, and then shrugged before she got an answer. "Don't bother answering. It doesn't matter if it is okay or not. It will have to do either way."

Edith chuckled. "You know it's better than okay. You look great as always. Was it George who bought this dress, too?"

Sofia sighed as pain went through her.

"I'm sorry for bringing him into our conversation again." Edith tilted her head. "You still miss him, don't you?"

"Very much," Sofia said.

"Even after all he has done to you. After everything he has taken away from you."

"Yes, Edith. If he came back now and apologized, I would take him back immediately. I miss him that much."

Edith didn't say anything for almost a minute, and then she gave Sofia a sad smile. "You have to put him behind you, Sofia. Try to get to know Jude as much as possible and open up to him so he can also get to know everything about you. I know you can be extremely charming when you want to, but you've changed so much since you and George broke up. You need to bring back that exuberant girl I knew."

"I don't know if I can, Edith. I think George was the one who brought out that part of me."

"That's a lie, Sofia! You were like that before you met George. Remember, I've known you since college. You need to forget about George completely and focus on your future. You have a bright future in front of you."

"Yes, a bright future married to stranger," Sofia

said sarcastically.

Edith burst out laughing, and Sofia frowned. "Please, Sofia, being married to a handsome guy like Jude cannot be that bad."

"Handsome and *poor!* Let's not forget that part."

"Yeah, I know you're used to the good things in life and a man taking care of you. But all that has ended. At least for now. You have to start taking care of yourself. Besides, I don't know why you're so worried. You will divorce Jude as soon as he gets his Green card."

"You don't know why I'm so worried?" Sofia narrowed her eyes. "How about the fact that all this is illegal and the government might come after me if it all goes wrong."

"Sofia, let's not think about that right now. Things will not go wrong if you know everything there is to know about your future husband. I feel as though Jude tried much harder to get to know you on your first meeting than you did. In fact, you didn't seem to try at all. You have to open up to him so..."

"Yes, yes! I know. You've said all that before."

"I mean it, Sofia. Give this a chance. Give Jude a chance."

Sofia did not answer. She grabbed her purse from the bed, opened it, and bought out her phone. She scrolled through her messages and found the address of the restaurant she was supposed to meet Jude at for their date. They hadn't even exchanged numbers when they met, so he'd had to send the message through Flynn.

"I think the restaurant I am supposed to meet Jude at for our date isn't far from your house," she said to Edith. She read out the address and the name of the restaurant and then looked up in confusion when Edith started to laugh. "What is so funny?"

"It's not exactly a restaurant, sweetie. It's a new fast-food place that just opened near here. I know you are used to only going to posh restaurants because of George, but welcome to my world."

Sofia grunted. She looked down at her black dress. She was probably overdressed, even wearing this simple LBD. "And you wanted me to wear that yellow dress. That would have been too much."

"Well, I didn't know you were going to have your first date in a fast food place. But I should have."

Sofia glared at her. "Just as I said... a poor husband." She slipped her feet into a pair of ballet flats instead of the pumps she had planned to wear.

Edith smiled at her. "Aren't you supposed to be heading out for your date now?"

She sighed. "I wish I didn't have to go."

She slung her purse on her shoulder and walked out of the room.

EIGHT

Sofia chose to walk to the venue of the date since it was not far from Edith's. She arrived about ten minutes later, and for a moment she stood in front of the brightly-colored, clearly new, fast food place. She tried to calm her anxiety by taking a few deep breaths.

You can go back and forget all about this, she told herself.

But then what? Flynn would insist that Edith throw her out of the house. She had no money and no job. As Edith had gleefully reminded her, she had nothing to her name.

She strolled into the fast food restaurant and looked around. Hopefully, Jude was here and she did not have to sit waiting for him. There was a crowd of people in the place, and it was quite noisy. She had not been in a fast food restaurant in years.

She saw a guy seated at the back of the building waving his hand at her. She sighed with relief when she saw it was Jude, but nervousness replaced her concern. Taking a deep breath, she told herself to calm down. She squared her shoulders and walked over to his table.

He smiled broadly as she reached him and stood up quickly to pull a chair out for her. She sat down, amused. She was pretty certain that most people here did not pull out chairs for ladies. But she had to admit to herself that she was impressed. That was another point for him. He was handsome and now she knew he was also a gentleman. Or maybe he was just trying to impress her because of what he wanted from her. Hopefully, he would not expect the same from her.

A waitress dressed in a bright green outfit came to take their order. Sofia was in no mood to eat, especially not in a fast food restaurant with all the grease and fat.

"Do you have a salad?" she asked.

"What kind of salad?"

"The healthy kind!" she said, and then decided not to be rude. The waitress didn't deserve that. "Sorry. Any kind of salad you have will do."

The waitress scribbled on her pad and looked at Jude. A bright smile appeared on her face, and there was a glint in her eyes. Sofia smiled, slightly amused. This waitress liked Jude. Sofia could see it in the girl's eyes. She turned to study Jude as he reeled out his order to the waitress. He had short cropped jet-black hair and a chin strap beard, very neatly trimmed. His dark brown skin shone, and his lips were so full that, for a brief moment, she imagined kissing them. She immediately brushed away the image from her mind and forced a smile when he turned back to her.

"So, Sofia, it's great to see you again," he said in a

foreign accent that sounded like he was singing in his deep baritone rather than talking. She smiled slightly as he continued. "I know this arrangement is strange, but even if it's just a business arrangement as you reminded me two days ago, it would be great if we could both try to give it our best shot."

She sighed and said, "Definitely." Two days ago, when they'd first met, she'd been trying hard not to freak out. It was after the meeting was over that she realized she'd been rude, but it had taken everything in her to come out to Edith's living room and meet him. Now, she had mostly decided to go through with this process and, just as he'd said, give it her best shot. It wasn't like she had any other choice.

"I am glad," he said. "We will go our separate ways once this is all over, but it doesn't mean we can't try to be friends... or at least friendly." He smiled. "Especially since we need to get to know each other really well."

She nodded. "I'm open to getting to know you better," she said. "I know your name is Jude, but what is your last name? I hope it's a good last name if I'm going to be taking it... at least temporarily."

Jude's mouth fell open, and he did not speak for a long moment. She pressed her lips together so as not to laugh. He finally spoke. "You're going to take my surname?"

"I might. Just to make the marriage more convincing to the immigration agents during our time together."

He smiled again. "Well, I don't know if you'll be able to pronounce it, but it's Shadamaraciah."

"What?" She stared at him.

He laughed out loud. "Okay, that's not my surname. I just wanted to see what your reaction would be. It's a boring English surname. Daniels."

"Daniels is easy enough." She smiled.

He laughed at her reaction. "Many people in my country have English surnames, and first names as well. Mostly biblical names." He tilted his head toward her. "So, what's yours?" He looked away from her when the waitress arrived with their food. They both began to eat, and then he looked at her again. "You still haven't told me what your last name is," he said, taking a bite of his cheeseburger.

She couldn't help studying him as he ate. When he raised his brows quizzically, she said, "Ross."

"Ross," he repeated in his deep accented voice. Her heart skipped a beat, and she frowned in confusion. She quickly put her away her emotions and said, "What country are you from, Jude?"

"Bakali," he said to her.

She shook her head. "I've never heard of that country before."

"It's a really small African country. I'm not surprised you haven't heard of it. Many people haven't. What actually surprised me was that when I first came to America, I found out that many Americans did not know some of the more well-known African countries. I have come across people here who think that Africa is a country."

He laughed again, and she chuckled. "Well at least I know that it is a continent."

He began to tell her about his country, and the more he did, the more she felt sorry for him. When he told her about the escalating violence there, she almost took his hand just to comfort him. She had never really looked past her small world. Yes, she and George had gone on multiple trips abroad, but it was usually to exotic locations. Even when they'd gone to any developing nations, they'd stayed in the best hotels and resorts.

He told her about his father, who had been somewhat well off and had sent him to school in America for his Masters degree. He had paid the tuition fees, but unfortunately, he'd passed away in Jude's final year.

"I'm so sorry," she said to him. "It must have been hard when he died."

"Yes. I had to get a work permit so I could meet my daily needs. Thankfully, I had paid for my tuition. The plan was for me to go back to my country immediately after my Masters program, but when all the killings in my country started, my father, who was a spiritual adviser to some of the government officials there, got caught up in all of it and was shot."

She winced. "I'm so sorry, Jude."

He sighed loudly. "I was devastated when I heard about it, but I have learned to just go on."

"And what about your mother?" she asked.

"She died when I was just eight."

"My mum passed away when I was around that age as well," Sofia said. "After that, I was left alone with my dad, who treated me as though I was not there. I think he just wanted to be single and without any responsibilities. I had to raise myself because he was usually absent. I left the house and the small town I grew up in once I got into college, and I have never looked back."

"I guess we have some things in common," he

said.

"So, I guess that's why you don't want to go back to your country," she said. "You can't because of the violence there and because your parents are gone. You are an only child, aren't you?"

"Yes. Just like you." He put down the fries he was eating, and for a few seconds he stared at the table. She could tell from the look on his face that there was something weighing on his mind. It was probably something about his country and his migrant status.

He looked up at her and said, "The violence in my country and the death of my dad are not the only reasons why I don't want to go back to my country."

She searched his face but said nothing.

"Before I left for America, I was engaged to my 'high school sweetheart,' as people here in America would say. We loved each other dearly, or at least I loved her dearly. I thought she loved me as much as I loved her." He turned his head to gaze out the window and then faced Sofia again. "Her favorite topic when we were in high school was coming to live in America one day. I didn't know how strong that desire was until a week or so before our wedding, when she broke up with me and the wedding had to be called off."

Sofia covered her mouth with her hand. "Oh, Jude, I'm really sorry. That must have been rough for you."

"Yes, it was," he said. "I was heartbroken. She was the girl I wanted to spend the rest of my life with. We had talked about getting married for so long, it came as a shock to me when she broke our engagement. I later found out that she had met an American man online and had somehow found a way to come to America on his invitation. The last thing I heard about her was that she had married him and was living in America with him."

Sofia shook her head, feeling really sorry for him. He looked incredibly sad. She wanted to reach out and take his hand to comfort him, but that would not be a good idea.

He continued. "When my dad suggested that I come to America for my Masters degree, I immediately agreed. I told him the standard of education here would be much better than the one I would get in our country, but I think the main reason why I wanted to come here was because of Keziah, my ex. It's funny to think about now, but I actually had an irrational belief that I would somehow run into her, in a country of over three hundred million people." He laughed harshly.

"You still love her?" Sofia asked.

Jude looked up with a thoughtful expression on his face and then looked at her again. "I don't really know. I miss her terribly. That I know. I wish I could just forget about her after what she did, breaking off our engagement two weeks before our wedding, but it's not so easy. It's been two years since she broke up with me, but I still think about her almost every day."

Sofia smiled sadly and touched his hand. And then she quickly withdrew it. She thought about telling him about George and, for a moment, she fought herself, not totally prepared to tell him so much about herself. But then she decided to. He had poured out his heart to her even though it was clearly painful for him to do so.

She said to him, "I understand how you feel, Jude. I broke up with a guy I thought I would spend the rest of my life with not too long ago."

She thought of telling him about her suicide attempt but held back on that. There was enough sadness to go around right now. She didn't want to compound it, and it was too early to tell him something so heavy.

"Your friend was talking about a guy called George the other day," Jude said. "Was he the one you broke up with?"

Sofia sighed. "Yes. He actually broke up with me. I also thought I was meant to spend the rest of my life with him. In fact, the day we broke up, I thought he was coming to my house to propose."

"I'm really sorry," Jude said.

Her heart felt heavy, and she remembered everything that had happened the day George had told her their relationship was over and kicked her out of his life and her apartment. She considered telling Jude about the fact that George's wife had come with him to throw her out of the apartment, but she decided not to. Maybe he would judge her the way most people did when they found out she'd been dating a married man. She was not in the mood for that. "In spite of everything, if George came back now, I would take him right back," she said.

He gave her a soft smile. "I would take Keziah back in a heartbeat if I saw her again as well." He shook his head. "This is the first time I am admitting it."

She looked down at her plate and then began to

eat again.

Silence reigned between them, but it was not an awkward silence like the first day they'd met. It was a thoughtful silence. She was sure that, like her, he was thinking about the fact that if either of their exes came back into their lives right now, this arrangement between them would be over immediately, and what the consequences of that would be. If George came back to her, she would end it. Jude would be the one to suffer the consequences if that happened. He would be deported out of the country if he couldn't find someone else. But even knowing that, she would still go back to George if he decided he wanted to mend their relationship and marry her. She felt slightly disgusted with herself over it, but it changed nothing about the way she felt.

She looked at Jude as he ate, while his eyes glanced around the restaurant. If in some crazy way his ex came back into his life, he had said he would take her back. That meant he would also end this arrangement, and she would be the one to lose. She would be kicked out of Edith's by Flynn and then where would she go? Who knew when she would be able to get a job and make enough money to get a decent apartment? She might end up having to sleep in a shelter or something.

She blinked when Jude suddenly turned to her and their eyes met. He gave her a smile that warmed her heart. "What were you just thinking about?" he asked. "You looked like you were somewhere else."

She told him.

He looked sober as he nodded. "Would you hate me if I prayed that your ex doesn't come back?" he asked with a smile in his voice.

She raised her brows. "I didn't know you believed in prayer? I have a friend who talks constantly about praying to God and all that nonsense." She thought briefly about Lily and then focused fully on Jude.

"Like I told you, my father was a pastor. I grew up in a very religious home, and I believed in prayer and all of that for a long time... until I stopped."

"You stopped believing in God?"

He shrugged. "Not really. I know God exists, but I don't think he cares one way or the other about us or if we pray or not. I don't believe that prayer makes any difference in our lives."

"Just try to tell my friend, Lily, that." Sofia sighed. "I miss that girl. She gets really exasperated with me sometimes, but I know she loves me." Sofia sighed once more, missing Lily. "I don't even know when I'll see her again."

"She sounds like a really good friend," Jude said.

"She is," Sofia said. "I have known her for only a short time, but she is now the closest person to me. The one person that I trust completely." Sofia smiled at him. "I think you came to America believing that somehow you would find your ex again even though it's almost impossible to. I think that is kinda sweet. In a way, I hope you do find her again. That is, after you have gotten your Green card and we've gone our separate ways."

He smiled widely. "You're right about it being impossible to find my ex. I don't even want to think about it. The mind is a strange thing. If I start to think there is a possibility of seeing her again, I will start to build my hopes up when I know it will probably never happen. I would wish the same for you, that you will get back with your ex, but somehow I just don't think he's for you. I don't think he deserves a girl like you."

Jude's eyes swept her face, and she felt herself blushing. *Settle down, Sofia. What is wrong with you?*

They soon changed the subject and began to talk about what they liked to do for fun. She told him that she enjoyed traveling the world above every other thing. Thinking about the many trips she'd taken with George brought an ache to her heart, but she pushed away the painful feeling. She listened as he talked about the many parties he'd thrown with his friend at their off-campus apartment. "It all sounds like a blast," she said, laughing as he told her one joke after the other about the parties.

His smile soon melted off his face, and he said, "The truth is that sometimes I just want to be alone, even when those parties are going on. Many times, I feel like going to the bedroom, sitting in the dark, and crying for my parents and my country."

This time she took his hand on the table and squeezed it. "I don't know what to say to make you feel better, except to say that in time it will get better." She smiled widely. "And also we need to hurry up this process so you can get your Green card and remain in this country." She blinked in surprise after she had spoken. She sounded eager to marry him, and in her heart the repulsion she had felt when she'd first heard the idea of marrying someone she didn't know in order to get him a Green card had mostly disappeared. She looked at Jude; really looked at him. She actually liked him and even felt comfortable with him. It would not be so bad, this proposed marriage. She felt much better now that she had gotten to know him more.

They continued to talk and laugh about their past. They talked a bit more about how she had come to Arizona and then about her old job. She still, however, didn't tell Jude that George was a married man.

Sometime later, she glanced at her wristwatch and gasped in surprise. "It's getting late, Jude. I have to go. It's already nine o'clock. We've been here for hours."

He stared incredulously at her and then glanced at his wristwatch. His eyes widened, and he looked up at her. "Wow! Nine p.m. It doesn't feel as if we have been here that long," he said.

She giggled at the expression on his face. "You look like a teenager who has gone past his curfew," she said.

He laughed. "In a way it feels like it."

They both stood up after they had paid for their meal and left the fast-food restaurant together. Outside the restaurant, she turned to him and said, "I had a great time."

"I did, too," he said, smiling at her. "Can we do this again? In two days' time?" he looked apologetic, and she tilted her head to study his face. "Normally I would ask to see a girl again for a second date days or even a week after our first, but this situation between us is different."

She smiled. "I understand. You don't have to apologize. We're in this together, Jude."

He looked surprised. "So you will go on another date with me... the day after tomorrow?"

"Of course," she said. "This time, though, I'll choose the place."

He looked back at the restaurant and laughed. "I'm sorry, Sofia. I knew from the first time I met you that this," he pointed at the fast food place, "would not be your scene. But I thought it might be a nice change for you." He gave her a sheepish grin. "And it was all I could afford for now."

"No, stop, Jude. I didn't mind coming here at all. And you were right. It was a nice change for me." She returned his smile. "But I have a better idea for a date."

He gave her another heart-warming smile. "What idea is that?"

"I won't tell you now," she said. She reached out to give him a brief hug, but he folded her into his arms and held her for a moment longer than she would normally allow for a first date. She did not pull away, however. Just as he'd mentioned a minute ago, their situation was different.

He pulled back and gave her another smile. "I'll call you tomorrow?"

"Yeah, no problem," she said to him.

Neither of them moved away from the entrance to the fast food restaurant until, at last, Jude chuckled and said, "Goodbye, Sofia. I'll call you tomorrow."

"Yes," she said, smiling. For some reason, she felt an overwhelming urge to take his hand. She resisted the feeling, however, and turned around again. She did not stop smiling as she walked away. For the first time since George broke up with her, she felt lighthearted. She had not expected to enjoy this date with Jude so much.

She was terribly grateful that she liked him, or this arrangement to marry him for a Green card and cash would be totally unbearable to her. She had thought she would be ridden with guilt after this date, but she was not just strangely lighthearted, she also felt hopeful of the future for the first time in a month. That was a good thing. That was a very good thing.

NINE

Sofia laid out the dress she was going to wear for her date with Jude on the bed. She opened her closet again and brought out a pair of black flats with silver and gold embellishments. She turned to the bed and picked up the floral dress she was going to wear for the date and inspected it. She put it back on the bed again.

The preparation for this date was so different from the last. On their first date, she had left off picking the outfit she would wear until about an hour before the date, but for this particular date, she'd picked out her dress after she came back from the first date with Jude.

She put on the dress and went to the mirror to look at her reflection. They were going somewhere casual, and although this dress was appropriate for their casual date, it showed off her every curve, and that was saying a lot as she wasn't exactly curvy. Would Jude think she was trying too hard? She looked closely at herself again and thought about taking the dress off and putting it back into the closet, but she decided to leave it on. It didn't matter if she put in a little more thought into what she wore today, and this dress, even though it was snug, felt just right for the date she had planned for them.

She began to brush her hair and then turned when Edith walked into the room.

"Getting ready for your date with Jude?"

"Yes," Sofia said. She turned to the mirror again and continued brushing her hair. She put it up in a ponytail and then changed her mind and put it down again. Sighing wearily, she turned to Edith, who was sitting on the bed looking at her. She blurted out, "Why am I looking forward to this date with Jude with such eagerness?"

Edith chuckled. 'Why not, Sofia? You're over-thinking this. It's a really good thing that you're looking forward to your date with Jude. Since you're going to marry the guy, it's good that he doesn't repulse you."

Sofia raised her eyebrows. "Repulse me?"

Edith smiled. "I know you, Sofia. Jude is typically not the type of guy you usually go out with, even though he's handsome. Just like you told me the other day, you like much older guys." Her smile widened. "With much more loaded bank accounts than Jude's."

Sofia glowered at her, but said nothing. Edith was talking about George. She blinked. Every single day for a month since she and George had broken up, she'd thought ceaselessly about him and the day he broke up with her. But when was the last time she'd obsessed over him? She knew exactly when. It was two days ago, after her date with Jude. She'd still thought about him, but she had not cried because of him. Somehow, the thought of losing him was not as painful as it had been before her date with Jude. She turned again to Edith and told her what she was thinking.

"That's good," Edith said. "I'm glad Jude is helping you get over your ex." She gave Sofia a mischievous smile.

Sofia frowned. "It's really not what you are thinking, Edith. I've only just met Jude. I think the whole novelty of this arrangement with him, and the fact that we have to get to know each other as much as we can in such a short time, has helped to distract me from focusing so much on George. Nothing more."

"Okay, then," Edith said. "But it's still a good thing that you are not spending your time obsessing over George. Instead you're thinking about Jude."

Sofia wanted to tell Edith once more not to read too much into what she had said about George and Jude, but she changed her mind. It wasn't like Edith really cared about her love life. All she was interested in was pleasing Flynn, who had something to gain by her marrying Jude.

Sofia inspected herself in the mirror again.

Edith walked over, put her hands on Sofia's shoulders and turned her around. She smiled. "You look radiant." She winked at Sofia. "And I thought you didn't care about making a good impression on Jude."

"I don't." Sofia shrugged and walked away from the mirror.

"You don't have to pretend not to care, Sofia. It's okay if you like Jude and want to make a good impression on him."

"I told you I like him, but not in the way you think. I still miss George. Besides, I cannot allow myself to become attached to Jude in any way, especially as we are going to get a divorce after all this is over. I won't forget that, and I hope you don't either."

Edith groaned. "George again!"

"Yes, George," Sofia said.

Edith stared at her. "You still believe he will return to you someday, don't you?"

Sofia shrugged. Edith was partly right. She wasn't exactly confident that George would come back to her, but she was hopeful. She loathed herself for wanting him to come back to her, especially after all he had done — all he'd taken away from her. But she could not help how she felt.

"Maybe you should just give this relationship you have now a chance," Edith said. "Who knows what will develop from it. Maybe you and Jude will develop real feelings for each other."

Sofia chuckled. "That will not happen, Edith. I cannot afford to get my heart attached to Jude's when we both plan to go our separate ways at the end of all this. Besides, he is still in love with his ex."

"And you are still in love with yours."

Sofia grabbed her purse from the bedside table and began to walk out of the room. She frowned when Edith followed her.

"Fine, Sofia. You're not going to allow yourself to develop feelings for Jude, and he is probably only thinking about getting a Green card, but at least try to get to know him as much as you can so this actually works out."

"Isn't that what I am already doing, Edith? I am going out on a date with him today."

"Yes, but don't close your heart to him. Let him in."

"You just said he's probably only thinking about a Green card. Why then should I not guard my heart?"

"Okay. I lied. I think this has the potential to be more than just a business arrangement," Edith said. Sofia sighed in exasperation, and Edith added. "Really, Sofia. I am serious. I like both of you together. Certainly better than your relationship with George. I am just saying that you shouldn't do anything to mess this up, okay?"

"Yes, ma'am," Sofia said. "Is there anything else you'd like to say to me?"

"If he leans in for a kiss after the date, just go with it, Sofia." Edith smiled. "And don't forget to tell me about the date and the kiss."

Sofia shook her head. "There's not going to be a kiss, so get that out of your mind right now." She touched Edith's arm and then, without waiting for Edith to respond, quickly walked to the living room and went out the front door. She sighed with relief when she got out of the house, thankful to escape having to hear more of Edith's unsolicited advice.

She walked in the direction of the park where she and Jude had arranged to meet when he'd called earlier today. She glanced at her wristwatch and blinked. It was still only noon. She was supposed to meet Jude at the park thirty-five minutes from now. She had left the house quickly in order to avoid Edith's continuous prodding.

She turned from the direction of the park and headed to the fast food restaurant she and Jude had gone to. The sun was blazing hot, and she could do with a cold drink right now. Walking briskly, she got to the fast food joint in no time and then went to find a seat at the back. The ones they had sat on their date were taken, so she chose another seat near there. A waiter came, and she began to order a tall glass of lemonade and then changed her mind. "You know what, I'll have a milk shake," she said. "And a double cheeseburger." She had not had any of these in a long time. George loved her very slim figure, and she'd tried her best not to add any weight in order to please him. Now they were not together anymore, she could have a burger... at least this once. The waiter began to walk away and she called back to him. "And fries," she said.

He nodded and left.

She felt slightly guilty as she waited for her order. And then smothered the guilt. Why couldn't she have a burger and milkshake once in a while? George was not here telling her how he loved her figure, how he hoped she stayed the same for him.

She pictured Jude in her mind. What kind of girl did he really like? Did he like the way she looked, or was she not his type?

She groaned. What did it matter what kind of girl he was attracted to? *Focus, Sofia. Remember what this arrangement is for.*

Her phone rang, and she dug through her purse to find it. Her heart flooded with excitement as she gazed at the screen. *Lily!* She immediately answered. "How are you, stranger?" she said. "How I have missed you!"

Lily laughed. "Have you really, Sofia? Didn't you tell me you were preparing for a trip soon? Knowing you, you are probably back from that and already getting ready for another one."

Sofia's heart sank. She would not be taking any more trips abroad. Those days were over. She usually took trips abroad with George, but sometimes she'd gone alone when he couldn't. However, he'd paid for all her trips. Now that he was not in her life anymore, there would be no more traveling to exotic destinations.

"Sofia, are you still there?" Lily asked.

Sofia injected a smile into her voice, ignored Lily's questions, and said, "How was your honeymoon? Did you guys have a great time, you and Taylor?" A small ache rose in her, mixed with a thread of envy. Still, it surprised her that she did not feel as bad as she'd thought she would when she finally had a chance to speak to Lily. She had thought the pain of her break up with George would increase when she spoke to Lily, considering her friend had gone on her honeymoon with her brand new husband. But it did not feel so bad.

"Our honeymoon has been awesome so far and we're still traveling, Sofia. We are not yet back."

"Oh, I thought your honeymoon had ended," Sofia said. "That's nice, Lily." Her heart ached as she remembered the day she'd tried to kill herself after George broke up with her. She had tried to call Lily without success. Perhaps if Lily had been there, she would not have done what she did.

Tell her what happened, Sofia.

She opened her mouth to tell Lily about her suicide attempt and then changed her mind. It might actually make her feel worse if she told Lily about her break up with George and Lily told her it was good riddance to bad rubbish. Not only had Lily not been a fan of her relationship with George because George was married, Lily had been so against the relationship that she had moved out of the apartment when George had come to spend the week.

"Sofia, is there something you're not telling me?" Lily asked. "You're not as talkative as you normally are."

Sofia laughed to cover up her roiling thoughts and said, "There isn't much going on in my life right now to talk about." It was a blatant lie of course, as there was a lot going on in her life, but she was definitely not going to tell Lily about it. She knew exactly what Lily would say about her arrangement with Jude and their proposed marriage. Lily would say it was wrong. She already knew what she was doing was wrong, but she did not want to hear it right now. Aside from the fact that she needed the money it would bring her, she liked Jude. She wanted to help him settle down in this country instead of leaving him to go back to his country, which, from all he'd told her, was a dangerous place to live in now. But Lily would not see it that way.

"Sofia? Are you still there?"

"Yes, I'm still here, Lily," she answered. She thanked the waiter when he brought her food and then said to Lily, "Tell me about your honeymoon. I want to hear everything that's happened so far."

"It's been great," Lily said.

"Is that all you're going to tell me about it?" Sofia smiled.

Lily giggled. "It's a secret."

In spite of herself, Sofia could not help laughing. "Well then, I'm glad you're having a great time with Taylor. Send my greetings to him." Her mind went to Lily's new husband, the handsome Taylor Dalton. He was everything a woman could dream of, Lily had told her before she met Taylor. When she'd met him, she had agreed to an extent. But she didn't like what most women did. Taylor was financially successful, which she liked, but he was too young and a bit too pretty. She did not want to have to compete with a guy when it came to physical looks.

And yet you're planning to marry exactly that. A pretty boy who is about your age.

Once again, she felt like telling Lily about Jude, but she held back the words forming on her lips. She continued to listen as Lily, in a voice full of excitement, told her about the places she and Taylor had already been and the places they were soon going to visit.

Lily sighed loudly. "Unfortunately, we will soon have to return to Fallow Creek because of the kids. We have to pick them up from Taylor's sister's house and then head back to California because Josh starts school soon."

"Josh?"

"Yes, Sofia. I told you about him. My stepson."

"Oh… yeah. You did." Sofia chuckled. "The one who doesn't like you."

"Sofia! He likes me now. He just really missed his mom and was afraid I would steal his father's attention away from him."

"So you are both good now?"

"Yes."

"And what about Taylor's business?"

Lily answered, "He took a break for our honeymoon, but he has to start working soon."

Sofia completely forgot about her sadness over her breakup with George as she remembered that Lily had been searching for her family. She asked, "What about your parents and sister, Lily? Have you guys found them?"

For a brief moment, Lily did not answer, and then she said in an emotion-filled voice, "We haven't found them yet, but we will continue to search for them."

"I'm so sorry, Lily."

"It's okay. I believe we will find them eventually. I won't give up searching for them, and Taylor is determined to find them as well."

Sofia liked the firm determination in Lily's voice. If only she could have as much faith as Lily did that everything would work out for her.

You know where that faith comes from, don't you? a voice in her heart whispered.

She shut out the voice and said, "When will you come and visit me, Lily? And by the way, what country are you in now?"

Lily chuckled. "We are in Greece now, specifically Santorini." She paused for a second and then said, "Taylor says hi. He went to get us some food, but he is back now."

"I'm super envious of you guys," Sofia said. She was not really envious of the fact that her friend was in Santorini or travelling the world. What she was envious of was that Lily was doing all that with the man she loved.

"And what about George?" Lily asked, sounding

hesitant. "You're still together?"

Sofia's heart skipped a beat. Did Lily know they had broken up? But how could she? *Calm down, Sofia.* Lily was probably just speaking her mind. As always, she clearly hoped they had broken up. She didn't know for a fact that they actually had.

"Sofia? Did you hear me?"

"Yeah, George is good," she said, and then changed the subject. "I asked when you're coming to visit me, Lily."

"I'm not sure when I can come to Tucson next. Our trip to Fallow Creek will be super quick as we will only be picking up Taylor's kids. It will probably be when Taylor is able to get away from California, or maybe when he has some business in Tucson. We'll probably stay at the apartment, and then we can get to see each other as much as we want, Sofia. That is if George is not around. We can have a mani-pedi party. I hate being away from Taylor, but maybe we can have an early afternoon party, and then I will go back to my husband."

Sofia sighed. Talking to Lily had made her partly forget how dire her situation really was. Lily thought she still lived in the luxury apartment building George had rented for her. Taylor had bought one of the two penthouse apartments for Lily before they'd gotten married.

She did not know what to say to Lily, but finally said, "A mani-pedi party sounds like fun, Lily."

"Yes." Lily giggled. She whispered something to someone and then said, "I've gotta go, Sofia. I hope I'm able to talk to you soon. We usually don't have phone service on the ship."

Before Sofia could say anything more, Lily hung

up.

Sofia lowered her phone and sighed. It was good to talk to Lily again. Her friend was having the time of her life with her new husband.

Once again, Jude's face appeared in Sofia's mind. Soon he would be her husband, even though it would not exactly be a real marriage. She shut her eyes briefly as she imagined with worry what Lily would say when she found out, and how different Lily's advice would be from Edith's. Guilt tugged at her heart.

You already know what advice Lily would give you, Sofia. Whose advice should you listen to? Edith's or Lily's?

She bit her lip and looked down at her burger and milkshake, which she'd almost forgotten now. Edith was brash, sometimes uncaring, recently unscrupulous, and her motives for the advice she'd given Sofia about marrying Jude were not exactly selfless. Lily had always been selfless. Even when they'd lived together, she was as caring as a good mother and as honest as they came.

Sofia knew exactly whose advice she was supposed to listen to. And yet, she had already made up her mind on the path was going to take.

She glanced at her wristwatch and gasped. *Oh no! What am I still doing here? I will be late for my date with Jude.* He was probably already waiting at the park for her.

She stood up, paid for her half-eaten food, and hurried out of the restaurant.

TEN

"Jude, come on now, man. I know the girl is not your type, but you have to admit she is very pretty," Ben said, putting his hand on Jude's shoulder. "It should not be so difficult for you to get to know her as well as you can and to marry her."

"I didn't say she wasn't pretty..."

"So you admit that she is pretty," Ben said, and then plopped down on the couch. They were in Jude and Samuel's apartment. Samuel, who was in his final year at the university, was attending classes, and only Jude and Ben were in the apartment. Jude sat down beside Ben and looked at him. "It doesn't matter if she's pretty or not. You know it's simply a business arrangement and nothing more. I can't afford to start thinking about how she looks or how her eyes sparkle when she's listening to what I am saying or how soft her skin looks..." He immediately stopped talking at the look on Ben's face and groaned.

Ben laughed. "Jude, you are already smitten, aren't you?"

"Smitten! Did I tell you I was smitten? No, I am not smitten, Ben. I'm just stating the fact. She is very pretty, but just as you said, she's not my type, and after all this is over, we will go our separate ways. I cannot allow myself to have any feelings for her. I don't even think we can be friends after I get my Green card. So I have to be careful. We will probably not even see each other again once all this is over."

Keziah appeared in his mind. He thought about her every time he was talking to someone about marrying Sofia. They would be married now if she had not broken off their engagement. He sighed and pushed her image out of his mind. He focused his thoughts again on Sofia. She was the one he was going to marry, and he really had to get to know her. She had called to tell him to meet her at the park some distance away from the house. Samuel had promised to come back before the time he was supposed to get there and drive him to the park. He looked again at the clock on the wall and frowned. "Where is Samuel? Why is he not back yet?"

"Maybe you should just go, Jude. You will be late for your date."

Jude groaned. "I've been waiting for so long that time has flown by. If I leave now, I might not get a taxi quickly, and then I will get to the park really late. I think I should wait at least five minutes more and see if Samuel comes back."

Ben's eyes searched his. "Wait, Jude! Are you sure you're not stalling?"

"Why would I stall?" Jude asked. "I have everything to lose if this date doesn't ultimately end in marriage."

"Yes, Jude, including your heart."

"What does that mean?"

"It means that, just like you said earlier, you are afraid to get attached to Sofia. I think you are developing feelings for her, and maybe you're unconsciously trying to stamp out those feelings by being late for your date so she thinks less of you."

"It's a good theory, but how will that stamp out whatever feelings you think I am developing for her?" Jude asked, amused.

"When she is angry with you for coming late to your date and curses you out, you'll end up fighting, and then all the feelings you have for her go out the window, just like that."

"You're crazy," Jude laughed, but he could not help wondering if there was some truth to what Ben had said. There was a huge part of him that not only knew that if he became attached to Sofia, his heart would be broken once they went their separate ways, but was also still slightly uncomfortable with their arrangement as it was not exactly legal. Maybe he was just self-sabotaging.

He stood up. The last thing he would allow to happen was for him to be deported back to Bakali, especially as the country wasn't safe anymore. The violence was getting worse every day. These days, he tried to block out any news of his country because it troubled him greatly. He could not go back there. He wanted to remain here, and he would do whatever he had to in order to make that happen.

"I'm leaving now," he said to Ben.

"Good," Ben smiled. "Remember to be the charming guy I know you can be. Make a great impression on her."

Jude walked to the door and then turned back to look at Ben. "I already made a great impression on our first date," he said laughing. He left the apartment, got out his phone, and called an Uber. He waited and waited for his Uber to arrive outside the apartment, but it curiously didn't. Glancing at his wristwatch, he saw he was already late and sighed. Just as he was about to call another taxi, his arrived. He got in and took a deep breath as his heart raced with worry and impatience.

As the car sped down the road, he thought about what Ben had said. He'd told him to make a good impression on Sofia. To make this work. It was the direct opposite of what his dad would have said if he were still alive. In fact, if his dad were alive and found out he was involved in this fake marriage arrangement, he would have thrown a fit.

"Dad, I miss you," he whispered, and looked out the window as the car navigated traffic. If his father were here, he probably would not be doing this anyway. And yet he was glad he had met Sofia, even if it was under some unconventional circumstances.

"You're smitten," Ben had said. He definitely wasn't, but he liked her very much. They had a lot in common, and she was easy to talk to. And yes, she was very pretty. But he definitely wasn't smitten.

He alighted from the Uber when he got to the park, paid his fare, and then trekked through the manicured grass until he found Sofia some distance away from him. She was sitting under a tree, her slim elegant legs crossed. She looked radiant in her floral dress, her dark hair falling in luxurious waves around her face. His heart skipped a beat as he neared her, and he frowned. She turned and gave him a smile that caused his pulse to race, and he sighed. *Be careful, Jude. Don't get attached.*

She stood up when he got to her and, without thinking, he reached out and gave her a tight hug. A sweet floral fragrance filled his nose, and he breathed it in deeply. She smelled as delightful as she looked. He pulled away, and his eyes swept over her. Before he could stop himself, he said, "You look absolutely beautiful, Sofia."

She grinned at him. "Thank you."

"I'm so sorry I'm late," he said. "My ride skipped town."

She raised her brows. "Your ride skipped town?"

He chuckled. "My friend Samuel was supposed to give me a ride here, but he did not appear at the apartment. Maybe someone captured him and tied him up somewhere."

Sofia blinked, and then she laughed when he gave her a corny smile.

He laughed along with her and said, "I hope I did not keep you waiting for too long."

"No, Jude. I really haven't been waiting for so long. Time ran away from me as well, and I've only been here for about six minutes." She smiled. "Let's go."

She began to walk, and he followed her. "So where is this secret place we're going?" he asked.

She gave him a small smile. "The only thing I can tell you is 'fresh fruit.'"

"Fresh fruit! What does that even mean? Is that a code for something?"

"Come on, Jude!" she said with mirth in her voice, and began to walk even faster. He matched her stride, and they walked to the road and then to the bus stop. When they settled in a bus to take them to wherever it was they were going, Sofia turned to Jude and said, "I cannot remember the last time I got onto a bus. I used to take a bus to where we are going with friends years ago." She had a wistful look on her face as she gazed out of the window. "I miss those days."

He tried to ignore the almost overwhelming urge he felt to touch her. She was sitting right next to him, and it would be so easy to reach out and tuck the wayward strand of hair whipping across her face behind her ears. He smothered the urge to do so and said with a smile, "I'm glad our date has introduced you to a couple of firsts, even a first in years." He studied her face. She didn't seem to be wearing a stitch of makeup, though he wasn't sure about that. What he was certain of was that she looked breathtaking and he could not take his eyes off her. "Where are we going exactly?" he asked. "Won't you tell me, Sofia?"

"Nope!" she smiled at him and then looked away again.

He turned away, but he could not keep his gaze away from her for long and looked at her again. She was still staring out the window. His eyes stayed on her shiny dark hair for a minute, and then it settled on her cheek. He threaded his fingers together so he would not reach out and caress it.

A smile tugged at her lips, and he wondered what she was thinking about. Everything about her looked like she was a girl from a privileged background, and yet he knew from what she'd told him that she wasn't. He could tell that she had definitely been exposed to a measure of luxury that he had never known, but clearly it had all been taken away because she was here with him. She still looked as luxurious as they came with her shiny, long hair, super smooth skin, and delicate figure. She started to turn around, and he quickly averted his gaze.

The bus ride took about half an hour. They alighted from the bus and walked side by side in a leisurely stride. She slowed some more as they continued to walk and, again, he matched her pace. He asked her where they were going, but she only smiled. Their shoulders and arms were only inches apart, and it took everything in him not to take her hand.

He lifted his brows as they approached a gate with the words, ABNER'S FRUIT FARM, engraved on it. Below were the words, 'pick your own fruit'. He turned to her, surprised, and said, "A farm? We are going to that farm?"

"Yes," she said in an amused voice.

He looked up at the sun. It was shining down mercilessly. He looked at Sofia again. "Why are we going to a farm, Sofia?"

"It's a pick your own fruit farm."

He chuckled. "I can see that. But why are we going to the farm? It's a blazing hot afternoon, and I am already starting to sweat."

They reached the gate and stood in a short line. A girl dressed in a red T-shirt and blue jeans was standing at the gate, collecting tickets and welcoming people to the farm. A few people had their kids with them. Jude and Sofia reached the girl, and Sofia pulled out two tickets from her purse and handed it to her.

Jude smiled and shook his head. When they went through the gate, he said to Sofia, "So, this is our date." He chuckled again. "You're going to make me work on a farm under the burning sun for our date." He laughed out loud when she nodded.

She took his hand and giggled. "It's a beautiful day, Jude. Come on." She began to skip forward while pulling him along with her.

He smiled, loving this fun-loving and cheery side of her. And to think he had believed the first time he'd met her that she was a brat who spent all day shopping.

They walked by rows and rows of trees and bushes laden with peaches, blackberries, strawberries, and apples. There were people everywhere, adults and children with baskets, plucking the fruits from the trees. Some just ate them, while others concentrated on putting them in the basket. Children ran around playing and laughing, and Jude felt like he could be a child again and join in their play. He turned to Sofia, who had a huge smile on her face as she watched the children running around. "You know... I did not take you for a farm kind of girl."

"I haven't done anything like this in a while, but I grew up in a farming community."

He committed the new information she had just disclosed about herself to his memory. It was another thing about her that he had just learned. "Did you ever come here with your ex?" he asked without thinking, and then immediately regretted asking as her face clouded over.

Before he could apologize and inform her she

didn't need to answer, she said, "George was never interested in this sort of thing. I told him about this place a few times after we met, but he always refused to go with me. He's definitely not a farm kind of guy."

Jude nodded, and his mind went to Keziah again. He did not know exactly how she would have felt about a date on a farm since they'd grown up in the city. But he had a niggling suspicion that she would not enjoy it as much as he was.

Is it really the farm you enjoy or Sofia's company?

Maybe both. Or maybe it was her presence that made everything seem so fun. Made him forget he had any kind of problems.

She began to talk about her ex again, and he sighed warily. He had thought she was through talking about the guy considering how sad she had looked when he'd brought him up. He should never have asked her about him.

Sofia said, "George was the one who introduced me to the finer things of life, like dining in the best restaurants, flying to different countries in business and first class, and staying in the best hotels." She shook her head and then looked at him. She looked like she was just emerging from a trance. She began to walk again and said, "Come on Jude. Let's go and get some baskets from that house. The earlier we start picking fruit, the better. We want to gather as much as possible before this place closes for the day."

They made their way to a small building that had a signboard in front with the words, *Abner's Blackberry and Strawberry Pies*, written on it. As soon as they entered the building, the tantalizing aroma of a variety of pies filled his nostrils, and Jude smiled.

"When we finish picking our fruits, we can come back here to get some pies," Sofia said, looking in the direction of the glass display where rows and rows of mouth-watering pies were sitting.

They picked up two baskets beside the entrance and walked out of the building again. They walked through rows of celery and broccoli and lettuce and finally reached the fruit trees. Sofia stopped in front of a row of bushes with strawberries so red and plump that Jude instantly reached out, plucked a couple, and popped them into his mouth.

A group of children ranging from about four to six years ran past Jude, laughing and playing, and Sofia's eyes followed them. She watched them with a wistful look on her face. When she turned back to him, he said "You like children."

She nodded but said nothing else about it.

He could not help wondering, as they plucked strawberries and then blackberries, what Sofia was thinking now; what more was hidden behind those long lashes. He wanted to know everything about her — all her trials and sorrows, her triumphs and joys. What exactly made her happy or sad.

Remember to guard your heart, Jude.

He dismissed his concerns. He was guarding his heart. But he had to know everything about her if they were going to pass the immigration interview when the time came. Fear suddenly gripped his heart as he thought about his immigration status. Yesterday, he'd heard again about a friend's relative who was deported. He was beginning to be extra cautious whenever he went out, afraid that at any time he would be apprehended and deported. Right now, he was ripe for ICE's plucking, just like the fruits they were plucking from the bushes.

Sofia reached out, plucked a particularly plump strawberry, and bit into it. For a moment, he forgot about his fears and watched her eat the strawberry, mesmerized. And then he blinked. *What is wrong with you, Jude?* He forced his eyes away from her, picked off a blackberry from another bush, and put it in his basket.

Sofia pranced from one bush to another, excitedly picking off fruit and putting them into her basket or eating them, a smile on her face. He tried not to watch her so intently, but he couldn't take his eyes off her. Maybe Ben was right. Maybe he *was* smitten.

But that was not a good thing. *I cannot be smitten.* He could not afford to risk his heart that way. This date was supposed to be about getting to know each other better so they could be convincing at their immigration interview. Nothing more.

She looked up at him just as a light breeze blew her hair across her face. She smoothed her hair back, tucked it behind her ear, and grinned at him, causing his heart to thud.

He sighed. Ben was definitely right. He was smitten.

He held back a groan. So much for guarding his heart. He hadn't done a very good job of it. He had to reign in his emotions now, because it would be devastating if he allowed himself to fall for Sofia knowing full well that they were going to get a divorce once he got his Green card. Even if by then he decided he didn't want a divorce, it was unlikely he could keep Sofia from getting one. And it would be wrong to try.

A little girl with pigtails came skipping in between them, her mother behind her. The little girl threw Sofia a smile, and Sofia smiled back. When they had passed by, Sofia looked at him, a wistful expression on her face.

He pressed his lips together as he gazed at her. What was she thinking about now? Maybe she was thinking about the kids she'd wanted to have with her ex. She'd probably been planning to build a family with the man. She clearly liked children, and it was clear she wanted a family of her own. Was their future marriage and his quest for a Green card going to prolong that desire? Would it keep her from her dream, even if for a short time?

Guilt flooded him, and he exhaled and pushed the guilty feeling away. He and Sofia would not be married for long. And then she could go ahead and find someone to have kids with.

The thought of her having children with another man made him sick with jealousy. *Maybe we could have children together after we get married.*

This time he groaned loudly. *Get yourself together, man.* What was he thinking? He was letting his imagination run away from him. This was nothing but a business arrangement. There would be no children involved. In fact, nothing would be involved except the reason why they were getting married, which was to help each other. She would help him get a Green card, and he would pay for that help so she could start her life over again.

He watched her again. Even though he had to keep in mind that this thing between them was just a business deal, he still wanted to find out everything he could about her. There was much more to know about her than what she had told him, especially concerning her break up with her ex. He could not wait to get to know her even better. Before he could ask her how she came to live with Edith and that scoundrel Flynn, she said, "Jude, could you tell me more about your relationship with your ex?"

He blinked and stared at her. Keziah was the last person he wanted to talk about right now, especially with Sofia. He sighed warily and looked away.

ELEVEN

Sofia watched Jude's countenance change. The smile melted off his face, and for a long moment, he didn't look at her.

"If you don't want to talk about your ex right now, I understand," she said softly.

He turned to face her again. "No, you need to know everything. That's why we are going on these dates, isn't it?"

She said nothing but kept looking intently at him.

"Keziah and I met in secondary school, what you Americans call high school." He had a faraway look on his face as his spoke. "Just like me, she was a pastor's kid, and her parents sent her to the high school I was already attending because it was a Christian school, and a good school too. She had been in another school, but transferred to mine in what you would call the tenth grade. Even though she was the new kid, she was vibrant and exuberant, and she soon became very popular. I, on the other hand, was very reserved and stayed away from the popular kids. Believe it or not, I was very quiet and shy in high school."

She chuckled. "No, I believe it. I can see you as the handsome, brooding guy who all the girls wanted but knew to stay away from because you just weren't interested in any of them."

He smiled and shook his head. "I don't know if you are just teasing me or being serious."

Sofia laughed softly but didn't say anything else. He continued, and she smiled as she listened to him talk about the popular and unpopular kids in his school. She was surprised at how similar his high school experience was to hers despite the fact that he'd lived in a country she'd never heard of until recently. She chuckled and said, "I guess kids are sort of the same no matter what country they live in."

He nodded and went on. "I had noticed Keziah a few times and was attracted to her, but so were a host of other boys in the school. Because of that, I did not think I had any chance with her. One day, I was walking down the hallway when I saw her walking toward me with a group of her friends. I tried not to look at her and kept my eyes averted because I didn't want to get mixed up with the popular kids and their problems. I was surprised when I felt someone come alongside me and turned to find she was the one. She kept walking beside me as though we were longtime friends who were just taking a stroll together. I remember the huge smile on her face, as though she had a secret that we both shared.

Sofia could not help grinning. She could imagine the look on his face when his crush began to walk down the hallway with him. "What did you say to her?"

"I was too dumbfounded to speak, and she didn't say anything to me. We just kept walking until I got to my locker. I felt awkward as I opened it because I could not think of anything to say. Everything in me was screaming for me to talk to her, to ask her out, but I could not bring myself to say the words."

Sofia laughed. "It reminds me of the first day we met."

He chuckled. "You're right. I felt almost the same way."

Sofia arched her brows. He had not been able to speak to Keziah because he had a huge crush on her, but did he feel the same way about her? Was that why he had said nothing for a long time that day. She had noticed how uncomfortable he'd been that day, and she'd been nervous as well, but now she wondered if his nervousness was because he'd liked her even though they'd just met. She sighed softly and forced herself to focus on his story again.

"I kept bringing out my textbooks and notebooks from my locker and putting them in my bag while I scolded myself for not having anything to say. Finally, I forced myself to speak. The thing is I cannot even remember what I said, but I know it was something stupid and incoherent."

"And did she say anything to you after that?" Sofia asked.

"She smiled brightly, and I remember my heart racing, and then she said I was very handsome and asked what my name was."

"Wow, she's a bold girl! At that age, I would have died rather than reveal to a boy I liked that I was into him."

Jude smiled. "That was Keziah. Very bold. When I told her my name, she asked if we could start hanging out every day."

Sofia smiled again as he continued. "I nodded dumbly, and I thought she was going to walk away, but she did not. She stood there talking to me and asking me a lot of questions until I opened up and finally became comfortable with her. Soon we became best friends."

"Friends," Sofia said. "So you did not start dating immediately?"

"No, our parents were very strict and did not allow either of us to date. We were not allowed to do anything about our clearly growing feelings for each other. But two years later, I finally asked Keziah out. That was in our final year of high school. When she said yes, I was ecstatic. We were inseparable and when our parents finally found out about us. They didn't make much of a fuss, which was surprising at first. But I later found out that they knew each other, as they were in the same ministry circles. Anyway, before we graduated high school, Keziah and I were already talking about getting married."

"And did you get engaged right after high school?" Sofia asked.

"Yes, but it was a private engagement. We were too young, at least in the eyes of the adults at that time, to be engaged. But it didn't stop us. It was around that time that Keziah's desire to immigrate to America became obsessive. She talked non-stop about it and constantly said she wanted to go to the US for college. I immediately wanted the same thing — not because I was particularly interested but because I did not want to be separated from her. However, her parents could not afford to send her to America to study. She tried to get funding and a scholarship, but it just didn't work out. We both went to different universities in our country but managed to stay in touch, and our relationship continued. Immediately after university, we announced to everyone that we wanted to get married and our parents were pleased."

Once again sadness overtook his face.

"We planned to get married in a few months and began to prepare for the wedding, but then I noticed that Keziah became more and more distant. Whenever I asked her what was wrong, she said it was nothing. She was just stressed out from the wedding planning. Soon, I noticed that she was disinterested even in the wedding planning, and I had to pick up a lot of things that she did not do. I became more and more worried, but I decided to believe that stress was why she stopped answering my calls. And then two weeks before the wedding, like I told you before, she broke everything off. It was one of the worst days of my life, probably the worst, except for the death of my parents."

"And when exactly did you find out that she'd left for America?" Sofia asked, her heart breaking for him.

"A few months later. The most heart-rending thing was hearing that she left to be with some guy who lived in America and was a citizen. She left on a fiancé visa, and the last I heard, they were married."

Sofia felt like reaching out and hugging him.

He had already told her some of what he'd just narrated, but now that she knew the full story, she understood why he'd said he still thought about his ex every day. He looked devastated. "I'm sorry, Jude. But she did not deserve you. You deserve much better. Someone who will love you no matter what." She remembered what he had told her days ago, that he had come to America partly because he had an impossible hope of seeing his ex again.

A weird feeling ran through her, and she frowned as she tried to pinpoint what it was. Was it jealousy she was feeling? And why was she jealous of his ex? The girl was not in his life anymore and, even if she appeared today, Sofia had no hold on him. She would be happy for him if he was happy his ex was back in his life. She liked him, but she could not afford to feel anything more for him. That would be asking for trouble.

She pushed away the confusing thoughts and changed the subject. "I'm hungry, Jude. I think we should go to that pie place and get something to eat."

The sadness on his face immediately lifted, and he smiled brightly at her. "That's a good idea," he said.

They made their way to the building where they sold the delicious-looking pies that had caused her mouth to water earlier on. They sat in the middle of the place with a few other guests — couples and families who had come to pick fruit from the farm. They both ordered blueberry pies and tall glasses of iced tea and tucked in.

Sofia began to tell him about her travels as she relished her pie. Soon they switched to talking about the fruit they had picked and how delicious and fresh it was. From time to time, her eyes went to the mounted TV on the wall. The sound was muted, but it was on a news channel and she wasn't particularly interested in what they were showing.

She continued to chat with Jude as they ate, and then she frowned slightly as her gaze fell on the TV screen again. They were now reporting on foreign news and, for a few seconds, she watched the images of burning cars and blown up houses, weeping women and children. And then she looked away and focused her attention on Jude, who had his back to the TV set.

A minute later, something else caught her attention on the television screen, and she glanced once more at it. She shuddered and her breath caught in her throat. Scrolling beneath the frightening images of violence were the words, "COUNTRY OF BAKALI IN FULL-BLOWN WAR."

She took hold of Jude's hand, but before she could stop him from looking at the horrid images from his country, he turned around. She immediately squeezed his hand. When he turned around again, he had a haunted look on his face.

"I'm so sorry, Jude," she said, searching his eyes. He bowed his head, and her heart broke for him again. Threading her fingers through his on the table, she watched him with tears in her eyes.

For a long moment, neither of them spoke. She kept squeezing his hand to show him she was here for him, even though she didn't know exactly what to say to comfort him. Thankfully, the news on TV about his country's frightful state had been removed, and a talk show was now on.

"I'm so sorry," she whispered again.

He finally looked up at her and gave a long, agonized sigh. "They are destroying everything," he said, his voice mixed with anger and sorrow. "It's not enough for them to take power — they have to destroy everything and everyone. Because of them, I don't have my father anymore, and they took friends of mine as well. Young men who all had a bright future."

She didn't know what to say to that. She had never followed the violence in his country. Until she met him, she hadn't even known such a country existed. The worst thing was that his father was one of the casualties of the senseless violence going on there. She could only imagine what was spinning through his mind. It was not just that his country was at war, but he had lost his father and friends because of it. She wanted to weep as he held his head in his hands, but she had to be strong for him.

"Jude, I cannot say I know how you're feeling, but know that I'll always be here for you."

He lifted his eyes and looked at her. "Thank you," he said, and gave her a sad smile.

She searched his eyes again. Seeing the sorrow and hurt in them filled her with pain. The images he had seen were heartbreaking. He couldn't go back there. She could not allow it. If he was deported, he might not survive for long.

"Jude, we should get married as soon as possible," she said. "You need to get your Green card quickly."

He gazed at her, his eyes boring into hers, and then grimaced.

She frowned, worried. "I'm sorry, Jude. I didn't mean to push you to get married sooner than we planned. I just thought, because of what we saw, it would be the best thing to do so you can get your Green card immediately. If that is not what you want..."

He shook his head. "No... I mean, yes. Of course it's what I want, Sofia. It's just that... I don't have the rest of the money to pay you yet."

She shrugged. "I don't care about that. You cannot go back to your country. Your life would be in danger. We can get married now, and then you can come up with the money later."

"Shaffar will not let us get married until I pay the money I owe," he said. "I gave him less than what he asked for the first installment. I doubt he will let us get married when I don't have the pre-wedding amount I owe him."

"Shaffar is not the one getting married to you. I am. We will get married now, whether you have the money or not," she said.

He looked overcome with emotion and gazed at their joined hands. She had forgotten that she was still holding his hand. She started to pull her hand away, but he held on. "You'll really do that for me?" he asked.

"Of course I will," she said.

He smiled widely. "Thank you, Sofia." His smile faded some, and he asked, "Are you sure it's what you want?"

"Very sure, Jude."

They began to eat their pies again as they talked about how and when she would file for his Adjustment of Status once they were married. Sofia knew very little of the process, if anything, and Jude did not know much about it either. But he knew more than she did. He told her that they would fill out separate forms and then be given a date to appear for the interview.

They talked about the kinds of questions they might be asked at the interview and even had a few laughs as Jude brought up one silly question after another.

"What is the name of your wife's sister's husband's father's child's friend's son?"

"Jude, stop it!" Sofia laughed. "How many strands of hair are on your wife's head?"

Jude did not laugh or even smile, and she said, "Well so much for trying to be funny."

"No," he smiled. "It's not that you weren't funny. It's just that it's so strange hearing those words. Your wife." His smile widened as he gazed into her eyes, causing her heart to skip a beat. "Imagine, we will be married soon and you will be my wife."

She studied him as he gazed at her. What was he thinking? Was he thinking about his ex? About the fact that his ex had been the girl he really wanted to marry — and from all he'd said — probably the girl he still wanted to marry but would never be able to?

Another thread of jealousy ran through Sofia, and she suppressed a groan. She had to remember why she was doing this. She sighed. It was supposed to be for the money, and yet she had told him she did not care about the money. And right at this time it was totally true. All she cared about was for him to be safe.

Is that really all, Sofia?

Once again, she pushed away the troubling thoughts in her mind and then turned her eyes away from Jude.

They finished eating their pies, and the waiter came and cleared away their table. They both remained in their seats as they continued to talk about their friends. She told him a bit more about Edith and then about Lily. He told her with an expression that held both amusement and what looked like shame about the parties and drunken fêtes he'd attended or held at his off-campus apartment.

"I could drink everyone under the table," he said, and then shook his head. "What am I saying? Samuel and my other friends will tell you that I probably still can. I partied months away in school, and I think that was why I did not pay particular attention to my immigration status. The day a friend of mine came to tell me that one of our mutual friends had been deported, I decided to slow down on all that partying. I leave it all to Samuel and the other guys now." He looked embarrassed, and she gave him a smile to know she was not judging him.

"I've had my own share of wild partying and just plain foolishness," she said. Once again, she thought of telling him about her suicide attempt, but she changed her mind. She just didn't feel comfortable telling him about that yet or the fact that George was married.

George! She hadn't really thought about him for the past few days. What was he doing now? He was probably with his wife, bowing to her every wish. She pushed George out of her mind and glanced at her wristwatch.

"Jude! We've been here for too long. I think it's time to go." She smiled at him and started to rise from her seat, then sat down again when he shook his head.

"We don't have to go now, do we?" he asked. "Do you have any other plans for this evening?"

She leaned back in her seat and shook her head. "I guess not," she said and smiled, pleasantly surprised that he wanted their date to go on.

He smiled back at her. "Well, since we are fast-tracking this relationship and we have to get to know as much of each other as we can, I suggest we play a game."

She stared at him and then chuckled. "A game? What kind of game?"

"I'll ask as many questions as I can about you. Rapid questions that you will have to answer in less than three minutes. Are you up for it?"

"Sure," she smiled.

He shot her one rapid question after another, and she tried to keep up. They were mostly fun, silly questions, like how many toothbrushes she had used in the past three months and whether she said bless you when someone sneezed. After some time, she laughed. "Jude! These questions are silly! Nobody is going to ask them, and they are unimportant."

He laughed, and she shook her head.

"We need to ask important questions," she said. "Maybe questions like what your favorite color is, or your best friend's last name."

"Okay then," he said, grumbling playfully. "If we must be so serious."

She laughed again. "They are not super serious questions." She searched her mind briefly for what to ask and said, "Okay, I'll begin." She asked him what his favorite movie was. He told her he liked the Transformers franchise. After that, he asked her what the name of her first child would be if she had a child now. She told him she had way too many names she'd picked out already and had never been able to settle on one.

Soon she was asking about his family and more serious questions. He shied away from none, answering every one of them. He also asked her similar questions. When he began to ask about George again, she grew slightly uncomfortable. She was even less willing to tell him that George was married now that she knew him better than when they had first met. She had not been exactly sure why earlier, but now she knew. She liked him a lot and she wanted him to think well of her. Knowing that she had dated a married man would probably not put her in his good books. It surprised her that she thought this way, especially since she had never really cared what anyone thought about her relationship with George, not even Lily.

She looked up when a full-bodied, kind-looking older woman walked up to them and told them hesitantly that she had to close up the place. Sofia looked around and blinked in surprise. Everyone had cleared out. She and Jude were the only ones here. She looked at him and he looked just as surprised as she was. She said to the woman who she was sure owned the place, "We are sorry. We will be on our way now."

The woman gave her a warm smile. "No problem. We close everyday by seven p.m., but we will be open tomorrow, and you are both welcome then." She walked away, and Sofia looked at her watch.

"It's seven o'clock already!" Jude said.

She nodded. They stood up, and she grabbed their basket of berries from the floor. A waiter had been kind enough to help them pack the berries into plastic boxes and wrap them with clear plastic before placing them in the basket again.

Jude took the basket of berries from her as they left the pie place. They walked through the farm together in silence, heading toward the gate. The place was mostly empty now except for a few people who were walking out of the gate. Once they were outside the gate, she reached out and hugged him. When she pulled back, he took her hands and stared into her eyes. Once again, her heart skipped a beat as his eyes searched hers. Without meaning to, her gaze settled on his lips and her mind filled with a picture of them kissing. She immediately pressed the image out of her mind and silently chided herself.

"Thank you, Sofia," he said, still staring into her eyes, his hands in hers.

"Can I ask when exactly you want us to get married?" she asked without thinking, and then hid a groan. Just days ago, she was dreading this arrangement, now she could not wait to marry him, an almost complete stranger. She had only known him for a few days. What was wrong with her? And what would Jude think of her?

He smiled broadly. "Whenever you want, Sofia."

"And do you want a big wedding ceremony so we can invite some friends, or should we just go to the court house alone?"

He answered, "We will do anything you want. You can choose a date you want us to get married and the venue, too." He smiled. "I'm just happy you want us to do it now."

"No, Jude. You choose the date."

He shook his head. "No, I want you to. It's your right, Sofia."

"Okay, then," she said. "We can get married next Friday." She inwardly winced. That was just a week from now. Would he think her too forward? But then, she wanted them to get married as soon as possible to keep him here in this country; to keep him safe. She hoped he would see that was why she wanted them to get married as soon as possible and not for some other reason.

Like the fact that you are falling for him?

She frowned and dismissed the stupid thought from her mind.

"Thank you." He smiled, still looking into her eyes. He lifted both her hands to his lips and kissed the back of her fingers. "Thank you, Sofia," he said again.

For a long moment, she did not know what to say. Her heart pounded as she gazed at him. Finally, he let go of her hand, and she sighed.

"So, can I see you again tomorrow?" he asked.

"Yes," she said, and then added, "But we should apply for a marriage license now."

"Okay. We can do that tomorrow or the day after." He reached out and touched her cheek lightly and then turned and walked away.

She watched him as he strode away, her emotions roiling. His spicy scent surrounded her, and she could still feel the imprint of his fingers on her cheek. *Get yourself together Sofia.* She exhaled, turned around, and walked in the other direction

TWELVE

"Jude, stop lying, man!" Samuel said, as he sat on the sofa and shook his head.

"I am not lying," Jude said. "I'm getting married in a week, Samuel." Jude plopped down beside his friend and sighed. "Why would I make up something like this?"

Samuel glared at him. "Who are you marrying? How come I have never met her?"

"You have been too busy partying and drinking to care what I've been up to," Jude grinned.

"So, tell me what you have been up to, Jude!" Samuel said. "I want to hear it all."

"Okay, but it's a long story. Do you want the long or short version?" Samuel narrowed his eyes, and Jude put his hands up. "Settle down, Samuel. Fine! I'll give you the long version."

He started by telling Samuel what Ben had told him at the party last week and then the call they had made. After that, he told him about meeting Sofia, the dates they had gone on, and the decision they had made on their last date to get married quickly.

He left out the personal parts and folded his arms when he finished.

"You're crazy, Jude," Samuel said.

"You know I'm not. I am only doing what I must since I have no choice."

"I guess you don't really have a choice, but still..." Samuel gazed at him, his expression full of surprise and amusement. "Well, do you have a picture of her so I can see if she's pretty?"

"What does the way she looks have to do with anything?" Jude said. It occurred to him that he did not have a picture of Sofia. He had to change that when they met up today.

Samuel laughed. "You don't have a picture of her, do you? That means she's as ugly as they come."

Jude smiled. "She's the very opposite of ugly."

Samuel arched his brows. "So she's gorgeous then? At least that counts for something. It would be doubly awful if the complete stranger you had to marry to get a Green card was also ugly."

Jude shook his head. "Samuel! Are you going to lend me your car or not?"

"And where exactly did you say you were going?" Samuel asked. "And what did you say you were going to do there again?"

Jude sighed exasperatedly. "I just told you. I have to pick up my fiancée from her apartment, and then I will drive us to the courthouse to get our marriage license."

"You are going to court to get legal documents? That means they will ask for your personal info. Won't that be a little risky, Jude, considering you're trying to avoid getting deported by the government?"

"I'll have to be careful. Hopefully, I will soon be married to Sofia and able to get my Green card."

Samuel's eyes searched his, and Jude frowned. "What?" He glowered at Samuel.

Samuel shrugged. "For someone who will soon be married to an almost complete stranger, you don't look particularly troubled about it. In fact, you look quite happy. Ecstatic, even."

Jude eyed him. "What are you going on about?"

Samuel laughed. "Well, don't tell me you have fallen in love with this girl you only just met?"

"Boy, what are you talking about?" Jude glared at him. He held out his hand. "You know what, don't bother answering that. Just give me your car keys."

Samuel was still staring at Jude. He finally looked up at the ceiling and said, "That girl has to be knock-down gorgeous for my man Jude to have fallen so hard already." He faced Jude again. "Tell me, does she have luscious curves like your ex, Keziah? Because I think she…"

"Stop it!" Jude frowned, annoyed. "Don't mention Keziah's name!"

"Okay, okay! I'm sorry."

"Samuel, are you lending me your car or not?" Jude asked, and glanced at his wristwatch. He still had some time to get to Sofia's and pick her up before they went to get their license, but he had to get going now, or Sofia would think he had a habit of being late. Samuel was still sitting on the sofa, and Jude sighed. "Well, I guess I'll have to take a taxi," he said, and began to head towards the door.

"Wait, Jude!" Samuel called out. "Let me get my car keys."

He left the living room, and Jude waited at the

door, tapping his foot impatiently. Less than a minute later, Samuel appeared again and handed him his car keys.

"So, when am I going to meet this fiancée of yours? Because I have to meet her before you actually marry her."

Jude turned around without answering Samuel's question and walked out the door. As he drove to Sofia's friend's house to pick her up, he thought about what Samuel had said. Had he really fallen in love with Sofia? And why did Samuel believe he'd fallen in love with her?

He grunted and then dismissed Samuel's words. His friend and housemate had a habit of over-exaggerating. He definitely hadn't fallen in love with Sofia. He hardly knew her. Yes, they had shared a lot between them the last few days, and he knew a lot about her life and she about his, but that did not mean they really knew each other. More than that, neither of them could afford to develop feelings for the other. He had to keep reminding himself that this was a temporary arrangement and that Sofia's heart still belonged to her ex. He would be getting into a world of hurt if he allowed himself to fall for her. And it would not be fair to her if she started to have feelings for him when he had not totally gotten over Keziah.

Involuntarily, he pictured Keziah clearly in his mind and groaned. Maybe he would never get over her. She and Sofia could not be more different in appearance, but they actually had a lot of similarities when it came to their personalities. They were both vibrant and exuberant.

You have to put Keziah out of your mind now,

Jude. He was going to meet up with the woman he would marry in a week's time, and it was wrong to still obsess over his ex. He focused his thoughts on Sofia again and was surprised how easily he managed to put Keziah out of his mind as an image of Sofia replaced hers. He and Sofia had a lot to do this week before they got married on Friday, even though they were just going to have a court registry without guests.

He finally got to Edith's house and knocked on the door. Edith immediately opened for him and smiled at him.

"Come in, Jude," she said. "Let me go and get your fiancée for you." She left the living room while Jude settled on the couch. He looked around the tiny, sparsely furnished living room. Sofia had not told him, but he was sure she had not lived in this house for long. He was certain she had lived in luxury for a long time before circumstances had reduced her to living in this tiny house with her friend. She needed the money he would pay her to marry him, but he didn't have the money now. She had said it did not matter, but it did.

Guilt tore at his heart. She was fulfilling her end of the bargain by marrying him — even more so because she wanted to marry him sooner than she needed to. But he could not even make enough money to fulfill his part.

He looked up as she stepped into the living room and embarrassment washed over him. And then his embarrassment was replaced with an intense attraction that took his breath away. She looked breathtaking.

He stood up and, without thinking, went to take

her hands. "You look gorgeous," he breathed as his eyes swept over her. She was dressed in a white dress with gold trim that went down to her ankles. Her hair was up, showing off a pair of dangling gold earrings, and she wore a bright red lipstick.

He gave her a teasing grin. "Wait, is today our wedding? Because I have probably forgotten. You look like a radiant bride while I," he looked down at his black pants and short sleeve blue shirt, "look like this."

She laughed. "I guess I just decided to wear something that will put me in the mood for the upcoming wedding," she said.

He linked his elbow with hers, and they walked out of the house together. A thread of pride ran through him as they walked to the car. He couldn't believe she was soon going to be his bride.

Calm down, Jude. Remember what this is really about. He pushed the thought away. That did not change the fact that they were soon going to get married and she would be his wife in just a week.

They chatted about mundane things as he drove them to the courthouse. They had to wait for about ten minutes and then went into an office, where a middle-aged woman in glasses sat behind a desk. She looked up at them and then told them to sit down. She asked for their IDs, birth certificates, and passports, which they gave to her. Sofia handed the woman her social security number.

She looked up from Jude's passport and said, "You're here on a visa?"

He nodded and his heart began to race. What if she said they couldn't get married? What if she called ICE and they came here and bundled him out to be deported?

He took a deep breath and forced himself to calm down. *You're being paranoid, Jude.* Everything would be all right.

But his heart did not stop racing as the woman began to ask them other informal questions. She handed them several forms to fill out, which they duly did. Jude paid for the license, which left him with only twenty-five dollars to his name. His anxiety increased, but he pressed it away. He would have to put in another extra shift at the factory to get more money. He'd been so consumed with the dates with Sofia this week, he'd done no extra jobs and now was low on cash.

He took a huge sigh of relief when, five minutes later, the woman told them they would get their license in a few days. For the first time in a long while, he said a prayer of thanksgiving to God, though not a long one as he had done in his teenage years, when he still was religious. He walked out of the office with Sofia, and then they grinned at each other in the middle of the hallway that led to the front doors of the courthouse.

"Thank God we have scaled through that," he said to her.

She tilted her head and looked at him. "What did you think was going to happen?"

He shrugged. "I don't know. I was afraid that something might go wrong and maybe ICE would storm in and take me away."

She laughed, and he said, "I don't know why you're laughing. It's not funny." But he soon joined in her laughter. "Okay, so I was feeling a little paranoid in there. But you can't blame me."

She stopped laughing. "I know. That is why we are getting married as soon as possible. So you can get your permanent resident card quickly and finally stop worrying." A sober expression appeared on her face, and she said thoughtfully, "Why are we waiting a week to get married anyway? Why don't we do it now? I mean we are already here, and nothing prevents us from getting married now."

He stared at her, surprised. "I would love to get married now, but aren't you forgetting something, Sofia? We haven't gotten our marriage license yet."

She shook her head and then burst out laughing. "What is wrong with me?" she said as he laughed along with her.

"I really wish we could get married today though," he said.

She took his hand, a huge smile on her face, and began to skip happily to the door. He chuckled as he watched her, feeling lighthearted and happier than he'd been in a long time. Her happy, carefree mood was infectious, and everything that had troubled him moments ago fled.

As they neared the entrance to the courthouse still holding hands, a brawny man that looked about his age opened the door and walked in. Jude blinked as the man came closer, and then his heart began to pound. The man looked like Felix, a friend of his from his country. But it couldn't be. Because he'd been told that Felix had been killed when the violence started a year ago. How on earth could he still be alive?"

The man's eyes grew wide as he approached, and then recognition lit up in them.

"What is it, Jude?" Sofia asked.

The man hurried up to them and put his hands on Jude's shoulders. "Jude? Jude Daniels!

"Felix!" Jude stared at his friend in wonder. "How is this possible? I heard you were... you were dead." Jude felt Sofia squeeze his hand as he continued to stare at the man before him.

"As you can see, I am certainly not dead," Felix said.

Jude's eyes flooded with tears. He had believed for over a year that his childhood friend was dead, and now here he was, alive and well. He reached out and hugged his friend fiercely.

Felix pounded his back good-naturedly.

Jude pulled back again and shook his head as he stared at Felix. "I feel like I am looking at a ghost," he said.

Felix laughed. "You know I am definitely not a ghost."

"I cannot believe this." Jude put his arm around his friend's shoulder. He felt Sofia's hand on his arm and then turned and smiled at her. "Felix, this is my fiancée, Sofia. Sofia this is my childhood friend, Felix, back from the dead."

Felix smiled and shook his head. "Back from the dead?" He turned to Sofia and greeted her warmly. When she held out her hand, he shook it.

"I'm so happy to meet one of Jude's friends from his country. Do you live in the United States now?"

"Yes, I just moved here," he said.

Jude put his hand on Felix's shoulder. "My man, how did that rumor that you had died spread? I'm not the only one who believes it, you know."

"It's a long story, Jude."

"I cannot wait to hear it." Jude punched his

friend's arm playfully. He hugged him again, overcome with emotion and unable to stop himself. "What about your father and brother?"

"Like I said, it's a long story. We have a lot to talk about."

Sofia put her hand on Jude's back, and he turned to her. "I should leave both of you to catch up. You definitely have a lot to talk about." She smiled at Felix. "It's been a pleasure meeting you."

"No, don't go, Sofia," Jude said. "We can all sit and talk. I want you with me." He cupped her elbow. "Besides, I drove you here. I have to drive you back home."

She smiled at him. "It's okay. I'll find my way home. You both need to talk alone." She began to walk away before he could say anything else. She turned briefly, waved at him, and turned around again. When she had left the courthouse, Jude faced Felix. "I think I saw a small restaurant somewhere near here. We can sit and talk there."

They reached the restaurant in less than three minutes and sat outside. Jude ordered iced tea, and Felix chuckled.

"What?" Jude said, smiling curiously.

"You've joined these Americans to drink their strange cold tea. That is not real tea. Whatever happened to our traditional tea and milk?"

Jude laughed. "Hot tea and milk, in the afternoon, in this heat? Felix!"

Felix shook his head and chuckled. "You had no problems drinking it in Bakali, Jude. And it's as hot as Arizona! Now it's a tall glass of iced-tea... whatever that is. Just stop it!"

Jude laughed out loud.

After his laughter died down, Felix said, "So you are engaged?"

"Yes," Jude answered. He hoped Felix would not ask him anything more about his engagement or Sofia. He did not want to talk about that right now. Besides, he wanted to find out exactly why Felix was here, alive and well, when most of the people they knew back home thought he was dead. Also, Jude wanted to know how he had come to live in the U.S. "So, tell me, Felix. How did the rumor that you had been killed start and spread so widely? And how did you get here?"

Felix folded his hands on the table and gave Jude a sad smile. "The day my father, my brothers, and I disappeared from Bakali, we were taken by some men sent by the government."

Jude blinked. "Men sent by the government?"

Felix stared at him. "Surely you have been following the news about everything happening in our country."

"Not really. I guess I block most of it out. All I know is that Bakali has been torn apart because of the greed and self-centeredness of a few power-hungry men."

"Yes, that will be the present government. Those same greedy and self-centered men kidnapped me, my father, and my brothers. You know my dad was a chieftain in the opposing party. When the violence started because people were crying out against the injustices of the present government, people began to disappear. People who were opposed to the government. My father, my brothers, and I were some of those people. We were taken to a tiny village that was virtually empty. We later found out that was where the ruling party was stockpiling their weapons."

Jude listened with his heart racing as Felix told him how the government had already gathered a sizeable militia who trained in that village when there was still relative peace in Bakali. Their countrymen had been lulled into a sense of false peace while the government had stockpiled weapons and gathered mercenaries in preparation for war.

"We were held in a small hut and tortured every day," Felix said.

Jude could not even imagine how much they had suffered. "I'm really sorry," he said.

Felix chuckled, but the expression on his face was hard as stone.

"And how did you manage to escape?" Jude asked.

Felix narrowed his eyes, his face a mask of rage. For a long moment he said nothing. Finally, he spoke. "One of the men who was delegated to guard our hut turned out to be a mole; one of my father's party supporters who had been recruited to infiltrate the ruling party. When he found an opportunity one day, he untied our hands and feet, let us out of the hut, and told us to run as fast as we could." He sighed loudly and his expression turned incredibly sad. "Unfortunately, the other guys caught wind of our escape and pursued us. My father and I were able to escape to the road, but my brothers did not make it. They were shot. The most agonizing thing was that we had to leave them in order to escape with our lives."

Jude moaned. It was one of the most awful stories he had ever heard. He'd known both of Felix's brothers. Even though he had believed them dead for some time now, hearing how they died pierced his heart. He took his friend's hand and squeezed it. He didn't know what else to say or do.

"We found a good Samaritan on the road, who called one of my father's friends. We were taken to the man's house, and later secretly taken out of the country by my father's party. We were taken to Rwanda, where we stayed for a long time, and then came to America about three months ago. What is going on in our country is shameful, Jude. And just horrible."

"I am sorry for everything that has happened to you," Jude said.

"And to you too, Jude. Most people have lost someone. Your dad was a great man. And he was the last person we thought would be targeted since he was just a pastor."

Overwhelming sadness threatened to suffocate Jude, and he could not take it anymore. He immediately changed the dreadful subject, but the next thing that came out of his mouth was almost as dreadful. "I've been an illegal immigrant in this country for a while and have been living under the fear of being removed from the United States. I cannot imagine being deported back to our war-torn country."

Felix blinked rapidly, surprise written on his face. "Is that why you're marrying that white girl?"

Jude hesitated, wondering how much he should reveal. He finally settled on the truth, at least a part of it. "Yes, I guess so."

"You guess so?"

"Okay, at first, it was nothing more than a

business arrangement — she helps me get a Green card, and I pay for her help. But I have come to like her very much. She's a great girl."

Felix waved his hand as though what Jude had just said didn't matter at all. "I saw Keziah, Jude."

Jude's heart stopped, and he froze for a few seconds, unable to speak. Finally, he found his voice and said slowly, "You saw Keziah? Are you sure?"

"What kind of question is that? I have known Keziah for years, and you know that. Of course I am sure it was her. I even spoke to her."

Jude's pulse began to race. Before he could stop himself, he blurted out, "Where did you see her? When did you see her?"

"I saw her about two weeks ago. A friend of mine who lives here in Tucson knows a few of the people in our country who moved to the United States. He was the one who connected me to Keziah. She told me she was divorced now."

Jude's jaw dropped, and he said in a shaky voice, "She is not married anymore?"

Felix nodded. "Yes. She and her ex-husband divorced about a year ago. She lives right here in Arizona, Jude. In Phoenix. She asked about you and she told me that she misses you terribly."

Jude could not breathe. Keziah lived right here in Arizona? And she wasn't married anymore. Most of all, she missed him. He felt overcome with conflicting emotions. And then, even though he knew he shouldn't ask since he was marrying another girl in a week, he asked, "Do you think she'd want to see me?"

"I am sure she would, Jude." Felix nodded. "I told her I did not know where you were, but that

I would ask our mutual friend if he had any idea where we could find you. She had tears in her eyes as she spoke about you. She told me she regrets not marrying you. She said she still loves you very much."

Jude shut his eyes as pain rippled through him. Why oh why was he hearing all this today? This was the wrong time to hear about this — that Keziah was single again and that she still loved him and wanted to see him. He took a deep breath to try to calm his nerves. He could try to forget everything that Felix had just told him about Keziah, but it would probably be impossible. He had to see her. He needed to. "I want to see her too," he said to Felix.

Guilt ran through him as he thought about Sofia. What would happen if he went to see Keziah and they got back together?

His heart began to pound. Surely Sofia would understand. He had told her he still had feelings for Keziah and would take her back if he ever saw her again. Besides, this whole arrangement — the dates, the wedding, all of it was really fake and also wrong. He would pay her the money owed for the first installment, even though she had told him she did not want it. It would be for the best. She would not have to marry someone she had only known for a week, and he would be back together with the girl he'd loved since he was a teenager.

But are you sure you are still in love with her?

Felix put his hand on Jude's arm. "I know it's a lot to process, especially since she broke up your engagement and married someone else. But she is really lonely now. She had no children with her husband and she lives alone. I believed her when she said she still loves and misses you."

Jude felt as though someone was squeezing his heart tight. With all his heart he wanted to see Keziah, but he did not want to hurt Sofia. He'd grown to like Sofia a lot, and the last thing he wanted was to hurt her in any way.

"Jude, what are you going to do?" Felix asked. "If you want to see Keziah, I can drive you to her house tomorrow."

Jude shut his eyes and laid his hand on his forehead. He had dreamed of getting back together with Keziah for so long. It was partly why he had come to the United States in spite of how impossible that dream was. Now he had a chance to see her. He could not pass it up.

And yet he had Sofia to think about. How would she feel when he told her he'd gone to see his ex? For that matter, how would she take it when he broke off their engagement, because that would most likely be what ended up happening after he saw his high school sweetheart again.

The thought of breaking up with Sofia when she had only just come out of a breakup that had left her heart in tatters seemed unsavory and a little cruel to him. How would he do that to her? But did he have a choice? He could not pass up getting back together with Keziah now that he had the chance to.

"Jude, do you want to see Keziah?" Felix asked again.

Jude groaned. If he did not marry Sofia, he would not be able to stay in America... unless Keziah was a permanent resident here and wanted to marry him and file for a spousal visa for him. He felt awful even thinking about all of this. Maybe it was for the best to leave Sofia. He definitely would be using her for a Green card even though he was paying, but he'd been in love with Keziah for a long, long time. Their union would be true, even if she could get him a Green card.

But are you still in love with her? the insistent voice in his mind asked again.

"Jude?" Felix looked into its eyes. "You're conflicted about all this, aren't you?"

"I'm supposed to marry Sofia so I'll be able to stay in America. If I go and visit Keziah and we end up getting back together, I might not be able to stay here, and then I will have to go back to Bakali."

"I'm not asking you to do anything but visit Keziah. I didn't say you shouldn't marry your Sofia."

"But it might be impossible to let Keziah go once I see her again."

"Then don't let her go," Felix said. "You can also marry Keziah and stay in the United States instead of marrying a girl you don't really know. I think Keziah has permanent residency here."

Once again, guilt ran through Jude as he thought about marrying Keziah rather than Sofia.

"Jude, do you want to see Keziah?" Felix asked again.

"Yes. Yes I do," Jude said, finally making up his mind. "You can take me to her house tomorrow?"

"Yes, Jude. I told you I would drive you there tomorrow. I will call Keziah and tell her that I'll come visit her, but I won't tell her you will be coming along with me. It will be a pleasant surprise for her. Unless you don't want that."

"That's okay," Jude said. "I'll surprise her." Overwhelming excitement suddenly flooded him as he thought about seeing Keziah. How long had he dreamt of being with her again? His dream would finally come true. But once again, guilt and uncertainty invaded his heart, tempering his excitement. In the dreams he'd had of Keziah where they were reunited, they had fallen into each other's arms and kissed passionately, vowing never to be separated again. But that would not be the case in reality because now there was another girl in the dream; a girl called Sofia who he was supposed to marry in a week's time and who he was growing to like more and more every day. He knew for certain that she also liked him. He dreaded hurting her, but that was exactly what would happen. He would probably end up back together with Keziah when he saw her tomorrow, but he was certain that he would live with the guilt of hurting Sofia. He would never forget breaking up with one of the sweetest girls he'd ever met.

He sighed as Felix began talking about Keziah, and for a minute, he only half-listened. Finally, he pressed the guilt in his heart away and allowed the excitement to take over.

THIRTEEN

For the first few minutes of the car ride with Felix to Phoenix, Jude's feelings alternated between guilt and excitement. He worried about how Sofia would feel when he told her a week before their wedding day that they would no longer be getting married, but at the same time the thought of seeing Keziah again filled him with heart-racing happiness. Finally, after they had driven for close to thirty minutes, his excitement completely took over.

He and Felix chatted, catching up on everything that had happened in their lives since the last time they'd seen each other. Keziah remained in the forefront of his mind. He hadn't seen her in years, and yet he could still picture her face clearly in his mind. It was etched in his memory, probably because he had stared at her picture for hours every day after they'd broken up. He had done so for months until he'd finally decided to give it up. He'd decided that the pain of seeing her picture every day did not exactly help him move on with his life.

He and Felix eventually stopped chatting, and

he looked out of the window. Memories of the years he'd spent with Keziah swept through his mind. He recalled clearly the day they'd first met in high school, their friendship that had grown to love, their long distance relationship in university, and the day he'd proposed to her; how happy he had been when she'd said yes. How carefully he had slipped the ring on her finger.

The familiar pain tugged at his heart as he recalled the day she'd broken up with him. He had tried calling her countless times after, but she'd never answered his calls. It wasn't long after that he'd heard she'd married someone else. Was he a fool to be so excited to see the woman who had caused him so much pain?

But he had forgiven her for all the pain she'd caused years ago. It was impossible for him to hold a grudge against her. But that had not lessened the pain he'd felt every time he remembered how much he had loved her and that she was married to someone else. But she wasn't married anymore. They had an opportunity to be together again. To start all over, to forget the painful past.

His excitement rose again only to be followed by an uncomfortable feeling he could not quite decipher. He pressed away the strange feeling, and then imagined how Keziah would look when she saw him. Felix had already called to tell her he was coming to see her, but as they had planned yesterday, he had not told her Jude was coming with him. She would be so surprised.

"Are you nervous, Jude?" Felix asked as they approached the road sign that read, *Welcome to Phoenix.*

"Just a little," he said and then smiled. "Actually, a lot. But it's a good kind of nervousness."

"I'm so glad you are going to see each other again. I was so surprised when I heard you two had broken up."

"We didn't break up, Felix. She broke up with me."

"I know," Felix said. "But I think you have forgiven her now. You wouldn't be coming with me to see her if you hadn't."

"I have forgiven her, but I can still remember how much it hurt when she broke off our engagement. I never want to feel like that again." Sofia's face immediately appeared in his mind. He knew how much it hurt to have someone break off an engagement, and yet he was going to do the same thing to her. He pressed his lips together and immediately suppressed the guilt he felt. It was hardly the same thing. Unlike his engagement to Keziah, which had been very real, his engagement to Sofia was just a business deal that could be ended at any time.

"... both of you were so in love, Jude. Everyone believed you were the perfect couple. It was the strangest thing when the wedding was called off."

"I definitely loved her dearly, and I thought she felt the same way about me."

"I am sure she did. I was around you two a lot, remember. I could see the way she looked at you. I don't know why she called off your wedding and ran off with someone else, but she regrets doing that now. When she said she wants to make things right, she looked really sincere. I hope you guys get back together."

Jude's heart thudded as Felix talked. Most of their friends did not know that Keziah had always had a dream of going to America, which was why she'd left him when she found a way to bring that dream to life. He did not blame her for doing so. It was just that when she had, she'd taken a piece of his heart with her.

Felix turned onto a street with identical bungalows lining each side and neatly manicured lawns. Jude's heart beat wildly as Felix began to slow down. He parked in front of one of the bungalows, and Jude took a deep breath. The pavement gleamed under the burning sun. They got out of the car, and Jude exhaled again as he followed Felix to the front of the house.

Felix rang the doorbell, and Jude tried to sort out the mix of emotions in his heart. Nervousness, guilt, and excitement battled for dominance. The door opened, and Keziah stood there looking as beautiful as he had ever seen her in a sleeveless purple shirt and black shorts. His pulse started to race as she smiled at Felix, her eyes fixed on him.

"Felix! You are an hour early," she said reaching out to hug him.

"We left early," he said.

She turned with a smile to Jude, and then her eyes grew round. Her mouth dropped open, and she stared at him for a long moment, astonishment and disbelief clearly written on her face. She blinked rapidly and then exclaimed, "Jude! Is it really you?"

He smiled broadly. "Yes, Keziah! It's really me."

She gasped. "How come you are here?" She opened the door wide, and Felix entered the house. She gazed at Jude as he stepped in, and then she shut the door. Her eyes remained on him and, for a long moment, they stood silently gazing at each other.

Felix stood up. "Let me give you some space to talk and catch up," he said. "I will be waiting in the car." He left the house.

Keziah said in a trembling voice, her eyes still planted on him, "Jude, I cannot believe you're here." Tears welled up in her eyes and ran down her cheeks. A huge smile suddenly took over her entire face, and she reached out and threw her arms around him.

He held her tightly and felt his shirt dampening with her tears. He rubbed her back and inhaled deeply as the familiar scent of lavender enveloped him. For a long time, they stood wrapped up in each other's arms as she cried, and then she finally pulled back. Her cheeks were streaked with tears as she smiled at him. And then the smile melted off her face, replaced by a look of shame. She bowed her head and sighed audibly.

He tilted her chin up so that he could look into her eyes.

"I'm so sorry, Jude," she said in a broken voice. "I'm sorry for everything. I regret what I did to you every single day. I know how much you loved me. I should never have broken our engagement." Fresh tears streamed down her face, and he wiped them away with his thumb.

"It's okay," he said.

She shook her head. "No, it's not. I hurt you terribly when I broke up with you. I know that. I'm just glad to have a second chance to see you and tell you how sorry I am. I made a terrible mistake." She bit her lips, despair taking over her face.

He wrapped her in his arms again and hugged her tightly, trying his best to comfort her and let her know he had forgiven her. She felt so familiar, and he smiled sadly. He was not surprised when she lifted her face, brushed her lips across his, and then kissed him fully.

For a long moment, she clung to him, kissing him. But he could not return her kiss. He felt nothing but guilt. Sofia's face was firmly planted in his mind, and he found himself holding on to it rather than trying to press it away because of how guilty he felt. He also found he did not welcome Keziah's kiss, but he could also not bring himself to pull away. She finally pulled back, and he could not hold back a sigh of relief.

She pressed her lips tightly together and then said, "I am so sorry, Jude. I should not have kissed you. I should not have assumed that you would just take me back." She bowed her head again, and once more he lifted her chin with his finger.

"There's nothing for you to apologize for," he said.

"No, there's a lot to apologize for," she told him. "I know it will take some time for you to come to place where you feel comfortable with me again and where you can kiss me as passionately as you once did."

He groaned. "I want to get back there, but I don't know how."

She took his hand and said, "I still love you, Jude. Very much. I've missed you so much, and there's nothing I would love more than for us to be together the same way we were years ago." She threaded her fingers through his. "Please, I know what I did was unforgivable, but please find it in your heart to forgive me."

He stared her without a word.

"I think you still love me, Jude, like I love you. I want us to get back together," she pleaded. "Don't you want that?"

Jude pushed away Sofia's face from his mind as his emotions roiled. He had never been more confused in his life. He sighed heavily, unable to sort through his feelings.

She held his hand tighter, intently gazing into his eyes, and then she blinked. "Ah, Jude, I did not even think to ask if there was someone else! There is, isn't there? You have a girlfriend or a wife."

He shook his head.

Her eyes lit up. "Then there's nothing stopping us from being together again," she said, and wrapped her arms around him once more. She pulled back slightly and asked, "Do you still love me, Jude? I love you with all my heart. The moment I called off our wedding, I knew that I had made the biggest mistake of my life, but it was too late to go back to you."

He felt emotionally weary from his jumbled thoughts and feelings. He didn't know what to say to her.

"Please forgive me and take me back," she pleaded desperately.

He sighed again.

She looked tense as she said, "Say you still love me, Jude." Her eyes filled with tears once more.

His mind filled with Sofia's smiling face. He recalled clearly how eager she had looked the day she'd told him they could get married as soon as possible; how happy she had looked after they had gotten their marriage license. Yes, their marriage was a business arrangement, but it was also more. He cared for her deeply. Most of all, he had made a commitment to her.

He shut his eyes and sighed as Keziah leaned in and kiss him again. She pressed her body to his, and then he responded and kissed her back. Their kiss reminded him of the many kisses they had shared and how heady they had felt.

She pulled back slightly. "I love you, Jude. You still love me, don't you?"

He searched her eyes for a few seconds and then took both her hands. "Yes, Keziah. I still love you."

Her eyes lit up, but he shook his head. "I still love you, but I am not in love with you anymore." His heart ached at the confused look on her face. He was still filled with confusion and conflicting emotions, but he was certain about his feelings. He was still greatly fond of her, but that passionate, all-consuming, intense love he'd felt when they were still together was not present any more. And it would be unfair to both of them if he led her on without telling her the truth.

"There's someone else, isn't there?" she cried.

"It's not that." He squeezed her hand.

"Then what is it? You still haven't forgiven me? I know what I did was very wrong, but can you not find it in your heart..."

"Stop, Keziah!" He sighed and said softly, "Listen, I have forgiven you, but we cannot be together. Your dreams of coming here to America were bigger than your love for me."

"I knew it. You haven't forgiven me."

"I have, but that doesn't mean we have to be together." he smiled sadly. "You think you love me now and want to be with me because you're lonely, but the next time you find someone who can fulfill some dream that you have, something that I might not be able to give you, you will leave me again. I don't want that. I'll never allow that to happen again."

She shook her head. "No, I won't leave you. I love you too much, and I realize now that we belong together."

"No, we don't," he said firmly. Once again, he pictured Sofia in his mind. He said, "You know what? You are right. There is someone else. A girl I plan to marry next week."

Her eyes grew round, and then she pulled her hand away from his. She looked shocked. "You are getting married next week? To another girl?"

"Yes," he said. He hugged her again and then pulled back. She looked miserable. "I am really glad I saw you today, Keziah. I wish you all the best." He started to pull away, but she held on to him.

"Please don't go," she said. "Is the girl you plan to marry an American citizen?"

"Yes," he said, gazing curiously at her. "Why?"

"I know many immigrants marry U.S citizens for a Green card, but you don't have to. I am a permanent resident now, Jude. We can get married, and I will file for your adjustment of status. You will get your Green card in no time."

He gave her a sad smile. "I would never do that to you, Keziah — marry you just for a Green card. You deserve to be with someone who loves you passionately and completely." He touched her arm and said, "I want you to know that I don't hold any grudge against you, Keziah. I want you to have every good thing in this life and more. I'll never forget you." He kissed her cheek and then turned around and walked out of her house.

Felix looked surprised when he opened the car door and got in. "Wow! That was fast, Jude. I thought you would stay with Keziah for much longer." He gave Jude a knowing look and grinned.

Jude did not smile back. "Let's go, Felix."

"And is everything good with you and Keziah now? Are you going to break up with that white girl?"

"I'm not breaking up with Sofia, my fiancée, if that's who you're referring to. And everything is good with me and Keziah, at least on my part. I've truly forgiven her, but I cannot give her what she wants."

Felix raised his eyebrows. "What are you talking about?"

"I know you think we are a perfect match, Keziah and I, but we are not. We are not getting back together."

"You're not?" Felix gazed at him with an astonished look. "Wow, I thought you still loved her."

"I still do, but I am not in love with her anymore. All these years I've spent fantasizing about the day I'll see her again. Now that I have, I know for sure that my feelings for her are not the same as they were years ago. I guess I needed to see her once more to realize that. I have idolized our relationship for so long, even the part where she left me just two weeks before our wedding and married someone else. I never blamed her for it. I believed at the time that she had no choice because she was going after her dream and had found someone who could provide that for her when I could not.

He sighed and shook his head at the strange way his mind had worked, at least when it came to his relationship with Keziah. "I actually believed it was right for her to pursue her dream even though she had hurt me terribly in the process of doing so. But now I know that when you truly love someone, they become an integral part of your dream. You don't just throw them away in the pursuit of your dream as though they were dirt that you get rid of. The difference between me and Keziah was that she was a part of *my* dreams. I wasn't a part of hers."

Felix sighed. "I guess you're right." He started the car and began to drive away from Keziah's house. "So, that girl you're planning to marry. Sofia. Are you in love with her?"

Jude looked out of the window and then faced Felix again. "I think so. But most of all, I made a commitment to her, and unlike Keziah, who broke our engagement, I intend to keep mine."

Felix drove slowly down the road, and Jude hit the dashboard in front of him. "Move this thing, Felix! I have to get to my fiancée as soon as possible. She'll be wondering where I am and why I haven't come to see her today."

Felix laughed. "Yes, sir!" He gave Jude a mock salute and sped up the car.

All through the ride back to Tucson, Jude could think of nothing else but getting back to Sofia. He didn't know when their arranged marriage had become more than a business transaction to him, but it was now. And there was no one he wanted to see more than her. He'd thought he would be back together with Keziah and planning to break up with Sofia, but he was now more certain than ever before that he wanted nothing more than to marry her. And to tell her that he loved her.

FOURTEEN

Sofia laughed as Jude showed her his painting of her. They were in an art class for couples, and the instructor had told them to paint a depiction of each other. She pointed at the caricature sketch Jude had painted that was supposed to be her and shook her head, still laughing. "Who is this, Jude? Do you have another fiancée, an ugly one hidden somewhere, because I know this certainly isn't me."

Jude chuckled and said in mock indignation, "What are you saying, Sofia? This painting of you is a masterpiece."

Sofia shook her head. "No, this painting is definitely not me."

Jude burst out laughing and then pressed his lips tightly together when a few of the couples in the class turned his way.

Sofia studied the painting again. "Well, at least you tried. You painted my bangs, but that is the only thing you got right about me in this painting. My bangs."

"Okay." He chuckled. "I agree completely. You

are infinitely more beautiful than this painting of you. Now, let me see the mess you made of me."

She shook her head again and shielded her canvas with her body.

"Sofia, let me see it." He tried to move her out of the way, but she shook her head and held her ground.

He reached his hand behind her back, but she laughed and moved her easel further away from him.

He chuckled as he went after her. "Sofia, show me!"

She shook her head again, feeling slightly embarrassed. He reached her but rather than try to grab her canvas again, he looked into her eyes, smiling. She stared curiously at him and then her heart melted at the warmth in his eyes. She smiled broadly and then gasped when, with lightning speed, he grabbed the canvas from behind her back.

She groaned. He had tricked her. She looked around the room. All the couples were showing each other their paintings and laughing. Maybe she needed to loosen up a bit and not feel so embarrassed by her painting of Jude.

He studied the drawing and his eyes grew wide. He looked at her and then looked at the painting again. "Wow! Sofia, this is amazing!" He grinned as he glanced at her again. "This is really good. Why didn't you tell me you could paint? You should have an exhibition or something."

"No," she said, waving him away. She turned away, embarrassed once more at how closely he was studying her painting. "It's no big deal, Jude. I'm not good enough to have an art exhibit."

"That is not true, Sofia. I'm telling you that this painting is really good. You should definitely have your own studio at least."

She shut her eyes, hoping he would stop making comments on her painting. She had simply come here with him because she thought it would be fun, but she did not want him focusing on whether she could paint or not. Apart from her father and George, she had never shown anyone anything she'd painted and had even stopped painting years ago, after she'd met George. She had painted as a teenager, but her dad had told her continuously that she was wasting her time and that she could be spending it on more profitable things.

George had seen one of her paintings, and though he'd said he liked it, he did not encourage her to paint more. In fact, the first time he'd come over to her apartment when she was painting, he had complained about how untidy she looked with paint all over her. He preferred her in finery — in the best lingerie when they were indoors and all dressed up when they were out. Soon after, he'd told her that painting took away the time they had to spend with each other. After that, she'd put away all her painting materials. Her easels and brushes and acrylic. When he'd gotten her the new expensive apartment, she'd given them all away.

"Sofia, did you hear what I just said?" Jude asked, looking up from her painting of him.

"Let it go, Jude. It's not my thing anymore. And you're just saying it's good because that's what you're meant to say as my fiancé." She smiled and waved her hand. "You know it's not that good."

"You painted me, Sofia. If this painting didn't

look like me, I would tell you." Before she could protest, he showed the couple nearest to them the painting.

She groaned. *Jude, what are you doing?*

Jude asked, "Doesn't this painting look exactly like me?"

The blond girl beside them and her full-bearded boyfriend studied the painting. The guy looked at Jude and said, "It really does. This looks exactly like you."

The blonde nodded. "This is really good." She looked at Sofia. "You painted this?"

Jude answered for her. "She did. I was just telling her how good it is, but she doesn't believe me."

The bushy bearded man said to Sofia, "It's really good. I wish I could paint like this." He turned to the blonde and smiled. "If I could, I would paint you every day, baby."

The girl grinned at him.

Sofia felt even more embarrassed than she'd been earlier. Were they saying all this to be polite, or were they really serious? She reached out to move her easel away from Jude, but he took her canvas and held it away from her. Before she could say anything, he raised his hand and beckoned to the art instructor.

"Jude, what are you doing?"

Jude ignored her and showed her painting to the instructor, a woman dressed in a tie-dye skirt and peasant blouse. Sofia turned away and sighed warily. She turned around again when the art director put her hand on her shoulder. "This is really good. You painted this?"

Sofia groaned inwardly and said, "I don't paint

seriously. I haven't painted in years, but I used to paint a lot when I was younger."

The art instructor looked really surprised. "You know, there is an art exhibition happening a month from now. If you have any pieces as good as this that you would like to show, I can get them in for you."

Sofia shook her head quickly. "No, I have no pieces to show."

The art instructor kept looking at the painting, and some other couples gathered around. Sofia sighed again. She did not like all the attention this was bringing her. She was used to drawing attention, but it was usually for her looks. She was comfortable with that. But she did not like this kind of attention. When the other couples praised her painting and told her to paint more, she felt even more uncomfortable. She could hear her father's voice in her mind telling her that her painting was no good and that she was wasting time doing it. She could see George's disapproving look when he saw her covered in paint. He had said that she was better at other things and then had pulled her into his arms and kissed her. Surely if she was that good, George had connections with many rich and wealthy people. He could have connected her to someone who owned an art gallery or something. When the instructor brought up the topic of the art exhibition again, she firmly refused and told the woman she would be busy with other things and could not commit to painting any pieces.

After another round of painting, this time of whatever inanimate object was before them, the class thankfully ended. She had painted the wine glass before her as roughly as she could, hoping not to draw any more attention to her work. She'd been relieved when no one had paid any attention to it.

She and Jude walked out of the art studio together. It was almost ten o'clock in the evening, and the studio was as brightly-lit outside as it was on the inside. The light illuminated the cars parked in front of the building. She followed Jude to his friend's car that he had used to pick her up from Edith's. They got to the front of the car, but rather than get in, Jude leaned his back against the hood and looked up at the sky. She smiled and went to stand next to him.

Without turning he said, "It's a beautiful evening." He grimaced and a look of agony crept into his face.

"What is it, Jude?"

"In times like these, just when I fully start enjoying being here with friends and relishing the life I have, that overwhelming guilt suddenly hits me as I remember that there's a war going on in my country and that people are dying." He turned to Sofia. "My countrymen and -women are dying."

She ran her hand up and down his back, hoping to soothe him. She didn't know what to say to him or how else to make him feel better.

"Sometimes I feel as though I'm a coward for wanting to remain here. As though I am jumping ship and abandoning everyone back in my country."

"But you're not abandoning anyone. You don't even have family in your country anymore."

"But I left friends back there."

"You left before the war began. You did not jump ship, and you are certainly not a coward."

A few other couples were standing near their cars, chatting. The blonde and bearded man who had worked close to them at the studio walked by and waved. Sofia smiled and waved back and then faced Jude again. She was worried about him. What if he decided to go back to his country on some ill-advised notion that that was the right thing to do? She shifted closer to him and linked her arm with his. When he turned to look at her, she gave him a wide smile so he would know she would always be by his side, no matter what.

"We're getting married in three days, Sofia," he said. "Can you believe it?"

She smiled with relief at his words. At least he was thinking about their marriage rather than going back to his war-torn country. "You're looking forward to marrying me?" she asked.

"Yes, of course I am." He turned fully to her and took both her hands. "The more time I spend with you, the more things I discover about you that I love. It's not a business deal to me anymore, Sofia. It's very real now."

Her heart began to thud. *Calm down, Sofia. Remember that you have to protect your heart.* She could not afford to fall for him.

And yet, as he searched her eyes and she studied his face, she yearned with everything in her to kiss him. His eyes moved to her lips, and her breath caught in her throat. Maybe he felt the same way. Maybe at any moment he would kiss her. She tilted her head and shut her eyes, anticipating his kiss, but he did not kiss her. Instead he said, "Sofia, I have something to tell you."

She sighed in disappointment but forced herself

to smile. "What is it, Jude?"

"I went to see my ex, Keziah, yesterday."

She felt as though someone had poured a bucket of cold water on her.

"My friend, Felix, the one we saw at the courthouse the other day, told me she lives in Phoenix now and that she was divorced. He said she'd told him that she missed me." He looked away for few seconds and then looked at Sofia again. "He asked if I wanted to see her, and I said yes."

Sofia shuffled her feet and looked down at the ground. Her heart raced with fear and uncertainty. What was he about to tell her? Was he back with his ex? Did he want to break off their engagement?

She dismissed the worrying thoughts. Jude had told her days ago that he was looking forward to marrying her. He wasn't the kind of person to change his mind. She was sure of that.

She blinked when he said nothing more and then looked up at him. "Is that all, Jude?"

He looked uncertain, and she knew there was something else he was not telling her. "I want to hear it all," she insisted. "We promised each other that we would disclose everything we could about ourselves in preparation for our interview once we get married."

He sighed audibly and looked intently at her. "Are you sure you want to hear it?"

Her pulse spiked, and she took a deep breath. She was sure whatever it was that he had yet to tell her, it was something that would be difficult to hear, and yet she wanted to hear everything. "Yes I do," she said to him.

"Felix and I went to see her, and she apologized

for breaking off our engagement and marrying someone else. She said she realized she'd made the biggest mistake of her life shortly after and that she wanted me back but knew it was too late. And then she said she still loved me and wanted us to get back together."

Sofia pursed her lips as worry flooded her, but she said nothing.

"When I told her there was someone else, someone I was planning to marry soon, she told me she was a legal resident in the U.S. now and could file for a spousal visa for me if we got married."

Sofia's heart crashed to the floor, and she fought the tears threatening to spill down her cheeks. That meant Jude did not need her anymore. She wanted to shut her ears so she would not hear the next thing he was going to say. But she didn't. She had asked him to tell her everything. She had to hear it all.

He sighed again. "She kissed me, Sofia. And I kissed her back."

Sofia shut her eyes as pain tore through her. So he was going back to his ex. Why then did he tell her now that he was looking forward to marrying her? Jealousy and despair flooded her, and she bit her lip. The thought of him leaving her for someone else hurt more than she had thought it would. If she felt such pain when they were not yet married, how would she feel if they got married and they later got a divorce? Maybe going back to his ex was the best thing for both of them. She looked down at her shoes as a tear rolled down her cheek.

"Sofia, look at me."

She refused to raise her head up.

He tilted her chin with his finger. When their eyes met, he looked deep into hers. "All through the time we kissed, I could only think about you. I realized I was not in love with Keziah anymore, and that it was you I wanted. I knew there was nothing more I wanted than to marry you."

She gasped and her heart soared. "Really?" she asked, joy sweeping through her.

"Yes. I adore you, Sofia." He took her face in his hands and kissed her.

She gave in to the heady sensations racing through her and kissed him ardently. She wrapped her arms around him as they kissed, completely shutting out everything around her. And then she recalled what he had said about kissing his ex and uncertainty flooded her. She drew back slightly and looked into his eyes. "Jude, are you sure you want to marry me and not your ex? You told me how much you loved her. Are you sure you still don't love her?" She wanted to ask him if he loved her now, because he still hadn't told her that he did, but she was scared of what his answer would be.

He placed a hand on her cheek. "Sofia, I made a commitment to you that I would marry you. I'm not the kind of guy who backs out on his commitment."

She shut her eyes as disappointment filled her heart. She did not want staid commitment. She wanted love. She wanted to feel secure knowing he loved her. He cupped her cheeks, clearly to kiss her again, but she stepped away from him. She could not stand here kissing him and giving up her heart, when she was not even sure how he felt about her. She also wasn't sure she had given up her feelings for George completely.

Take a chance, Sofia. Open up your heart to him.

But she resisted. How could that be the right thing to do when he had kissed his ex just the day before and told her now that he was going to marry her because he was committed?

"Are you okay?" he asked, gazing at her with a look of concern.

"Yeah, I'm fine," she said. Why did she feel so jealous, and so afraid?

She knew why. She'd let her guard down and started to fall for Jude. But she had to protect her heart now, to remember that this was a business transaction and, if either of them weren't interested in moving forward with it, they could walk away. He had paid the introduction fee and she had received her share. Since they had not gotten married yet, he didn't owe her anything else. He didn't have to marry her for commitment's sake. They owed each other nothing. He could go back to his Keziah, who he was still probably in love with. When he married Keziah, he could get the Green card he needed and also be with his childhood sweetheart.

"Sofia, are you sure you're fine?" he asked again.

She nodded. "I think I'm just tired. Can you take me back to Edith's now?"

"Sure," he answered. He gazed at her with a question in his eyes, and she looked away. She opened the car door and got into the passenger seat.

They said nothing to each other as he drove her back to Edith's house. When he parked in front of the house, he reached out and hugged her. When he pulled back and looked at her lips again, she knew he was going to kiss her. She turned her cheek to him just before their lips met.

"I'll see you tomorrow," he said as she got out of the car.

"Yes," she said slowly, and then strode to the front door with a sigh and went into the house. She made her way to her tiny spare room, changed into her pajamas, grabbed her phone from her purse, and got into the narrow bed.

She had turned off her cell phone just before she and Jude had entered the art studio for their date. She turned it on to see if she had any messages or missed phone calls and blinked in surprise. She had missed calls from George. She scrolled through her messages, and her heart skipped a beat. George had left a message for her. She read it and then shut her eyes as her emotions roiled. Opening her eyes again, she re-read his message, which basically said he was so sorry for breaking up with her. He wanted to meet up at their favorite restaurant for dinner tomorrow. He also had something important to ask her.

She shook her head and groaned. Why had this message come now? She felt utterly confused. Once more, she read the text message and bit her lip. Just a week ago, she would have been on her feet by now, already searching her closet for what to wear to George's planned dinner. But now, after spending a full week with Jude, she wasn't sure she wanted to meet with him. She wasn't even sure she wanted to see him ever again. But then again, she was curious. What exactly did he want to tell her?

You know there's a part of you that still wants him.

She sighed. He had apologized. He probably wanted to get back together with her. But was that what she wanted now?

Jude's face filled her mind. What if she went to see George and all her feelings for him returned and she decided to get back together with him? Maybe it was best she didn't go to dinner. But had Jude not gone to see his ex? She owed it to herself, and maybe to George, to see him and get some closure.

But she could not make up her mind as she lay in bed. She tossed and turned, trying to find peace and to make the right decision, but she felt restless and unable to arrive at any firm decision.

Two hours later, with her head and heart full of conflicting thoughts and emotions, she finally fell into a fitful sleep.

FIFTEEN

Sofia felt tense as she dressed for her dinner with George. She'd chosen a strapless red dress that hugged her every curve. It was a dress she had bought on one of her few trips abroad without George. She slipped on a pair of black, sky-high sandals and went to stand in front of the mirror. Swiping on a red lipstick that matched her dress, she put on a pair of gold chandelier earrings. She glanced at herself in the mirror. She looked exactly the way George liked her to look when they were out together — slinky and sophisticated.

What are you doing, Sofia?

Her heart knocked as she picked up her black clutch from the bedside table. She had told herself that she would go and meet George today, just to get some closure on their relationship and tell him that she was moving on, but now, looking at herself in the mirror and the way she was dressed, she wasn't so sure that was going to happen.

Her thoughts traveled to her last date with Jude. How would he feel if he knew she was going to see George? Guilt ran through her, and then she remembered that he'd gone to see his ex and had even kissed her. She squared her shoulders and pressed away the guilt. He had gone to see his ex; she could go to see hers.

She heaved a sigh as she walked out of the room. It was only two days until her and Jude's court wedding. He had told her yesterday that he did not see their upcoming marriage as a business transaction anymore, and it was the same for her.

So why are you going to see George?

She had no clear answer for that. All she knew was that she was going to get some closure. She had been in a relationship with George for years. They had history together. She had only known Jude for less than two weeks.

Edith came out to the living room and stared at Sofia. "Wow! You look amazing! You have a fancy date with Jude today? Where are you going with you all dressed up?" She grinned. "To the Oscars?"

"I'm going to see George," she said slowly and then regretted speaking.

Edith stared at her for a long moment and then said, "You're going to see who?"

Sofia turned away from Edith. "He sent me a message last night. He said he had something to tell me."

"Didn't you tell me that was exactly what he told you when he broke up with you? You thought he was going to ask you to marry him, but he walked into your apartment with his wife and took everything you had away from you."

Sofia shook her head. "He didn't take everything."

"Really? He took your apartment, your car, your

job…"

"He wasn't the one who took those things. His wife did."

"Keep lying to yourself, Sofia. George does not care about you. And why would you want to do this to Jude?"

"I'm not doing anything to Jude. This is not about him. I'm not going to get back with George, if that is what you are thinking. I just want to find out what he wants to say to me and get some closure. It's not easy to just forget about someone you spent years loving. You can ask Jude about that. He visited his ex two days ago and even kissed her."

"What? He did?" Edith looked surprised. "Did he get back together with her? Did he break up with you?"

"No, he said he didn't love his ex anymore and he wanted to marry me because he was committed to me."

"Well…" Edith looked at her. "So is that what this is? You want revenge? Since Jude went to see his ex, you decide to go see yours? Just don't do anything stupid."

"I am not planning to."

"And this talk about it not being easy to forget someone you spent years loving. Remember George is married. He should be easier to forget than most."

"That makes no difference. Our relationship was real to me even though he is married."

Edith glared at her. "At least Jude did not get back with his ex when he went to visit her. Just remember he is counting on you when you go and meet George."

Sofia shrugged. No matter what happened, Jude

would be all right. He would still get his Green card if they didn't get married. Keziah was prepared to marry him and get that for him. "Jude will be just fine," she said.

Edith stared at her but said nothing.

Sofia went to the door to open it just as the doorbell rang. She flung the door open, and her heart skipped a beat. Jude stood at the door, looking at her with a confused expression on his face.

"Where are you going, Sofia?" he asked, studying her. "I've been calling you since this morning but could not get through to you. What happened?"

"Oh… I turned off my phone before I went to bed. I was tired and wanted to sleep without interruptions." She looked away after she'd spoken. That was a lie. She had turned off her phone so he would not be able to reach her. She'd been afraid that the truth would spill out of her and she would tell him about her planned dinner with George. She did not want to have to deal with his reaction. She dug her hand into her purse, brought out her phone, and turned it on.

Edith smiled at Jude and said, "Let me leave you two to talk." She left the living room quickly.

"So, where are you going, Sofia?" Jude asked. "I thought we were supposed to spend this evening together right here."

She turned away, and to avoid answering his question, she said "I'm going to the bathroom. I will be right back." She hurried away before he could say anything more.

She got to her room and stared at herself in the mirror. Taking a deep breath, she tried to calm her nerves. Why had Jude come right now when she was just about to go out? Maybe she should not have turned her phone off. She could have given him an excuse as to why she could not spend this evening with him. She glanced at her wristwatch. She would be late for her dinner with George if she did not get going. But how would she get rid of Jude without raising his suspicions. She still hadn't answered his question. Without a doubt, he would ask her where she was going again once she came out to the living room. She had to come up with a convincing excuse.

She took another deep breath and went straight to the living room. She would tell him she had a girls' night out and was meeting up with some friends. Guilt flooded her heart at the thought of lying to him. But he would be hurt if she told him she was going to see her ex.

She began to approach him, and then she frowned. He was holding her phone, staring at it with a look of distress and confusion. For a few seconds, she stood still, unable to move, and then she forced herself to walk up to him.

He looked at her and, in a voice full of hurt, said "Sofia, when were you going to tell me that George contacted you?"

Her hackles immediately rose, and she grabbed her phone from him. "Why did you go through my messages?" she asked angrily.

"A series of messages came in, and I just checked to see..." He blinked rapidly. "You haven't answered my question, Sofia. When were you going to tell me your ex called you and asked you to meet up with him? That is where you're going, isn't it?"

She bristled. "You went to meet with your ex and

kissed her," she said, feeling defensive. "What do you care if I go and meet my ex as well."

His mouth tipped, and he said, "I can't force you not to go and see your ex. But please be careful, Sofia." He looked her in the eye. "Do you still love him? George?"

She turned away from his perusal.

His voice sounded haunted as he asked, "Sofia, are you having second thoughts about us? Do you want to go back to George?"

She shrugged. "I don't know. I have to go now, Jude."

She started to walk past him, but he took hold of her arm. He pulled her to him and gathered her into a hug. At first, she resisted, but he held on and she settled her head on his chest. "Yesterday I knew I said something wrong after we kissed," he whispered in her ear. "You were withdrawn, and I kept wondering what it was that I said that made you pull away."

"Jude, stop it." She tried to pull away from him, and he released her.

He took her hand before she could leave. "I kept trying to figure out what it was I said, and then I realized the exact moment you pulled away was when you asked if I was sure about my ex. I told you I was committed to you, to marrying you." He gazed into her eyes. "I think you thought I was saying that I still love my ex but wanted to marry you because of the commitment I made. But that was not it at all."

She groaned.

"What I meant to say was that you were the one I wanted to marry — not just because of a commitment I made to you, but because I know that I am starting to fall in love with you."

She gasped and gazed at him, not knowing what to say. Her heart began to thud like it might burst out of her chest at any moment.

They stood looking at each other, and then his gaze shifted from her face to her lips. She could not remember how to breathe as he drew her closer, knowing he was going to kiss her again. She tilted her head up to receive his kiss and then started when her phone rang. She pulled away from him and grabbed her phone from the table. It was George.

She let the phone ring without answering, but she gave Jude an apologetic smile. "I'm sorry, Jude. I have to go. George will be waiting for me at the restaurant."

As much as she wanted to stay here with Jude, she wanted to see George more. She wanted to know what he had to say to her.

She started to sweep past Jude, but once more he took hold of her hand. She groaned as his eyes searched hers. "Listen, Sofia, I will understand if you decide that you want to get back together with your ex after today, but just know I will be waiting right here for you to return. I won't give up on us." He let her go, and she sighed as she walked out of the house.

George was already sitting at their favorite table when she reached the five-star restaurant. He had asked for Edith's address in the text message he sent her, saying he wanted to pick her up and take her to the restaurant, but she had refused. She had told him she would come by herself because she did not want Edith or Flynn to see him. She didn't want either of them to find out she was having dinner with George. Unfortunately, Edith had found out. So had the last person she'd wanted to know about her and George's dinner date — Jude. She sighed, put her concerns away, and wore a smile for George. She hurried to the table and thanked him when he got up and pulled out the chair for her.

She sat across from him and studied him. He looked the same. He still had the sprinkling of grey hair at his temples, the smile lines at the corners of his eyes and mouth. But then again, the last time she'd seen him was barely two months ago. Her gaze swept over his face. His distinguished look had been part of what attracted her to him, but now she could not help comparing him with Jude.

He took her hand on the table and kissed it. "You look stunning, Sofia. As always."

She said nothing. He had called her here because he had something to tell her. She would let him do all the talking.

He beckoned to a waiter and then reeled out his order. He ordered for her as well, just as he always did. When the waiter left, he turned his attention to her. "Sofia, I made a big mistake letting you go. I'm truly sorry. You are the one I want to be with forever."

She shook her head. "And yet you broke up with me." She snapped her fingers together. "Just like that."

"My wife and I are getting a divorce. We are no longer together."

Sofia blinked, surprised. All through the time they dated, he had constantly promised to divorce his wife, but he never had. Now that they'd broken up, he'd finally decided to leave her.

He took her hands again and wove his fingers through hers. "We belong together, Sofia. Please tell me you'll take me back."

Her heart beat rapidly. She could have what she had been dreaming about for a long time now that he and his wife were no longer together. "But what about your job and your wife's threats? You could lose your job and everything you have?"

"I don't care about any of that anymore," he said. "As long as I am with you, I know everything will be all right."

She shut her eyes briefly, feeling conflicted. Jude was in Edith's house right now, waiting for her to return to him.

George squeezed her hand and leaned forward. "I promise you, Sofia, as soon as my divorce comes through, we will get married."

Her mouth dropped open and she shook her head, surprised. "Really?"

"Yes." He kissed the back of her hand again. "Please say you will take me back, Sofia."

What am I going to do now?

She wanted to say yes, that she would take him back, but she could not stop thinking about Jude.

George squeezed her hand again and pleaded once more. Clearly reading how hesitant she was to give in from the expression on her face, he said, "You told me a couple of times that your dream wedding would be a destination wedding in Venice. We could have our wedding there and honeymoon in that hotel we stayed in the last time we were in Venice. Or we could have our honeymoon in a different country, if that is what you want."

"But if you have left your wife, she has probably carried out her threats, hasn't she? You don't have a job now. How will you afford all that?"

"Sofia, yes, I don't have a job now, but I still have savings and investments, more than enough for us to live on until I get a new job. Don't worry about all that. Just say you will marry me."

She bit her lip, still uncertain about what to do.

He pressed her again. "Say yes, Sofia. Say you will marry me. Please."

She sighed. *Isn't this your dream, Sofia? Isn't this what you've wanted for years?* She heaved a long sigh again and gathered up a smile for George. She said, "Yes, George. I will marry you."

He grinned and clapped his hands in the peculiar way he had whenever he was excited about something. "Thank you, Sofia!" He laughed and stood up, pulling her up with him. "Let's get out of here!" he said jubilantly.

She frowned. "What about our food?"

He shrugged. "Don't worry about that. We have to go."

"Where are we going?"

"To a fabulous five-star boutique hotel I discovered recently. It just opened, and it's not far from here. I already booked a room for us to celebrate in the event that you accepted my proposal. We will order room service and it will be just you and me."

An uncomfortable feeling settled in the pit of her stomach. She hesitated for a beat, and he turned to look at her.

"Sofia, what is it?"

"Umm... nothing." She smiled and brushed away her concerns.

He hurried out of the restaurant with her, holding her hand firmly. His Mercedes was waiting in front of the building. Len, his driver, opened the car door for them, and she got in. George got in beside her and the driver shut the door.

She wanted to ask George how come his official driver was still his chauffeur if he wasn't working for his father-in-law's company anymore, but she changed her mind. Len had probably decided to become George's personal driver, fully loyal to his boss of many years. There was no need to doubt George.

They reached the posh hotel, and while George checked them in, she stood next to him, her emotions raging with a mixture of guilt, confusion, and hope. As they rode the elevator to their room, she asked herself if this was what she truly wanted, but she had no ready answers.

Thirty minutes later, she lay on the bed beside George, listening to his quiet snoring. Guilt threatened to suffocate her, and self-loathing washed over her. She could not get Jude out of her mind. He was probably still at Edith's waiting for her to return, while she was here in a hotel room with George. There was no way she could go back to him now. Not after she'd slept with George again. He would know when she didn't return tonight. There would be no wedding. At least not with him. She would marry George and try to forget about him. George was right. They belonged together.

She struggled to sleep like George, but she couldn't. She could not erase Jude's face from her mind or forget the kiss they'd shared yesterday. She pictured him, the sincere expression on his face when he'd told her he was falling in love with her and would be waiting at Edith's for her. She began to weep softly and could not stop as tears fell down her face in torrents and soaked her pillow.

Why am I crying so much? George was right beside her. Wasn't he the one she had always wanted? She had only known Jude for a month.

Pain rippled through her as she thought about Jude. She felt torn. How would Jude feel when he found out she was back with George? He would be terribly hurt, she was sure.

She took a long deep breath and then wiped her tears with the duvet. She had to let go of Jude. He would be fine. Thankfully he would not have to go back to his country. After he accepted the fact that they would not be together, he would get back with his ex, marry her, and get his Green card. She, on the other hand, would marry George and be content with him. That was exactly how everything was meant to be.

George shifted on the bed and pulled her close. She snuggled up to him and settled into his arms, her head resting on his chest. Fresh tears formed in her eyes as Jude's face appeared in her mind again. She forced his face away and wiped her tears. She had to be content with what she had now. Most of all, she had to try to forget about Jude completely.

SIXTEEN

Jude could not sit still. He kept pacing his living room as he stared at his cell phone on the table. It took everything in him not to pick it up and dial Sofia's number.

He groaned and raked his fingers through his hair. *Sofia, where are you?*

Once again, he reached out to pick up his phone and call Sofia, and then he withdrew his hand. He had to wait for Edith to call him. He had already dialed Sofia's number more than a hundred times in the past night, but she had not picked up once. It was unlikely that she would answer his call now.

He stopped pacing and stood in the middle of the living room. For a long moment, he placed his hands on his head as he thought about Sofia and what she had told him yesterday. He could not bear the thought of her spending the night with her ex, but his mind would not let that possibility go. If she hadn't spent the night with George, she would have answered his calls or called to let him or Edith know where she was. His heart pounded with fear. Unless something bad had happened to her. Something really bad.

He groaned and shook his head, and then looked at his phone again, willing it to ring. But it did not. His mind traveled again to his confrontation with Sofia yesterday. She had looked torn when she'd told him she was going to see George. He had kissed her, hoping it would make her change her mind and stay with him, but now he chastised himself for doing so. Maybe that had contributed in chasing her further away. Maybe she thought he had come on too strong. Before she'd left, he had told her he would wait for her to return, and he had. He had worried continuously as he waited in Edith's living room; every hour she was away had left a thorn in his heart.

Flynn had returned to the house, clearly drunk, at about one a.m. and asked him what he was still doing there. He'd told Flynn he was waiting for Sofia to come back. Flynn had stared at him as though he'd lost his mind. "You are plumb crazy," he'd said, and then staggered away.

He was grateful for Edith. She had come to the living room and sat with him while he talked about Sofia. He kept asking what was keeping Sofia, why she had not returned, all the while calling her phone. Edith did not answer any of his questions.

By two o'clock, his thoughts had begun to alternate between Sofia being in the arms of her ex, and her lying somewhere on the street, hurt or dead. Both scenarios made him feel sick.

"Maybe something bad has happened to her," he had said to Edith at about a quarter past three. Edith only shook her head. Ten minutes later, she stood up and told him to go home. When he refused, she shrugged and told him she was going to bed. She left and once again he picked up his phone and called Sofia's number. Again, she did not answer. He finally sat down on the sofa and folded his arms while he tapped his feet impatiently, still hoping Sofia would call him back.

Another hour later, Edith had returned to the living room. She sat across from him and said, "Jude, what are you still doing here? You know Sofia is with her ex right now." She had pointed to the clock on the wall. "Look at the time. It is clear that she's spending the night with him."

He felt sick at the thought and told Edith that it might not be the case. He didn't want to believe that Sofia had really gone back to her ex and was spending the night in his arms. But if she wasn't with her ex, then where was she? It would mean she was definitely hurt or worse, and that, he could not stomach either.

Soon, he grew sleepy and then felt himself dozing. What seemed like a short time later, he woke up with a start when someone tapped his shoulder.

"Jude, you're still here," Edith said, looking down at him. "You should go home. I am sure Sofia is safe."

He had told Edith that he would not leave until Sofia returned and he was certain she was okay.

Edith had sat next to him on the sofa and thrown him a sad smile. "She might not return. At least not today."

He frowned. "Aren't you worried about that? Maybe she's hurt or something." His heart squeezed with fear for Sofia. Once again, he prayed, asking

God, who he had not spoken to in years until recently, to protect her.

Edith shook her head. "Jude, do you want to know the truth?"

He narrowed his eyes. He did not want to hear what she was going to say.

"I am going to tell you anyway," Edith said. "You already know what the truth is, Jude. You need to accept it. Sofia is back with George. She has been with him for years, and even when I and some of her other friends warned her about him, she still stuck to him. She spent the night with him. There is no doubt about it."

He wanted to ignore everything that Edith had just told him, but it was impossible. He'd refused to believe that Sofia had slept with her ex, even though deep down he knew it was true. Still he said to Edith, "Sofia would not do that. We are supposed to get married in two days' time. Before she left, I told her I loved her."

Edith sighed loudly. "And did she tell you she loved you?"

He shut his eyes and tried to convince himself that Sofia did love him and that she was not now with her ex, but he knew Edith was right. He did not know what he was going to do or how all this would turn out, but he felt as though his heart was being torn to shreds, just like when Keziah had broken up with him weeks before their wedding. *Why is this happening again? Why would she do that to me?*

He groaned. He had told Sofia before she'd left the house that he would understand if she decided to go back to her ex, but now, sitting here, imagining her spending the night with that George guy, he knew it was a lie. He did not understand and never would. It hurt like crazy. Why had he allowed himself to fall in love with her?

"Jude, you should go home," Edith repeated.

He shook his head. "I can't. I promised Sofia I would be here waiting for her."

Edith raised her brows. "You really love her, don't you? You will stay here waiting for her even when you know she spent the night with another man?"

Pain tore at him again, but he nodded.

The hard look on Edith's face disappeared, and her eyes softened. She said to him, "You're so good for Sofia, Jude. I wish she wasn't so stupid… leaving you here to go back to a man like George." She looked into Jude's eyes. "Fight for her, Jude. Don't give up. Let me tell you something Sofia might not have told you. George is married."

Jude raised his brows. "Married?"

"Yes! It was why they broke up. His wife came with him to the apartment he'd rented for Sofia and basically evicted her, took the car George bought her, and forced George to break up with her. Sofia was also fired from her job because she was working at the time for one of his wife's father's companies. I cannot imagine why Sofia would go back to him after all that."

Jude tried to process what Edith was saying to him. George, the man Sofia had told him about, who she'd been totally enamored with, was a married man? "Why was she dating a married man?"

He did not know he'd asked the question out loud until Edith said, "Your guess is as good as mine. Maybe he called her to tell her he would leave his wife for her. He's done that before, but he did not leave."

Jude said in a tortured voice, "Maybe this time he truly has." He could imagine a man, any man, married or single, leaving everything for Sofia. She was that kind of girl.

Edith said again, "Go home, Jude. I will call you when Sofia comes back."

"And what if she doesn't?" he asked.

"If I hear anything from her, I will let you know. There's no point in you staying here and torturing yourself like this." She picked up his phone from the table and began to punch in a number. Her phone rang on her lap and she picked it up. She gave him back his phone. "You have my number now, and I have yours. I promise I'll call you as soon as Sofia comes back."

"We are supposed to get married in two days' time," he said, more to himself than to Edith. But he decided to heed Edith's advice. He glanced at his phone. It was a few minutes past five o'clock. Reluctantly he stood up and staggered to the door, emotionally weary. He had gone back to his apartment and had been pacing the living room ever since.

He glanced at the clock on the wall. It was eleven o'clock now, and Edith still had not called him. He sighed and picked up his phone, unable to resist any longer. He dialed Sofia's number. Just as he'd expected, she did not answer. He dialed Edith's number and scrubbed his face with his hand as he waited for her to answer. When she did, he asked if Sofia had returned.

"She hasn't, Jude. I told you I would call you as soon as she comes back." There was a long pause on the other end of the line, and then Edith said, "Wait, Jude, someone is at the door. It might be her."

Jude's pulse raced. "Please, let it be her," he whispered, and relief flooded him when Edith told him Sofia had just walked into the house.

"I am on my way right now," he said, and hurried out of the apartment.

He took a cab so he could get to Edith's quickly. He kept looking out the window, willing the cab driver to go faster than he was. At the slow pace this driver was going, Sofia would have left again by the time he arrived at Edith's house.

The driver finally arrived and parked in front of Edith's. Jude jumped out of the cab after paying his fare. He ran into Edith's small house and found her in the living room.

"Where is she?" he asked Edith.

Edith pointed at a door to the left of the living room. "She's in there, packing her things. I tried to talk her out of it, but she refused to listen to me. Maybe she will listen to you."

He immediately went into the bedroom Edith had pointed out to him. He found Sofia standing near the closet, throwing her clothes into a suitcase. She looked up at him, and a look of shame filled her face. She looked down again and continued to pack her clothes into the suitcase.

"Sofia, what are you doing? Why didn't you come back yesterday?"

She did not answer.

He went to her and took her hand before she could throw another dress into the large suitcase.

He looked her in the eye. "What happened, Sofia? Why didn't you come back?"

She looked embarrassed and there were tears in her eyes. "I'm sorry, Jude. I truly am."

He held her hands. "What are you sorry for?"

She looked down, and he tilted her chin up so she would look at him again. "George and I have reconciled," she said in a small voice. "We're getting married soon."

He felt like someone had slapped him. "You are getting married to George? I thought we were getting married, Sofia. Our wedding is in two days. And how can you marry your ex when he's already married?"

She blinked and stared at him with a look of surprise. "Edith told you George was married," she said.

"Sofia, we are supposed to get married in two days. How can you marry your ex?"

A shadow fell over her face. "George has left his wife, and once his divorce is final, we will get married," she said. She looked him in the eye. "Jude, you know it's for the best. You remember the day we were talking about our exes, and I said I would go back to mine if he ever came back? You remember you also said you would do the same."

He felt his heart shredding into pieces. "That was before I fell in love with you," he said.

She looked down again. "I'm sorry. Maybe you think you love me now, but we have only known each other for a few weeks. I've known George for years and you have known your ex since you were teenagers. I think the best thing would be for both of us to go back to our exes, Jude."

"But I don't love Keziah, and I don't want to be with her. I love you and I want to marry you."

"No, Jude. This whole thing between us is nothing but a business transaction."

He cried, "You know it isn't! At least not for me. Not anymore."

"Jude, Keziah can get you a Green card. You won't lose anything by not marrying me. I'll go back to George and you can marry Keziah, and then she'll file for a spousal visa for you. You will get your Green card in no time."

Frustration consumed him. "I don't care about the Green card! I want you!"

"Jude, stop it!" Tears fell down her cheeks, and she dashed angrily at them. "I have to go." She locked up her suitcase and started to pull it out of the room.

He held her hand, stopping her. "Sofia, look at me." She refused to look at him, and he turned her face to his. "I love you, Sofia. Deeply." He folded her in his arms and felt her melt into him. He sighed with relief as she wrapped her arms around him, and then he winced when she pulled away abruptly.

"Please, Jude, stop trying to stop me from leaving. I have to go."

"Sofia, I love you," he said brokenly.

"You think you love me now, but our relationship started because you needed a Green card and I needed money. We are both in love with other people, but we got carried away with the novelty of our situation."

"That isn't true," he said.

"Yes it is. And you will realize it one day." She pulled her suitcase out of the room.

He followed her to the living room. "Don't go, Sofia. What about our wedding?"

"There will be no wedding, Jude. At least not between you and me. I'm getting married to George, and you will ultimately marry Keziah. That's the way it's meant to be."

She got to the door with her suitcase and he leapt forward, desperate to stop her from leaving. He stood in front of her, blocking her way. "Sofia, tell me the truth. I will let you go if you tell me you don't feel anything for me."

A trail of tears ran down her cheek, and he wiped it away with his thumb. "Please let me pass, Jude," she pleaded. He stayed where he was and she sighed. "Please, Jude!"

She looked at Edith, who was standing on the other side of the living room. "Please tell him to let me pass," she said.

Edith shrugged.

Jude sighed, his heart heavy. It was wrong for him to try to force her to stay, no matter how much he loved her. He finally stepped out of her way, and she opened the door and walked out of the house, taking his heart with her.

He collapsed on the sofa and held his head in his hands. He had lost every single thing that was important to him. Sofia had walked out of his life, leaving his heart in tatters. He was an illegal immigrant and it would not be long before he was driven out of this country. Not only had he lost Sofia, he would have to go back to a war zone. He definitely couldn't go back to Keziah as Sofia had suggested because, not only did he not love her but he would be using her simply to get a Green card if he went back. That just wasn't him. He stood up and went to the door, feeling numb.

"What are you going to do?" Edith asked.

He turned around and said, "I have to go and pack. Who knows when I will be dragged back to my country. I have to be prepared for it."

He had no money to buy a plane ticket. It was amusing in a terrible way that the only way he might be able to get back to Bakali would be through his deportation.

He opened the door and walked out of Edith's house, surrendering himself to the excruciating distress he felt at the fact that he had been dumped once again, right before his wedding. Whatever awful fate awaited him when he went back to his war-torn country might not be as bad as that.

SEVENTEEN

Sofia yawned as she turned on the bed and snuggled up to George. She blinked and opened her eyes. George was not on the bed anymore. Hearing footsteps behind her, she turned and saw him shrugging into his business suit. He smiled at her as he picked up his gold wristwatch from the dresser and clasped it on his wrist.

She started up on the bed and stared at him. "Where are you going, George? I thought you said you'd lost your job because your wife's father fired you. But it looks like you're going to work."

He walked up to the bed and smiled at her. "I was fired, but I need to get another job. I need to meet up with business associates and acquaintances; anyone who can help get me another job."

She suddenly remembered that today was supposed to be the eve of her wedding. She would have been getting married to Jude tomorrow if she'd not decided to stay with George. Now the wedding would not take place. Her heart squeezed with pain, but she brushed the thoughts aside.

There was no use dwelling on what would have been. The decision to stay with George rather than marry Jude had been a tough one, but she'd made her decision and she would have to be content with it. George was her future now. She looked up at him. "So you are leaving me all alone in this hotel room? What am I supposed to do with myself all day?"

He leaned down on the bed, cupped her cheeks, and kissed her. "I'll be back this evening," he said, stepping back again. "Hold tight." His gaze swept the length of her, and then he winked. "When I get back, we can order room service again and spend more time together."

She looked around at her luxurious surroundings and groaned inwardly. George was going to leave her here and go off to do whatever he had planned for the day. He expected her to wait for him until he came back to sleep with her.

An uncomfortable feeling rose up in her, and she felt a little cheap. She knelt on the bed and wrapped herself with the duvet. "I cannot stay in this hotel room all day doing nothing, George," she said to him.

"I promise, Sofia. I will be back as soon as I can."

"Can we go out when you return instead of staying in the room?" Without thinking it through, she said, "Maybe we could go to an art class?"

She winced as suffocating guilt enfolded her. Her date with Jude at the art studio had been memorable. In spite of how uncomfortable she'd been about the attention her painting had garnered, she had had a lot of fun. Was she trying to recreate that date with George? Jude had praised her painting skills. Would

George do the same if they went, or would he still be indifferent? She quickly brushed all thoughts of Jude aside and focused on George. He was looking at her with a curious expression on his face.

"Can we go to an art class?" she asked again, wanting to know what he would say if he saw her painting again. It would definitely not be to the same art class she and Jude had gone because bringing another guy just days after she and Jude were there would be really strange.

"An art class? Whatever for?" he asked. He brought her his tie and, she leaned forward to tie it around his neck for him. When she finished, he stepped back and buttoned his business suit.

She studied him. He looked as dapper as always. Jude's face appeared unbidden in her mind. Unlike George, who lived mostly in business suits, Jude sported jeans and T-shirts almost all the time. But he always looked gorgeous, even dressed casually every day.

Stop thinking about him, she chided herself. She said to George, "It's an opportunity to spend time together creatively instead of just staying in this room. We can draw random stuff and have fun doing it. Jude said I was a good painter and that I could have my own studio and hold an exhibition." She winced after she had spoken and pressed her lips tightly together.

George frowned. "Who is Jude?" He shrugged before she could say anything. "We're not going to an art class, Sofia." Once again, he winked at her. "I'd rather do something much more enjoyable with you when I return." His eyes swept her body. "Besides, by the time I get back, I'll be too tired to go out."

She opened her mouth to protest again, but he put his finger over her lips, stopping her words. "Order anything you want to eat for breakfast and lunch, Sofia, and charge it to my card." He kissed her again and then picked up a file from the bedside table. "I'll see you later." He stepped back from the bed and left the room.

She huffed and sighed wearily. *Great! George is gone.* What would she do with herself now?

For a short moment, she sat staring at the door, and then she got out of bed and shrugged on her silk robe. She wore her slippers and padded out of the bedroom to the living room. This particular hotel suite George had booked for them reminded her of the one they had stayed in when they'd gone to Prague. It was luxurious but minimal at the same time. She opened the curtains, stretched, and looked out the window at the view of the city.

A while later, she called to order a large breakfast and then went to take a long, soothing bath. She shut her eyes as she immersed herself in the bubble bath and immediately Jude's face appeared in her mind. She groaned. She hadn't stopped feeling guilty since she'd left him at Edith's yesterday. It did not escape her that this was the second time a fiancée had broken up with him days to their wedding.

She bit her lip as she thought about Jude. If only things were different. But they weren't. She was destined to be with George, and he with Keziah. It was why fate had brought his ex back into his life despite how slim the probability had been of that happening. And it was why he had gone to see her and kissed her days before their wedding.

But he did not spend the night with her like you did with George, she scolded herself.

She moaned. She had to stop thinking about him! She climbed out of the bath and dried her body. After putting on her clothes, she made her way back into the living room and turned on the television to try to distract herself from her guilt. She flipped through one channel after another and then got up when the double doorbell rang. She opened the door and smiled at the waiter as he rolled her breakfast into the room.

After she'd eaten, she sprawled on the sofa and soon fell asleep. She awoke sometime later and began walking around the suite, completely bored. She flipped through a stack of magazines on the coffee table, dozed once more, and then woke up again.

She glanced at the clock on the wall. It was a few minutes past one. Her stomach rumbled in spite of the large meal she'd eaten this morning. She thought about calling and ordering lunch and then changed her mind. If she stayed cooped up in this suite alone for one more minute, she would lose her mind. She had to get out.

She put on a pair of jeans and a loose top and left the suite. Riding the elevator down to the lobby, she considered going to one of the restaurants in the hotel for lunch, and then an idea came to her. She strode out of the hotel and began to walk down the street, looking this way and that, hoping to find a fast food restaurant. She clearly recalled her date with Jude and the delicious hamburger she had tried the next day. She wanted another one. She hadn't had a burger in years, except for that day.

She found a McDonald's, entered, and ordered a double cheeseburger. She sat down at a table near the window and began to consume her burger. George would not be happy if he saw her in a fast food restaurant eating this cheeseburger. She had spent her years with him dining on expensive gourmet foods. He never went to fast food restaurants and he had influenced her to never eat junk food. She would probably have to give it up again now that they were back together.

As she ate, she thought about Jude again. She clearly recalled their first date. How nervous and cautious she had been before the date, but how relaxed and comfortable she'd felt by the end. She'd discovered they had a lot in common, and before she knew it, Jude had swept her off her feet.

Do you love him, Sofia?

She squeezed her eyes shut for just a second. She didn't have an answer to that question. She cared greatly for him, but how could she love him and love George at the same time?

And do you still love George?

She immediately dismissed that thought. Of course she loved George. They had been through so much together over the years, and she had stuck with him despite the ups and downs of his marriage and the pressure it put on their relationship. He had promised on various occasions to leave his wife so they could be together, but he had not. She'd still stayed with him. Thankfully, he had finally come to his senses and left Elena. She was going to marry him soon. Of course she loved him.

Her heart ached as she recalled for the umpteenth

time what Jude had said to her yesterday. He had pleaded with her and told her he loved her. She sighed as the same question arose in her heart. *Do you love him?*

She could not think about that right now. Even if she did, there was no point dwelling on it. Just as she had told him, their proposed marriage had been nothing but a business transaction and they would eventually get divorced. This way was better.

For who?

She groaned and pressed the unsettling question out of her mind. Hurriedly finishing her burger, she left the restaurant. She still didn't want to go back to the hotel suite, so she strolled down the sidewalk aimlessly. She continued to walk until she got to a commercial area with businesses and corporations. She looked into the windows of a few clothing stores and then continued to walk until she approached George's former workplace.

She started to walk past the investment company and then blinked in surprise when she noticed George's Mercedes parked at the side of the building.

Why is George's car here?

She stopped beside the car and looked up at the building, wondering if George was here. She sighed and told herself she was overthinking things. Even if George was in the building, he was probably here to get his things from his former office. She started to walk away, but curiosity got the better of her and she turned around and walked into the building.

She had been here a couple of times to see George and knew her way around. She rode the elevator up to his office and stepped into the reception area.

Caroline, the girl who manned the front desk simply smiled and nodded at her. She continued on until she got to the front of his secretary's office. Sheila, his fifty-something-year-old secretary, looked up at her as she walked in. The woman always looked stern and she had never spoken more than a few sentences to her. Today, she frowned and narrowed her eyes.

"Good afternoon, Sheila," Sofia said politely. She pointed at George's former office. "Is George in that office now?"

Sheila looked at her as though she were the stupidest person she had ever met. "Of course he's in his office."

"So why is he there?"

Sheila stared at her with a look of distaste. "Because that is his office! Where else would he be?"

"I don't understand," Sofia said. "Is he here to get his things? He was fired, wasn't he?"

"What on earth are you talking about?" Sheila glared at her. "Who told you George was fired? He is the CEO of this company."

"But... he told me the chairman..." Sofia's heart began to race. So George had lied to her. Why, oh why would George lie to her? "Can I see him?" she asked Sheila.

"No!" Sheila said emphatically. "His wife and daughter are in there with him."

Sofia's heart stopped. "His wife and daughter?"

"That's what I just said." Sheila looked like she wanted to stand up and bundle Sofia out of the building. "I think you should leave before they come out."

Sofia's stomach burned with rage. She wanted

to barge into George's office and confront him, but she would probably be escorted out of the building by security. She had to get herself together. She squared her shoulders and looked at Sheila. "I'll wait for him." She went to sit on the sofa facing Sheila's desk.

The secretary gave her an amused smile, as though to say Sofia waiting here would be at her own risk, and shrugged. "Your call," she said, and went back to her work.

For a long time, Sofia waited, simmering with anger. She hoped with all her heart that there was some reasonable explanation for why George was in his office, still working for a company he had told her he'd been fired from, and with a wife who he had purportedly left. She tried to think of a good reason why everything he'd told her seemed to be a lie, but she could not come up with any. Still, she kept telling herself to calm down and not to overreact. There had to be a good explanation for this.

She crossed and uncrossed her legs, took deeps breath, and kept waiting. Finally, George stepped out of his office with his wife and their sixteen-year-old daughter, Allie. Sofia's anger turned to rage when George kissed his wife fully on the mouth. Without thinking, she shot up from the sofa, marched over to George and the woman that had influenced him to throw her out of her apartment, and faced off with him.

His mouth dropped open, and his eyes widened in astonishment and then fear. He started to shake his head and Sofia narrowed her eyes in anger.

"George! You liar!"

His wife turned around and glared at Sofia.

"Please, Sofia. Not here. Not now. Please, let's talk later."

Elena turned to him. "George, what is this? I thought this tramp was out of your life for good."

Sofia burned with fury, but she refused to react to Elena's insult. It was not the woman's fault after all. George was to blame for everything. He had lied to her and to his wife over and over again. He did not want her to make a scene in here? She would destroy everything he held dear, just like he had destroyed her life. "So you lied to me and told me you had left your wife and were going to divorce her and marry me. But all the while, you were lying to me and to her."

"Please, Sofia," George pleaded.

Elena stared at George and asked coldly, "What is she talking about? Did you tell her we were getting a divorce?"

He began to plead with his wife, but Sofia was not through with him. So what if his daughter was here? She might as well hear what sort of person her father was. "We spent the night together," she said to his wife. "Yesterday."

His daughter shrank back, and his wife gave him a death stare. "You told me you had to work all night at the office," she said. "So you were with your mistress all along."

Before he could answer, Sofia nodded. "Yes. He was with me. And he told me he had been fired by your father because he asked you for a divorce."

"Sofia, please not here," George pleaded again. "We can talk about all this later."

"No, we will talk about it now," Sofia said. "You

told me you would marry me; that you didn't love your wife and had finally left her. But it was all a lie." She laughed harshly. "I was a fool. Everyone warned me about you, but I did not listen."

George said to her, "I love you, Sofia, but I couldn't just walk away from my wife. I could not afford to lose everything I have."

His face turned red as his wife slapped him hard. "Well, that's too bad," Elena said. "Because you are going to lose everything you have. You can have your mistress now, but know this — by the time I'm through with you, you'll not be able to find work anywhere. And you want a divorce? I will give you one, but I will make sure I fight you for sole custody of all our children and win." She turned to their daughter. "Allie, let's go!" Turning around again, she marched out of the secretary's office, Allie right behind her.

George looked like he was going to melt into a puddle. He gave Sofia a pleading look, but she turned around and marched away, fuming. Anger, pain, and shame ran through her as she exited the building. She thought about Jude and felt like breaking down right on the sidewalk.

What have you done, Sofia?

She had pushed away the man who loved her and a chance for a great future with a guy like Jude for someone like George. A cheat and a liar.

But you were a part of it all, Sofia.

Once more, guilt threatened to suffocate her. She had ignored everyone who'd told her it was wrong to be with a married man. She had made constant excuses for George every time he promised he would leave his wife but never did. Why had she let him talk her into going back to him? But she could not blame him alone. She shared a large portion of the blame.

She got back to the hotel room and packed up all her things. Why had she believed George's lies? It was not the first time he had lied to her. Why had she chosen to believe that he would suddenly become honest?

Oh, Jude! He would never forgive her for this. He was probably back with his ex already, while she would be left to rue losing him and making the biggest mistake of her life.

She finished packing and rolled her suitcase out of the suite. What future did she have now? She was going back to stay with Edith and Flynn, but it would not be long before Flynn convinced Edith to send her packing. Where would she go then? She still had the money Jude had paid for the first installment. Flynn and his friend had gotten part of it, but the little she had would be enough to rent a tiny apartment and live on for a short while. It was better to find an apartment of her own than go back to Edith's only to be thrown out.

Congratulations, Sofia. You have ruined your life in a matter of days.

The overwhelming hopelessness that she had felt when George had broken up with her and taken everything from her settled over her again. For a short moment, she embraced it, wishing she could end her life. And then she shook it off. Even feeling like this was pointless. Trying to escape the awful way she felt now, which was a direct consequence of her stupid choices, was the coward's way out.

She had never taken control of her life and had

depended on others — George, Edith, and in some ways even Jude — to do that for her. Now, she had to find a way to live independently. She didn't know how she would do it, but it had to be done. Great difficulty awaited her in the future. She would constantly live in regret for letting go of Jude, who she could now admit she loved, but she would have to find a way to go on and dig herself out of her problems. She had to try to make some sort of life for herself, no matter how hard it would be.

She got into a taxi outside the hotel, still thinking about Jude; about the awful mistake she had made in letting him go. She remembered what Lily always said whenever she had a problem: *Ask God to help you. He will.* Sofia couldn't remember the last time she'd prayed. Maybe it was when she was a kid.

She prayed with uncertainty. Not for herself, but for Jude. She asked God as best as she could that everything would ultimately work out for Jude and that he would be able to marry his ex so he would not have to go back to his country where his life would be in danger. Most of all, she prayed that one day he would find it in his heart to forgive her.

EIGHTEEN

"Man, I'm telling you, there will be no wedding!" Jude said, pressing his cell phone to his ear. "The deal is off."

"What do you mean there will be no wedding!" Shaffar yelled on the other end of the line. "Listen, Jude, you owe me money, and you're going to pay up!"

He pushed aside some of his clothes, which were all over the bed, and sat down. Shaking his head, he said exasperatedly, "I am not marrying Sofia anymore, Shaffar. That means I don't owe you any more money."

He began to pack his clothes into his suitcase, holding his cell phone between his ear and shoulder. He frowned as Shaffar swore loudly and insisted once more that he had to pay the rest of the money.

"Man, you are crazy!" he said to Shaffar. "How can I keep paying you when I'm not getting married?" A thread of pain went through him as he thought about Sofia and the fact that their wedding was off.

"Listen, I don't care if you're getting married or not. We had a deal, and you have to pay!"

Jude sighed wearily. How was he supposed to explain to this unreasonable guy that this "deal" had not worked out, so he did not have to pay?

"I know exactly what to do if you refuse to pay!" Shaffar said. "ICE is only a phone call away."

Jude shook his head and hung up on Shaffar. The guy's threats meant nothing to him at this point. Not when his heart was hurting and he was going to leave the United States in a few hours. He had a flight booked to Guinea, and Ben had promised to take him to the airport in about an hour. A friend of Ben's who lived and had contacts in the Guinean government had kindly promised to host Jude in his home temporarily so he didn't have to go back to his war-torn country. Ben and a few friends had lent him money for his plane ticket. Of course he would not be able to stay in Guinea indefinitely.

Though it was a temporary arrangement, it had given Jude some hope. At least he was sure to survive, even if it was just for now.

Overwhelming sadness settled over him as he continued to pack his clothes into his suitcase, and he told himself to look on the bright side. But at this moment it was almost impossible for him not to dwell on what he'd lost. He and the woman he loved would have been married if not for circumstances beyond his control. She would be married to someone else in no time, and he would be miles and miles away from her.

Samuel walked into the room as he continued to pack. Sitting on the bed, he looked at Jude and said, "I cannot believe you're leaving today. I'm going to miss you."

Jude reached out and pounded his friend's back affectionately. "I will miss you too, man."

"Will you ever come back?" Samuel asked.

"I don't know," Jude said. "But I will definitely not be allowed back into this country if I am caught and deported. In fact, since I overstayed my visa for months, I don't know if I will be allowed back… at least for a long time."

Samuel said, "I'm really sorry about how everything ended, you know, with Sofia."

Another wave of pain hit Jude at the mention of Sofia. He sighed and tried to focus on his packing. "I can't think about her right now, or I will start to drown in self-pity. I have to concentrate on finishing my packing and making sure I leave for the airport on time."

"We've had a blast in school together, haven't we?" Samuel smiled at him.

Jude chuckled. "Yes. We had some good times."

"We had a lot of fun, Jude."

"Yes," Jude said. "I just wish I'd had less fun and concentrated more on my immigration status. Maybe, just maybe, I would not be leaving America now."

"Stop blaming yourself, dude. Everything that happened was out of your control. Your father's death, the war in your country… Sofia's betrayal. How would you have known that everything would turn out the way it did?"

"I should have taken responsibility when things started to go bad and realized I needed to do something so I could remain in this country." He shook his head. "Anyway, it's all too late now. I will miss everything. My life here..." He wanted to say Sofia, but stopped himself at the last minute.

They talked about school and their friends and studies until he finished packing. He left the room, rolling his suitcase, and Samuel followed. Before he could sit down in the living room, a loud knock sounded at the door. He looked up at the clock on the wall.

"Who is it?" Samuel called out.

"Probably Ben," Jude said. "He is thirty minutes early, though." He strode to the door, opened it, and blinked in surprise. Edith was standing there, looking at him with a worried expression on her face.

His stomach flipped with concern. "Hey, Edith! What is it?"

"It's Sofia, Jude."

Fear gripped him. "What about her?"

"I really don't know. I have not been able to reach her since yesterday. Normally I would not worry about it, but I received a troubling message from her saying that she had lost everything dear to her and that she wasn't sure she could go on living anymore."

He winced and his heart began to race.

"I am worried about her, Jude."

Before Edith spoke again, he dug his hand into his pocket, brought out his phone, and dialed Sofia's number. It did not ring. He looked at Edith. "Her phone isn't ringing."

"I told you I've been trying to call her, but her line is not going through," Edith said. "I am terrified that she may have done something to herself."

Jude blinked, confused. "What do you mean?"

Edith sighed. "She has tried to kill herself before."

Jude stared at Edith in horror. Fear snaked itself around him, and for a moment, he could not breathe.

"She didn't tell you?" Edith asked with a surprised look.

He shook his head.

"Just before you met, I went to her apartment and found her lying on the floor, lifeless. She had taken some pills to end her life. If I had not arrived and called 911, she would be dead."

Jude began shake his head. "No, no! Edith, we have to find her!" He felt like the wind was being sucked out of him, but he took a deep breath to try to gain control of his emotions. They needed to act.

"I'm so worried about her, Jude," Edith said. "But I really don't know where to start looking for her."

"We need to start somewhere; anywhere," he said. "We have to go right now." He swept past Edith.

"Where exactly are we going?" she asked.

Jude turned to her. "I don't know... Someone has to know where she is." He looked up thoughtfully. "I have never met her other friends and acquaintances. Do you have any of their numbers? Their addresses?"

"We have a few mutual acquaintances and I have their numbers," Edith said. "I have called some of them, but we can call more."

"And George?" Jude asked. "Do you have his number or do you know where he lives? She might still be with him."

"I don't have his number or his address," Edith answered.

He shut his eyes briefly as another wave of terror went through him. *Sofia, where are you?* He opened his eyes again. "Let's start calling all your mutual acquaintances while we look in your house for any clues of where she might have gone."

They started to leave Samuel's apartment together, and Samuel called, "Jude, what about your flight? Ben will be here any moment now."

"I need to find Sofia, Samuel," Jude said. "I need to find her right now." He hurried out of the house, with Edith on his heels.

"You drive while I make the calls," Edith said, handing Jude her car keys. He got into the driver's seat of Edith's car while she sat next to him on the passenger's seat. She called her and Sofia's mutual acquaintances as he sped down the road toward her house. Every call she made ended in disappointment, as none of the acquaintances knew where Sofia was and none had George's phone number or address.

Edith called a final acquaintance, and the girl told her she did not know where George lived, but she knew where he worked. She texted Edith the office address, and Edith showed it to Jude.

Jude nodded and changed directions.

The traffic light above turned red, and he bit his lips and nearly screamed in frustration. He thought about running the light, but it would be a really bad idea, especially considering his immigration status. The last thing he needed was to be pulled over by a police officer. He kept looking out the window, hoping the light would turn green. Sofia's face was etched in his mind, and he felt like throwing up as an image of her lying lifeless on the floor appeared.

Once again, he prayed silently that she would be protected and that she would not harm herself.

The light turned green, and he heaved a sigh of relief. He raced down the road until he finally reached George's office, a huge building with the words, "Impact Investments" emblazoned at the top of it. As they walked into the building, anger raced through Jude. This was where George worked, the man who had evicted Sofia from her apartment and taken her job. But Sofia was not without blame. The man was married, and in spite of everything he'd done to her, she had still gone back to him. Jude gritted his teeth. It was beyond his understanding.

Settle down, Jude, he told himself. He was not here to fight with George. All he wanted to know was that Sofia was okay, even if she was still with the man.

At the front desk, they asked the receptionist if they could see the CEO of the company. The girl was on the phone and seemed distracted. She nodded at them and pointed at the elevator. "His office is on the last floor," she said, and went back to her call.

Jude got into the elevator with Edith and rode it up to the top floor. When they exited, they walked straight through a long hallway into the office of a grumpy-looking middle aged woman sitting behind a desk, speaking on the phone. As they came to stand in front of her, she looked up at them and pointed at the sofa across from her. Jude tried to speak, but she shook her head and held up her hand. "I will be right with you," she said firmly, and turned away from them.

They both sat, and Jude tapped his feet

impatiently, clenching and unclenching his fist. *Sofia, please hold on. God, please don't let her hurt herself.* He looked at the secretary who was still on the phone and forced himself not to yell at her.

She finally got off the phone, and he stood up and walked over to her again. "We need to see George Davidson, now."

She arched her brows and stared at him and Edith. "George Davidson does not work here anymore," she said angrily.

Jude blinked. "We were told this was his office…"

The woman cut in. "This used to be his office." She pointed at the door to her left. "But as I said, he doesn't work here anymore."

Jude groaned. "Do you know where he lives?"

"No!"

"What about a phone number?"

"I'm sorry, but I cannot help you!" the woman said belligerently. She turned away from him as her phone rang and picked up the receiver.

Jude turned to Edith. "Where are we going to look for her?" he asked as worry flooded him. "Should we go to the police?"

"She has not been missing for twenty-four hours," Edith said. "I don't know if the police will be of much help."

"I think we can call and file a report," he said.

She nodded as they left the angry secretary's office and went to the end of the hallway to place the call. She came back to Jude a minute later, and he asked, "Where else can we search for her?"

"I am out of options," Edith answered.

They asked a few other employees rushing past them if they knew where George lived. Everyone looked like they were in a hurry and none of them had George's address or offered a phone number. Jude finally left the office building with Edith.

Outside, Jude stood in front of the building, his arms folded across his chest, his heart beating wildly with fear. "This is not good, Edith." He shook his head slowly. "This is really not good. What did the police say?"

"That they are on it."

"That is all?" he frowned. "Maybe we should actually go to the police station. They might take our report more seriously if we come in person." His phone rang, and for a brief moment, hope soared in his heart. He plucked it out of his pocket and answered immediately.

"Jude, where are you?" Ben's voice came over voice the line. "I'm at Samuel's, and he said you left the house, just like that. You need to get back here."

"Ben, Sofia is missing. I am looking for her now. I cannot come back until I find her."

"Jude, I'm sorry about that, but you have to get back. We have to leave for the airport or you will be late for your flight."

"I can't come right now, Ben. I'm sorry."

"What are you saying, man? You know you have no choice. We have to leave for the airport this minute. Remember what will happen if you don't leave the country. It's only a matter of time before you get deported."

"I cannot leave without making sure Sofia is okay," Jude said.

"Jude, listen, you cannot afford to be arrested by ICE. I hear that some people are detained in jail for weeks on end before they are finally deported back to their countries. You don't want that to happen to you."

Jude shut his eyes and shook his head. "I'm not leaving until I find Sofia." He ended the call and stuffed his phone into his pocket. It rang again, but he ignored it.

"Let's go to your house and see if we can find any clues to where Sofia might have gone," he said to Edith.

They got into Edith's car, and he began to drive to her house. His phone rang again, and he took it out of his pocket and turned it off. He was well aware of the risks he was putting himself in by staying in the United States, but Sofia was more important than any of those risks. Right now, he did not care what happened to him as long as he knew she was fine. That was all that mattered.

They reached Edith's house and went straight to Sofia's tiny bedroom. They searched everywhere for any clue that could lead them to where she was, but they found none. They went around the whole house searching, but they found nothing. At last, Jude stood in the middle of the living room, his hands propped on his waist, troubling thoughts racing through his mind. They were out of options. The only thing they could do was go to the police in person. He told Edith what he was thinking.

She opened her mouth to say something, but he shook his head. "I know you have already filed a report police, but as you said, she hasn't been missing for more than twenty-four hours. They might not take your report seriously and we cannot stay here with our hands folded, doing nothing." He pressed his lips together as another wave of terror went through him.

Sofia might be seriously hurt. He did not want to say it out loud, but she might be dead. He felt like weeping, but he knew he had to hold it together.

"I am going now," he said to Edith. He strode to the door and then turned around when Edith did not follow. "Are you coming?"

She sighed loudly and then followed him out the door.

NINETEEN

Sofia slowly sat on the old couch in the run-down apartment she had rented yesterday. She stared at the bottle of pills for a full minute and then poured a handful into her palm. She lifted her hand to her mouth to swallow the pills and then put her hand down again. She looked at the pills in her hand once more and glanced at the bottle on the couch. The last time she'd taken some pills, she had not succeeded in killing herself. She had to take all of them and hope this time she would not awaken.

She emptied the entire bottle into her palm and once again raised the pills to her mouth.

Don't do it, Sofia!

She inhaled and stifled the warning voice inside her. It hurt too much to be alive. She had to end the pain. There was nothing to live for. She had made a complete mess of her life. But worse than that, she had made a mess of the lives of those around her — George, his wife, their kids... Jude... She cried out as she thought about Jude. Overwhelming shame filled her, and she felt even more determined to end it all. She lifted her hand with the pills and opened her mouth to swallow them. Her phone rang and she jumped, causing the pills to spill to the floor.

She blinked in surprise and stared at her phone on the coffee table. She had switched it off yesterday when she'd left George's office and she was certain she had not switched it back on. How on Earth was it ringing now?

She groaned as she looked at the pills that had fallen and were scattered across the floor. She looked at her phone again and frowned. Moaning, she began to gather the pills from the floor, placing them in her palm again. Just as she finished gathering them, her phone rang again, startling her and causing the pills to spill right back to the floor. She screamed in rage and frustration and then grabbed her phone from the battered coffee table in front of her. "Yes, who is this?" she asked in annoyance.

"Sofia, is everything okay?"

"Lily!" She immediately gathered herself together. She'd been trying to call Lily to talk to her for a long time without success.

"Sofia, how are you? Are you okay?"

Sofia slipped down to the floor, her heart aching and tears falling down her face. Maybe Lily was right all along. Maybe there was a God above who truly cared for her, because what were the chances of Lily calling her right when she was about to end it all? And her phone being on when she was certain she'd turned it off was inexplicable.

"Sofia, are you there?" Lily asked. "Are you okay?"

Sofia could not hold back anymore and she blurted out, "No, Lily. I'm not okay."

"I knew something was wrong," Lily said, sounding worried. "Taylor and I arrived in Fallow Creek yesterday. This morning, I felt a constant urge to call you. Tell me what's wrong, Sofia."

Sofia gripped her phone. "Everything is wrong, Lily," she said. She began to tell Lily about her first break up with George; how his wife had come to her apartment, kicked her out, and fired her from her job. Shame flooded her as she said, "You warned me about George, Lily. I should have listened. I should never have ignored your words."

She continued to talk about the pain she'd felt after she and George had broken up.

"No, Sofia," Lily cried when Sofia told her she had tried to kill herself after George had left her the first time. "You did not!"

"My friend Edith came just in time, or I would be dead," she said. She continued on about getting back with George.

"Sofia, you went back to him? Why?"

"I feel so stupid now," Sofia said. She talked about George; how she'd found out that he had lied to her. She could not bring herself to tell Lily about Jude. It felt too painful to talk about him and what she had done to him. Most of all, she did not want Lily to judge her because she had chosen to marry Jude for money or to judge him because he'd planned to marry her to get a Green card. Lily would not understand that things had changed later on and that they had developed feelings for each other. She didn't want Lily to think badly of Jude in any way.

"When I confronted George in his office, he told me he was sorry, but he had not left his wife because he did not want to lose his job and everything that mattered to him. I was so mad at him that I told his wife everything he had said to me. His wife asked him for a divorce right there. At first I felt great about that, but later on I just felt awful."

She told Lily about trying to swallow a fresh bottle of pills. Her break up with Jude was a big part of how she felt and why she tried to kill herself now, but she still could not talk about him with Lily.

"Sofia… no! No, you did not try to kill yourself again." Lily sounded on edge.

Sofia began to sob. "I feel so empty… like I have nothing to live for anymore."

"Listen, Sofia," Lily said, still sounding worried, "I know you've never wanted to hear me talk about Jesus, but you know He loves you. If you give your life to him, you will have something to live for. Now and for the future. You will have someone who loves you unconditionally and completely."

Sofia shut her eyes and listened as Lily talked about Jesus and his love and offer of salvation. She drank up everything Lily said, desperate for hope; for true love and for redemption. She sobbed loudly as Lily asked if she wanted that love in her life — a Father who would love her unconditionally and would always be there.

"I do, Lily. How do I receive His love?"

"By asking Jesus to come into your heart. Would you like to pray and ask Him into your heart?"

"Yes. I would like that," Sofia said, and then prayed with Lily, repeating the words that Lily told her to. She asked Jesus into her life and then her heart began to feel as though someone was opening it up and taking out all her despair and sorrow and the sins she was terribly ashamed of. Even those she had told no one about. Hope like she had never felt before descended on her, and then overwhelming joy flooded her. She could not stop crying. Not from sorrow this time, but from overwhelming happiness.

Lily stopped talking, and Sofia laughed out loud. "I cannot explain how I feel, Lily. I feel as though I could take on the whole world and that no matter what happens from now on, I will be okay." She laughed again. "No, not okay. I will be glorious."

Lily laughed. "Glorious! This is the first time I've heard you use that word."

"I don't know why I said that," Sofia chuckled. Her heart felt as light as a feather.

"Sofia, I will come and see you as soon as possible," Lily said, sounding worried again. "Please, don't ever try to hurt yourself again."

Sofia stood up, held out her hand, and spun around, laughing. She held the phone to her ear and said, "I would love for you to come and visit me, Lily, but I won't try to kill myself again. You don't have to worry about that."

"Are you sure?" Lily asked.

Sofia gathered the pills from the floor once more, but this time she put them all inside the bottle. She walked to the tiny bathroom in the single-room apartment, poured the pills into the toilet, and flushed them down. "Did you hear that, Lily? I flushed all the pills down the toilet. I'm too happy to even think properly, let alone try to kill myself."

Lily chuckled, but she still sounded uncertain as she told Sofia that she would come to Tucson to see her as soon as she and Taylor could get away. "We still have a few things to do in Fallow Creek, but hopefully, since we are in Arizona I can convince Taylor to come to Tucson with me so we can see you before we go to California."

"Okay, Lily," Sofia said. She asked if Lily had found her parents and sister, and Lily said she hadn't.

"There are a few trails we are following up," Lily said, "but I'm not sure they're going to lead to anything. Josh will soon start school, so we have to get back to California as soon as possible. After he's enrolled in school, we will continue to search for my parents and my sister."

"I hope you find them soon," Sofia said. "Don't worry, Lily. I'm sure they're safe wherever they are."

They changed the subject and started to talk about Taylor's kids. Lily could not stop talking about them and about Taylor. Sofia could hear how excited she was to have a new family of her own in spite of her worries about her parents and her sister. She felt thrilled for Lily.

A sliver of envy went through her as she thought about Jude. She could have been looking forward to starting a family with the man she loved if she had not messed it all up. She took a deep breath as she realized she had finally admitted to herself that she did love him.

"Sofia, are you still there? Are you sure you're okay?"

Sofia smiled as a heart flooded with joy again. "How can I not be when Jesus is in my heart now?" she said. "I'm so happy you have a family of your own, Lily. I knew that Taylor was a keeper when I first met him."

Lily laughed. "And I'm happy for you too, Sofia. You're now a part of God's forever family, and I can truly call you my sister now."

Soon, they changed topics again and talked about Sofia's present situation. She told Lily she had temporarily rented a tiny apartment and she had begun to try to find a job. Lily felt sorry for her, but Sofia told her not to. "I feel so happy, I might as well be living in a palace."

Lily chuckled.

They kept talking about Sofia's plans for the future and then the call finally ended. Sofia bent over the sink and washed her face, wiping away the tears that streaked down her cheeks. She stared at herself in the mirror. She looked a total mess, but she could not help smiling.

You need to call Edith.

She blinked. The words she'd heard now had been her thoughts, and yet they felt like they weren't. She sighed. She definitely needed to call Edith. Her friend would be wondering where she was and worrying. Edith was the one who had found her lying on the floor when she'd tried to kill herself. Maybe she was afraid that the same thing had happened to her.

She went to the living room again, sat on the couch and dialed Edith's number. An otherworldly peace settled in her heart as Edith answered on the first ring.

"Sofia, where on earth are you?" Edith exclaimed. "I've been trying to reach you. Are you okay?"

"I'm fine." She gave Edith the address of her new apartment.

"I will be right over," Edith said before Sofia

could tell her not to worry. Edith clicked off and Sofia put her phone aside and raised her eyes to the ceiling.

"Lord, what now?" she stood up and walked aimlessly around the tiny apartment. There was really not much to look at. It was just the single living room with a small kitchenette at the far end and a bathroom to her right. There was no bedroom. Still, she could not help smiling. She had rented the apartment with the little she had. Hopefully, it would be a temporary home. If things went well, she would soon get a job and save enough to rent a better apartment.

She suddenly remembered that Lily had spoken often when they lived together about studying her Bible, but she had no Bible. And then she recalled the day Lily had told her she wanted to read her Bible only for her to pick up her phone. Sofia had asked where Lily's Bible was. She had not been around any Christians for years, and she was surprised when Lily told her she had downloaded the Bible app on her phone.

Sofia picked up her phone, went on the internet, and then found a Bible app that looked appropriate. She downloaded it on her phone and then gleefully started to read from the very beginning. She was fascinated by the creation story. She hadn't read it since she was a child, and now that she had invited Christ into her heart, she felt an overwhelming sense of gratitude and awe that the God who had made the whole world was now her friend and father.

She was on the fifth chapter of Genesis when a loud knock sounded at her door. She stood up and went to open the door knowing it was Edith. And then she gasped. Jude was standing right next to Edith! Her pulse raced.

She looked down in shame and then started in surprise when he grabbed her and hugged her. He let her go and she bit her lips.

"I was so afraid that something bad had happened to you," Edith said.

Sofia let Edith pull her into the apartment, but her eyes stayed on Jude as he walked in and closed the door behind him. She was surprised he was here and had even hugged her, but she bowed her head in shame, knowing that nothing she said now would ever make up for what she had done to him. She had done the same thing as his ex, leaving him so close to their wedding. He was too good for her. She knew he was here because Edith had probably told him about her first suicide attempt and had made him come here to see her. Even when she'd hurt him, he still cared about her. He might never take her back, but she hoped that one day he would forgive her.

Her eyes grew wide with astonishment when he gathered her in a tight hug again. He pulled back and smiled at her, the warmth and love in his eyes taking her breath away. "Thank God you are okay, Sofia," he said. "I don't know what I would have done if you weren't."

TWENTY

Jude's heart pounded as he held Sofia in his arms. His emotions raged between despair, happiness, and uncertainty. He held her tighter, kissed the top of her head, and then held his breath, hoping she would not pull away. When she didn't, he sighed with relief.

She rested her head on his chest, and he could feel her tears wetting his T-shirt. He finally held her slightly away from him and looked into her eyes. "You're crying Sofia," he said. He wiped her tears away with his thumb and studied her face. He touched her hair and put his hand on her cheek. Waves of relief flooded him. He had been so afraid that she had hurt herself. Seeing her now, alive and well, he felt as though he had just been released from a dungeon. He longed to kiss her, but knew he couldn't. She had told him clearly that she was getting back with her ex and was going to marry him.

Once again hopelessness flooded him, but he immediately pushed the negative feelings away to concentrate on her. Relief filled him again at the fact that she was okay. He said softly. "I'm glad you're fine, Sofia. But why did you turn off your phone? Edith and I were so worried about you."

"It's a long story, Jude," she said.

His stomach flipped at the look in her eyes. She was looking at him as though he meant something to her, and he wondered why. If he did not know better, he would say she wanted to kiss him; to be with him. But she had told him in no uncertain terms that they did not have a future together. His heart hurt, and he wished she would stop looking at him the way she was. It only made the fact that he was leaving soon that much harder.

He sighed sadly and took her hands. He had to leave the country. He doubted that he would ever be at peace knowing that she might try to hurt herself the way she already had. He searched her eyes and said, "Please, Sofia, please promise me that you will never try to hurt yourself again."

She gave him a sad smile. "It will never happen again," she said. "I promise."

They stood holding hands and staring into each other's eyes. His heart flooded with love for her, and he sighed as an overwhelming urge to kiss her washed over him. Hopelessness settled over him. Today would have been their wedding. They would have been married by now if everything had gone as he had thought they would. But now he had to leave her, probably forever. He felt like someone was slicing his heart open.

She looked away from him and looked down at the floor but not before he saw an expression of shame creep into her face. He tilted her chin up so she would look at him again and then stepped back from her as the urge to kiss her increased. He turned to Edith and said, "Please watch over her. Don't let her hurt herself again. I wish I could be here, but I'm already late for my flight."

Sofia cried out, "Flight? What flight?"

He turned to her. Her eyes were filled with panic, and he frowned. "Ben found a way for me to move to Guinea temporarily since I can't stay in this country any longer."

He blinked. She looked devastated, and he quickly said, "I will be fine, Sofia. At least I will be safe there until the war in my country stops." He was somewhat relieved that she at least still cared about his well-being, but sad that she didn't care enough to stay with him and marry him.

Tears fell down her face, and he blinked. "Are you leaving America with your Keziah?" she asked in a voice laden with emotion.

His frown deepened. "No, Sofia. Keziah and I are not together." His heart beat wildly at the look of hope on her face.

"You are not?"

"No." He gazed at her in confusion. Why did she look so relieved when she was now with George? She said nothing, and he searched her eyes, trying to find the truth in them. Finally, he said slowly, "I guess I'll be going now. I wish you and George all the best. Please remember what I said about not hurting yourself, Sofia."

He wondered if George was the reason she had tried to harm herself again. And where was he now anyway? Jude looked at his wristwatch and let go of her hands. If he stayed another minute longer, he would not be able to leave today. And who knew if the flight Ben had booked for him was non-refundable. He could not afford to miss his flight unless Sofia…

He blinked in surprise when she grabbed his hand. She gave him a piercing look and she said, "I'm not with George anymore, Jude. I broke up with him because he is a liar and a cheat." Shame crept into her face again, and she looked down but only for a second. She looked up at him again. "But I also now realize that I wasn't any better than him. I was so deep in sin that I didn't even care that he was married, and I convinced myself that I loved him." She had a glow in her eyes as she said, "But now I have Jesus; I have a love that surpasses everything I could ever imagine. And His love has helped me recognize true human love as well. I know I didn't know what that meant at all until I met you."

He couldn't breathe as he listened to her.

"You truly love me, but I treated you badly, Jude. I know an apology will never make up for what I did to you, but I am truly sorry. I hope you can forgive me one day. I know you might not want to get back together with me, but…"

He could not hold back any longer and swept her into his arms again, joy flooding his heart. He kissed her hair, her temple, her cheeks, and then her lips. He hugged her fiercely and then pulled away slightly.

She looked up at him and said in a trembling voice, "I love you Jude, more than I have ever loved anyone before."

He swayed lightly on his feet, delirious with joy. Smoothing back her hair, he said, "You don't know how long I've wanted to hear you say that." He kissed her again and again, and then sighed when someone touched his shoulder. Pulling back reluctantly from Sofia, he turned to Edith.

"Guys, you can continue kissing later on," she said with a goofy smile on her face. "Today is supposed to be your wedding day, remember."

How could he have forgotten. It was impossible. It had haunted him since the day Sofia had told him she would not marry him anymore. It was all he could think about since then.

Sofia gasped loudly. "Edith, it is, isn't it?" She smiled broadly at him. "We can still get married today, Jude, and then you won't have to leave." She suddenly looked uncertain. "That is if you still want to marry me."

He touched her cheek. "Of course I still want to marry you. I want nothing more than to be your husband, Sofia." He glanced at the clock on the wall. "But the courthouse is probably closed by now."

"That's true," Edith said.

Sofia looked disappointed, but Jude's heart filled with hope. "We will get married tomorrow. I already got the marriage license in the mail. We can schedule a time to get married online." He could not help grinning. "Once we get married, Sofia, we will be together forever." He turned to Edith. "You will be our witness at our marriage, won't you?"

Edith nodded.

He sat on the couch and lowered Sofia onto his lap. He put his arms around her waist and she leaned back against him. Edith sat next to them and they talked about the arrangements they had to make and what they might have to buy before their court wedding tomorrow. Edith asked Sofia if she had something suitable to wear, and she told Edith that she did.

They continued to talk, but from time to time he tilted his head up to kiss Sofia. About half an hour into their conversation, Sofia leaned down to kiss him again, and then he could not stop kissing her until Edith snapped her fingers and cleared her throat.

"Focus, guys!" Edith said, as Sofia smiled and brushed her nose against his. "We need to make sure you have everything you need before we go to the courthouse tomorrow."

He focused on what Edith was saying, but held Sofia tighter, his heart threatening to burst with happiness.

About ten in the evening, Edith finally got up to leave. She stretched and yawned. "Okay, I am tired. I have to call it a night, but I will call you guys tomorrow morning."

Jude took Sofia's face in his hands and kissed her lips. He gave a long sigh and said, "I guess it's time for me to leave as well."

Sofia stood up from his lap, and he rose from the couch. Edith stared at him and Sofia with a surprised look on her face. "I thought you were going to stay here with her, Jude."

Jude turned to gaze at Sofia, his heart pounding with longing. "I would love to spend the night with you, Sofia, but I want to be respectful of you. I would like to wait until we get married tomorrow, and then we will be together forever." He smiled. "But if you want me to stay here with you, I will."

His pulse quickened as he gazed at her and, then

he looked around the tiny apartment. As far as he could see, there was no other room, which meant that she had no bedroom. He added, "I could sleep on the floor while you sleep on the couch." He remembered again what Edith had told him about her suicide attempt and he became worried once more. "You know what, maybe I should stay." He began to sit on the chair again, but Sofia shook her head.

"No, Jude. If you're worried about me, I will be fine. I told you that I had an encounter with God that changed my life."

He raised his brows and asked curiously, "What encounter?"

She shrugged. "I'll tell you all about it later, but just know that I will not try to hurt myself again. And you are right. It's better we spend the night separately... to avoid any temptation. Once we are married tomorrow, we will have the rest of our lives to spend together."

He took her hand again and looked into her eyes. "I can't wait for tomorrow when we are finally married, Sofia."

"Me too," she said, smiling brightly.

"You two are acting like lovesick teenagers who have been caught making out and have to be separated forever. You're going to see each other tomorrow." Edith waved her hand. "Come along, Jude, since you're not going to spend the night here. You will see Sofia again in a couple of hours."

"Tomorrow morning?" Jude asked, hopefully.

"No, in the afternoon," Edith said. "You both have to be in the courthouse and inside the doors before five p.m. If you are late, the doors will be shut and you will be shut out."

Sofia raised her eyebrows and gave Edith a knowing smile.

Edith grinned. "Don't ask me how I know all this. I've been waiting for Flynn to propose for years now. That boy is completely clueless about my desire to settle down." She sighed, opened the front door, and walked out.

Jude kissed Sofia again and reluctantly let go of her hand. "Tomorrow, Sofia. We will be married tomorrow," he said.

She squealed. "I'm so happy, Jude. And thank you for forgiving me and taking me back."

"No, I should be the one thanking you." Once again, he gazed longingly at her and then he moved to the door. "I should leave now or I never will." He opened the door and walked out. Edith had already gone down the stairs, probably waiting for him by her car. For a short moment, he leaned his back against Sofia's door. Waves of happiness went through him, and then he mellowed a little when he thought about Ben. Since he had missed his flight, he would have to refund Ben the full amount for the plane ticket if it was a non-refundable ticket. For now, he had very little money.

He sighed. He would have to deal with that problem when the time came. He smiled, his heart filling with joy again. For now, he had a wedding to prepare for.

He turned and stared at Sofia's door again and then shook his head. *Tomorrow, Jude. Wait until tomorrow.* He hurried down the stairs before he would change his mind and go back into her apartment.

TWENTY-ONE

Sofia yawned, stretched, and stood up from the couch. She had a crick in her neck, but she smiled widely as excitement and anticipation ran through her. Today, she would be marrying the man she loved. She felt like standing and dancing for joy. She glanced at the small clock on the wall. It was still only six a.m. She had not slept much at night, tossing and turning with excitement.

She glanced at her phone on the table and immediately felt an overwhelming desire to read her Bible again. She picked up her phone and immediately went to the Bible app. She felt ecstatic. Today was the happiest day of her life because she had received Jesus into her heart and now she was going to marry Jude.

She was unable to stop smiling as she continued reading her Bible from where she had stopped the day before. She read one chapter and then another. She told herself to stop so she could go and lay out the outfit she would wear to her wedding, but still she read another chapter. She had read four chapters before she finally closed the app. Her suitcase was leaning on the far end of the room near the kitchenette. She dragged it to the middle of the small living room and opened it.

She began to search the suitcase for the outfit she wanted to wear for her wedding. She finally found it and laid it on the couch. It was an expensive white pantsuit with wide lapels and gold buttons. She had never worn it, but the day she'd bought it, she had tried it in the store and it fit her perfectly.

She searched through her suitcase again for the white and gold shoes that would go perfectly with it, and then something occurred to her and she groaned. She looked at the pantsuit again as she recalled clearly the day she had bought it. She'd been with George in Milan. She had seen it from afar through the display window of an upscale clothing store and she had immediately wanted it. George had told her she could have it, and they had entered the store. When she'd tried it on and it was the perfect fit, George had paid for it and she had been ecstatic. Now she just wanted to toss it into the trash.

She put it back in her suitcase and search through her clothes, trying to look for something else to wear that would be equally appropriate. She brought out a cream wrap dress she had worn only once and then remembered once again that George had bought it for her for her birthday. She groaned and tossed it on the floor.

She kept searching through her clothes for something to wear, but found nothing. She had way more clothes than she could wear, but all of them were either bought for her by George or with

George's money. She could not imagine wearing any of them for her marriage to Jude.

Ten minutes later, she looked at the heap of clothes now on the sofa and frowned in frustration. They were all expensive and sophisticated. George had expensive taste and he liked to buy her expensive things. She thought about how different he was from Jude. In spite of all his perceived sophistication, he could not hold a candle to Jude. She would rather live a thousand years in a hovel with Jude than spend another day in luxury with George.

She sighed again as she stared at all her clothes. *What am I going to wear for my wedding?*

Her eyes fell on a simple knee-length dress. It was white and inexpensive. It was one of the few items she owned that had not been bought with George's money. She'd had it as long as she could remember, and it was nowhere near new. She picked it up and inspected it. A few weeks ago, she would never have imagined wearing something like this to an occasion so important, but today, she knew it was exactly the right thing to wear. She had bought it with her own money. She would feel comfortable wearing it for her wedding. Most of all, Jude would love her in it. Unlike George, who always liked her to be decked out in expensive clothing, Jude would not mind what she wore. He loved her for her and not just because of the way she looked.

Her heart flooded with joy again, and she stood up and danced around her small apartment. "Lord, thank you for Jude." A thought occurred to her — that Jude did not yet share the faith she now had, but she pressed the thought away. Until yesterday, she had avoided God; even resented him, but now she loved him with all her heart and it was because of her relationship with Lily; because Lily had not given up on her. Jude had told her he'd once shared the faith of his pastor dad. She would stick with him and love him until he came back to Christ. And she was certain it would not be long before he did.

She chose a simple pair of black shoes that she had also bought with her own money and then she looked around her apartment. Jude would move in here with her after their wedding. There was no bed here and just a single couch. They would have to sleep on the floor until they could buy a mattress at least. Rather than feel gloomy about that, she smiled gleefully, amused by the idea of them having to sleep on the floor because there was no bed.

She stooped down to look for earrings that would go with her outfit and then looked up when her phone rang. She grabbed it from the coffee table and looked at it. "Lily!" she smiled, and immediately answered the call.

"Hey, Sofia," Lily said, sounding breathless.

"Lily, hi!" Sofia said, surprised that Lily had called as they had only spoken yesterday.

"I am in Tucson," Lily said. "Taylor and I arrived yesterday."

"What?" Sofia shook her head. "How come?"

"I told you we arrived not long ago in Fallow Creek. After our call yesterday, I was really worried about you, and I convinced Taylor to come with me to Tucson since we were in Arizona. Thank God he agreed to come with me immediately. We are at the apartment he bought for me. Text me your new address, so I can come see you."

"I can come and get you, Lily," Sofia said, still surprised that her friend was in Tucson, but extremely excited to see Lily after so long.

"No, I'll come to you," Lily said. "Just send the address to me."

Lily ended the call, and Sofia stared at her phone and then chuckled. She immediately sent Lily the address of her apartment via text and then quickly gathered her clothes and put them back in her suitcase. Lily was a neat freak and she was sure to complain if the apartment wasn't tidy. Sofia looked around the empty apartment and smiled in self-mockery. It wasn't like there was enough in this apartment for it to be cluttered. It was virtually empty and it didn't take much to make it neat again.

For a short while, she thought about what she and Jude would live on. Jude had a job, but since he was an illegal immigrant and didn't have a working permit yet, she would have to insist that he stopped working until she could help him get his Green card.

She looked down at the outfit she had chosen for the wedding, which she had placed carefully on the sofa, and she felt slightly uneasy. Lily was bound to find out about Jude and the unusual circumstances under which she had met him. What would Lily say? It was why she had not told Lily anything about Jude. She respected Lily's opinion, especially now that she had committed her life to Christ and they shared the same faith. Lily was further on this journey with God than she was. What if Lily said it was wrong for her to marry Jude?

"Oh, Lord, please help," Sofia whispered, growing worried. Yes, at first their decision to marry had only been a business arrangement, and an illegal one at that, but now, she truly loved him and he loved her. She could not imagine living without him. Their feelings for each other were real and strong, and their marriage would be very real. Surely, Lily would understand when she told her about it. Surely, the Lord did.

She pressed her concerns away and went to hang up her outfit on the curtain rail. A niggling doubt remained in her mind, tempering the overwhelming joy she'd had just minutes ago.

Half an hour later, a knock sounded at her door, and she hurried to open it. She smiled broadly at Lily and they fell into each other's arms. She pulled Lily into the apartment and grinned at her. "Well... you are glowing, Lily! Marriage looks good on you."

Lily's eyes bored into hers. "You know, for a girl who was in utter despair just yesterday, you look amazingly happy. I will say you're also glowing, Sofia. I was worried about you as I came here, but I see you are clearly feeling great."

"Yes, Lily, I feel great. Thank you so much for telling me about Jesus."

Lily took her hand. "You look radiant, Sofia. Is there something else you're not telling me?"

It was on the tip of her tongue to tell Lily about Jude, that she was getting married to a man she loved with all her heart, but she immediately felt nervous and pressed her lips together. She could not bear the thought that Lily might not support her decision to marry Jude. If Lily was against the decision she'd made, it would not change her mind in anyway, but it would definitely hurt. With all her heart, she wanted Lily to be on her side and be happy for her. Telling Lily that she was going to marry an illegal immigrant was not the image she wanted Lily to have of her marriage, or of Jude.

She changed the subject and asked Lily how her honeymoon was.

Lily looked around the apartment and faced Sofia again. "This place reminds me of the cheap apartment I was living in before Taylor came and dragged me out of that place." She waved her hand. "Anyway, my honeymoon was great. We had such a great time." She sat on the couch, and Sofia sat down next to her. "Taylor is so funny, Sofia. I did not know that about him when we got married. But he makes me laugh all the time."

Sofia smiled. Everyone who saw Lily from a mile off would see she was clearly in love. Did she look the same way? As though Lily could read her mind, she took Sofia's hand and said, "You look really different, Sofia. I know you just asked the Lord into your life, but there's something more, isn't there?"

Sofia sighed. "Well, I guess you'll find out eventually," she said. "I'm getting married, Lily. Today."

"What?" Lily's eyes grew as round as saucers. "And you are just telling me? Who are you getting married to?"

"His name is Jude..." She hesitated for a few seconds, and then it all poured out of her. She told Lily everything, starting from the day she was introduced to Jude to yesterday when he left her apartment after they had made a decision to get married today. When she finished, she looked down at the floor and then looked at Lily again, feeling uncertain. She said in a shaky voice, "I know he's an illegal immigrant and all, but I'm not doing anything illegal now. We truly love each other, and I would move to his country with him in a heartbeat if it weren't for the fact that they are in a war right now. Please, tell me it's okay to marry him."

"Well, I can't say I know much about any of this, but you seem to truly love this Jude and, from all you've said about him, I believe he loves you too. I think that your relationship is very real and your feelings for each other are too. I can also understand why you two are getting married as soon as possible. I do not know what the government will think, but I have no problems with your relationship."

"So, you are not angry or disappointed in me?" Sofia asked, looking at Lily.

"No! I am ecstatic for you, Sofia. First, I'm happy you have left George and found someone you truly love and who truly loves you. I can see how in love you are because your eyes are sparkling. They didn't sparkle when you were with George."

Sofia giggled. "So, will you be my maid of honor?"

"Of course I will!" Lily looked around the room and said, smiling, "Or do you have another best friend hiding somewhere who is also in the running for that position? I am ready to fight that person for it."

Sofia laughed. "You are so silly, Lily!"

Lily chuckled and said, "I don't have anything to wear, though. All my clothes are in Fallow Creek. Maybe we can go shopping today."

"There is no time," Sofia said. "You're about my size, Lily. Don't worry about it. I'll find something for you to wear."

Lily's eyes lit up with excitement. She took Sofia's hand and pulled her up from the sofa. Putting her arm around Sofia's shoulders, she said, "Then what are we waiting for? Let's go try on dresses for your wedding." Lily pulled Sofia out of the living room into the bathroom. She looked confused as she glanced around. "Where is the rest of this apartment?"

Sofia laughed. "Where do you think it is? This is it."

Lily's eyes widened in clear surprise, and then she laughed out loud. "Wow! This place is really small. And you said Jude will be moving in here with you?"

"Yes," Sofia answered. "Once we get married."

Lily looked up thoughtfully and then a wide smile broke out on her face. "I have an idea, Sofia. Why don't you and Jude move into our penthouse apartment until you get a better place than this? You know the apartment is fully furnished, and it's not like Taylor and I are using it. It's just sitting there. We probably won't be in Arizona for more than two weeks in a year, if that, so we don't really need it."

Sofia stared at Lily, shocked. The penthouse apartment Lily was talking about was in Sofia's old apartment building. Her own apartment had been expensive enough. The two penthouses in the building were the most expensive.

Lily laughed. "Say something, Sofia. Will you accept my offer?"

"Lily, that apartment is really expensive! Are you sure?"

"Of course I am," Lily said. "You are my very

dear friend, and this is something I can do to show you how much I love you."

Sofia squealed and then reached out and hugged Lily tightly. "Thank you so much. You don't know what this means to me. Jude will be really happy, I am sure."

Lily smiled and then winked at her. "It's the least I can do considering you saved my life."

Sofia nodded and grinned. "I did, didn't I?"

"Yes..." Lily chuckled. "But remember you also nearly took it first."

Sofia laughed again. "But think about it. If I had not run you over that day, you would not have met Taylor in Tucson, and you wouldn't be married today. So I actually saved your life twice."

"You are crazy, Sofia," Lily said shaking her head and laughing.

Sofia felt like weeping for joy. She thanked Lily again and then took her hand and pulled her out of the bathroom. She pointed at her living room and said, "This, my dear friend, is both the living room and the bedroom. You can see that my suitcase is right over there."

Lily shook her head. "And where are the rest of your clothes... because I know that suitcase there cannot hold half of it. You would need a shipping container to hold all your clothes."

Sofia grinned. "Well thank you for telling me that I have way too many clothes. I left some of them at a friend's house."

"Okay then," Lily said. "Find me something to wear for your wedding."

They walked over to the suitcase, and Sofia opened it up. She rifled through, throwing out one outfit after another and shaking her head. "No, George bought this for me,"

she said when Lily pointed at a black and white dress. "I can't let you wear it."

Sofia held out another green knee-length dress and then immediately withdrew her hand. "No, you cannot wear this. It's not good enough." She brought out a Lilac jump suit and said, "I bought this in Paris, but George paid for it. You can't wear it."

When she held out a beautiful shift dress that Lily knew would look good on her, Lily asked, "What about this one?"

Sofia looked at it for a few seconds and then shook her head. "It was bought by George... for some special occasion he wanted us to attend." She straightened and sighed. "Most of the clothes I have were bought by George," she said, giving Lily an apologetic smile. "I really have to get rid of them. I don't see myself wearing them now that I am going to marry Jude."

"I understand," Lily said. "I agree you should get rid of them if you don't feel comfortable because George bought them for you." Lily smiled. "We should go shopping."

"I don't have any money, though," Sofia said.

"You don't need money, silly," Lily chuckled. "I have money. Let's go." She took Sofia's hand to pull her out of the apartment.

Sofia laughed. "Wait, let me put on something decent at least." She shook her head and grinned at Lily. "Marriage has made you impatient, my friend." She pulled on a white T-shirt and blue jeans and then left the apartment with Lily.

At the first store they stopped at, Lily did not find anything appropriate to wear. They found a lovely turquoise short-sleeved dress at the second store, and Lily promptly bought it. She held up a blue fitted dress to Sofia and said, "This will look great on you, and it's the kind of thing you like to wear. Why don't you try it on?"

"No," Sofia refused. "I shouldn't." But she could not take her eyes off the dress. Lily was right. It was exactly the type of dress she liked and would have bought if she had any money.

"Try it on," Lily insisted.

Sofia did, and it was a perfect fit.

"We have to buy it," Lily said and went to pay for it before Sofia could protest again.

They left the store and went back to Sofia's apartment, tired but happy. Sofia glanced at her wristwatch. "My wedding is in just a few hours," she said, smiling, her heart filled with joy.

"In a couple of hours, you will also be a married woman like me." Lily beamed at Sofia. "Maybe we can get pregnant at the same time."

Sofia laughed. "At this time, Jude and I are not thinking about that." But as she thought about what Lily had said, she grew increasingly excited. Maybe Jude would agree to start a family sooner rather than later. Because now that she thought about it, there was nothing she wanted more than to have a child with Jude; a baby that would be a part of her and him.

"Lord, please speed up the time," she said giddily, looking at her watch again.

Lily giggled.

Sofia sighed happily. Everything seemed to be

coming into place for her and Jude. First, God had restored their relationship, and now, they were getting married. Lily had given them a place to stay, and Jude would get his Green card soon. They had a bright future together as a couple, she was certain of that.

TWENTY-TWO

Jude whistled happily as he looked at himself in the mirror to fix his tie. He could not help smiling widely as he thought about Sofia and the fact that he was getting married to her today.

"You have not stopped smiling since you came back from Sofia's apartment yesterday," Samuel said to him.

"My lips are hurting from smiling so much," Jude said, his smile widening. He pointed at his suit jacket on the bed and asked Samuel to hand it to him. He shrugged it on when Samuel did and buttoned up the suit.

"You look great, man." Samuel grinned at him. "I wish I could come with you, but I have classes in an hour."

"I know. No worries, bro. Sofia and I decided we want our marriage to be intimate," he said. "Edith will be there of course, and Sofia called to say an old friend of hers would also be there. I wish you could be there too. However, I think we will have a small reception in the future and invite our friends."

Samuel pounded his back affectionately. "So by the end of today, you will be a married man. I am happy for you. Just yesterday you were miserable because you had to leave the United States and be far away from Sofia. Today, you're going to marry to her."

"I love her so much," Jude said. "I can't wait to make her my wife."

Samuel smiled. "Well, since I can't be there, kiss your wife for me."

Jude laughed. "Well, I will definitely be kissing my wife today, but it will not be for you, Samuel."

Samuel laughed and shrugged. "You're a lucky man," he said. "Sofia is gorgeous, and I know she loves you in spite of the problems you both have had the last few days."

"I know," Jude said.

"So, will you be moving into her house immediately after you get married, or will you wait until you both get somewhere bigger?"

"I have waited enough," Jude said, grinning. "I'll be moving in with her as soon as we are married."

Samuel smiled broadly.

Jude glanced at his wristwatch. "It's time for me to go." He put his hand on Samuel's shoulder. "I'll miss living with you, bro," he said. "I'll come get my things tomorrow." He left the room after picking up his marriage license from the bedside table and walked to the living room, Samuel behind him. His heart raced with excitement as he opened the door to go out.

Samuel said, "Jude, what about Shaffar's threat? Please be careful." Samuel grinned again. "I definitely don't want to visit you in prison."

Jude laughed. "I'll be careful, Samuel. I promise. Thankfully, after today he won't be able to do much."

"Hopefully, Sofia will file for your residence visa as soon as possible."

Jude shrugged. "Even if she decides never to do that for me, I would still marry her. Again and again."

Samuel raised his eyebrows and laughed. "Oh… so romantic," he said, giving Jude a teasing smile. "But then that will mean you will be deported and not be able to be with her."

"That's true," Jude said. He shook his head. "Why are we even talking about all this? Today is my wedding day. I am not about to start thinking about Green cards and deportation." Joy flooded him again as he pictured Sofia in his mind. He said to Samuel, "I have to get going." He opened the door, waved to Samuel, and walked out of the apartment.

He made his way down the stairs, jangling Samuel's car keys as he went. He was grateful that Samuel had agreed to lend him his car again. Sofia had asked him to stop working until he got a work permit. Right now he had no permission to work in the U.S., and he'd been working illegally. Hopefully, once he was able to start working again after he got his Green card, he would be able to save enough to buy a car and then a better home for himself and Sofia.

He felt as light as a feather as he hurried to Samuel's car. But just as he opened the door, a truck veered toward him and stopped right in front of Samuel's car. He watched in alarm as two men in black suits got down from the vehicle and walked toward him. His eyes widened as he stared at them, and a thread of fear ran through him when he noticed the guns partly concealed by their jackets. They stopped right in front of him and one of them said, "You have to come with us."

"Who are you?" he asked. But he had a niggling feeling that this was Shaffar's doing. They were probably from the government, here to deport him.

"Come with us quietly," they ordered again, and then one of them went around him and pressed his gun to Jude's back.

"Now," said he said.

Jude's heart thudded as fear ran through him, but he took a deep breath, pressed down his fear, and said, "I am not going with you. Today is my wedding day. That is very important to me." He groaned after he'd spoken. If they shot him right now, that would be the end. There would be no wedding. Why had he said what he did?

The one with the gun to his back cocked his gun. "You will come with us now, or you will be shot right here. Your choice."

Jude looked around him. There were no other people nearby, but a few pedestrians walked some distance away. He wasn't sure these men were from the government anymore. Maybe they were men from Shaffar's illegal agency. If he tried to make a run for it, they might not only shoot him but other people around might be in the line of fire and he did not want to put anyone in danger. He followed the men to their truck and got in.

As they drove away, he thought about nothing else but Sofia and how she would feel when he did not appear at the courthouse today. Once again, he found himself praying. He prayed that she would not think he had developed cold feet and run off.

He became more and more distressed as the vehicle sped down the road. He vowed to God that he would come back to Him if God got him out of this and reunited him with Sofia. He knew he was a prodigal son who had left his father's house and he had no right whatsoever to God's protection or help, but he continued to pray, asking for deliverance, not just for himself, but because of Sofia; because he could not bear the thought of her being miserable and believing he had willfully left her on their wedding day. He knew how that felt. All he wanted was to see her again and, because of that, he desperately wanted to live. But he didn't know who these people were, but whoever they were, without God's intervention, he would probably never see Sofia again.

They continue to drive on, and though he was sandwiched between two of the men, he looked out the window. They were now driving on a long dirt road with no one anywhere around; no cars or houses. They continued to drive and then, from a distance, he saw a small plane waiting on a narrow strip.

Curiously, he focused on the plane, wondering what was going on. Who was on that plane? Was it the plane he would be deported on? Why a private plane? They stopped a few feet away from the plane, and the men got out. They ordered him out of the car.

He got out, and two of the men came and stood beside him. One of them pointed at the plane. "Move," he ordered. Jude sighed and walked toward the plane.

And then his eyes widened in shock as Felix descended down the stairs. Felix reached him, and Jude shook his head. "You! You sent these men to kidnap me, Felix. Why?"

Felix glared at him. "Someone is waiting to speak with you on the plane, Jude."

"Who?" Jude stared at the guy he had thought was his friend.

"You'll see," Felix answered, and nodded at the men. They took hold of Jude's arms and pulled him toward the plane. He glowered at them and then at Felix. "I can walk by myself," he said.

Felix nodded at the men again, and they let him go of him.

Jude huffed and walked toward the plane and climbed up the steps, his heart knocking. Felix followed behind. He entered the plane and saw a woman standing in the middle of the aisle, her back to him. But he immediately recognized her. *Keziah!*

She turned and looked at him. "Jude, you're here," she said. She walked up to him with her arms open wide as though this was simply a cordial visit between friends rather than a staged kidnap. He stood rigidly as she hugged him. When she pulled back, he narrowed his eyes and said, "What is all this about? Why was I brought here by force?"

Felix patted his shoulder, and Keziah said, "We're sorry we had to send those guys." She pointed at the two men who had brought him here. "We knew if we did not bring you here by force, you would never agree to come willingly. Plus, we needed to show you just how serious our proposition was."

"So you had me kidnapped... on my wedding

day," he snapped. "Listen, I don't know what all this is about, but I need to get back. I am getting married to the woman I love today, and nothing in this world or out of it will stop me from doing so."

Keziah frowned, and Felix took hold of his hands. "What we have to discuss with you, Jude, is way more important than this marriage of yours. We brought you here because we've been recruiting several of our countrymen who are scattered in different parts of this world. Not all, but the educated ones who clearly have leadership qualities. People who have what it takes to help us win the war for our beloved country and be part of the leadership that will take Bakali to great heights in the future."

Jude stared at him in confusion. "What on earth are you talking about, Felix?"

"Our party, Jude. The opposition. We belong to an organization within our party comprised of patriots like me and Keziah. People who want to wrest power from the present government and restore our country's glory. We brought you here to help us fight our cause."

"What cause?" Jude asked in annoyance, staring at Felix and then at Keziah.

Felix sighed, a look of exasperation on his face. "Have you not been listening to everything I just said? We are part of an organization that fights the leadership of our great country. We want to remove the corruption and evil that has been taking place in our country and put in their place men who want better for her. People like you, Jude. We need you back there now to help us."

Jude stared at them, wondering if they were both

out of their minds. "Whatever you are up to, I want no part of it."

Keziah said, "We will get married, Jude, and together we will do great things for our country."

Jude blinked. "Are you both mad? So, you're part of the people who brought war to our country. All the killing and madness that has been going on there is because people like you want to take control of the country. It's all about power, isn't it?"

Keziah shook her head slowly. "It's not just about power, Jude. We want to sanitize the country, and if there is a little bloodshed in order to do that, then so be it."

"Can you hear yourself?" Jude stared at Keziah. He could not imagine that he'd loved this woman who could speak so callously about power and bloodshed. He laughed harshly. "A little bloodshed. Is that what you call the full-blown war going on in Bakali? You call all the violence and killings 'a little bloodshed?'"

Felix shrugged, while Keziah stared at him as though he were a recalcitrant child.

Jude shook his head slowly. "This is all madness. I have no interest in whatever organization you both belong to or in helping out your mad cause in any way. In fact, I am completely against it. The war in our country is because people are fighting for power and, the innocent suffer because of that. I cannot have any part in it. Your men will take me back to where they found me so I can go to my wedding."

Keziah took Jude's hands and said, "Forget about that woman you are about to marry. We have known each other since we were teenagers. We will get married as soon as we get to Bakali, and then…"

"Stop it!" Jude snatched his hands from hers. "Never! I don't love you anymore, Keziah. I love Sofia. And after all you've both told me, I want absolutely nothing to do with either of you." He started to walk out of the plane, but the two armed men came and blocked his path. He tried to force his way past them, but they grabbed him and pushed him back.

"Let me go!"

"Jude." Keziah placed her hand on his arm. "Think about this. Why would you stay in a country that is not your own instead of coming to be part of the leadership of your home?"

"I have no interest in leading anything," Jude told her angrily. "All I want is to marry the love of my life. Now, please let me go."

"We cannot do that," Felix said.

Jude struggled to get out of the plane, but the men in black suits held him back again. "Please, let me go," he said desperately. He turned to Keziah. "You told me you were sorry for breaking our engagement that day I visited you. So you know how it feels. I cannot do that to Sofia. If you ever loved me, please let me go."

She sighed, looking weary. She looked at Felix. "He's not going to cooperate until we show him the video."

Jude frowned. "What video?"

Felix looked at Keziah and then at Jude. He shook his head and said, "We hoped you would not have to see this, at least not now. But we have no choice." He nodded at one of the men in suits. "Bring the laptop."

The man went to the back of the plane and appeared a second later with a laptop. Felix turned it on and the screen came to life. His fingers moved quickly on the keyboard, and then he said to Jude, "Look at this.

Jude stared at the screen. A man sat on a chair, tied up. He groaned in pain and there were bruises all over his body. Another man dressed in black stood beside him, a gun pointed at him. Jude blinked as he moved closer to the laptop, his eyes fixed on the man in the chair. And then his mouth dropped open and he gagged in horror.

"My father!" He looked up at Felix and Keziah in revulsion. "Why are you showing me this? Why do you want to show me how he died?"

Felix shook his head. "No, Jude. He's not dead, but he will be soon, unless you agree to come with us and do as we say."

"What kind of sick joke is this?" Jude asked.

Keziah looked at him. "It is not a joke

Jude felt like someone had punched him hard. "Why would you lie just to get me to do what you want me to? You know my father is dead."

Keziah pointed at the video. "Look at this, Jude. What date and time is this?"

Jude squinted as he read the date and time on the screen. It said July eighth, six fourteen p.m.

Keziah showed him her watch. "You know what today's date is, don't you? And this is the time. It matches exactly."

His heart pounded, and he stepped back in fear. "No! It cannot be! You did something to this. I don't believe it."

"It's true," Felix said.

"No, it is not." Jude shook his head.

"It is," Felix insisted. "But even if it wasn't, are you going to trade your father's life and take that risk?"

Jude screamed. "You are both liars!"

Felix shrugged and said, "Fine, you can choose not to believe and go back to your Sofia. We will let you. But what if this is true and your father's life is in danger? Will you let him die or will you come and fight with us? Your father's life is on the line."

"Why would you do this to me, Felix? And you, Keziah. Why was I told he was dead when he wasn't?" Jude felt like someone had snatched his heart out of his chest. "He has been your prisoner all this while?"

"Not exactly our prisoner... but the party's. When we decided we could use his imprisonment as a bargaining chip, he was given to us."

Jude felt sick. How was it possible that he had once been close to people capable of such cruelty? And how could his father be alive all this time and he had no idea? He didn't want to look at the video again, but he did. Still, he refused to believe his father was alive. It was too hard to stomach. His father could not have been alive all these years when he thought he was dead. Was he being tortured all this while? It could not be true, and yet the video was right here, and the time on the screen was exactly the same time as now. Maybe it was doctored, but what if it wasn't?

"Why would you hold him prisoner for so long?"

"Your father betrayed our country and was working with the leadership," Felix said. "He's only alive because you are my friend, Jude."

Jude glowered at him. "I am not your friend! I could never be your friend after all this!"

Felix shrugged. "Fine. Are you going to help us or not?"

Jude groaned as he thought about Sofia. He said, "But I cannot help you in any way. I am not a politician or a fighter."

"You are all that and more, and you don't even know it," Keziah said. "I've known you for a long time, Jude. You are one of the people we need for the future of our country."

Jude said angrily, "And is this how you go about intimidating people to join your cause? Kidnapping and killing and ruining people's lives?"

"We do what we must," Felix said. "Make your decision, Jude. Your father's life is on the line. That Sofia woman will be fine if you don't marry her, but your father on the other hand..."

Jude shut out Felix's words. No, Sofia would not be fine. She had tried to kill herself twice because she broke up with her ex. She might try again, and this time she might succeed.

He looked at the video again and nearly threw up. If his father was truly still alive... tears formed in his eyes. It meant someone was holding a gun to his father's head right now and only he had the power to free his dad.

He groaned. When he prayed for God to deliver him on their way here, this was not what he'd had in mind. This was much more dangerous and confusing than he'd ever thought it would be. He had thought his own life was in danger, but this was even worse.

God, help me.

"Jude, you have just fifteen minutes to make a decision," Felix said. "We have to leave this country right now. Are you going to save your father's life, or should I give the order to end it?"

Jude groaned. He could call their bluff, and maybe, just maybe, they were lying about his father. But if it was true and he had the power to save his dad, his father's blood would be on his hands if he didn't.

But what if Sofia harms herself?

"Twelve minutes, Jude," Felix said. "You have twelve minutes to make your decision."

TWENTY-THREE

Sofia paced the hallway of the courthouse, her heart drumming with worry. Around her were happy brides-to-be holding hands with their future grooms, waiting to be married, but her own groom was nowhere to be found. She turned to Lily, who paced the hallway with her and asked, "Where is he, Lily? Where is my Jude?"

Lily took hold of her hand and squeezed it encouragingly. "I'm sure he'll be here any minute. Stop worrying so much."

Sofia sighed and placed her hand on her forehead. "Everyone is supposed to be here way before five o'clock, Lily. It's not like him to be this late. The doors will be shut soon. And once they are, we will not be able to get married today. He has to be here." She looked at Edith, who was sitting on a chair in the corner of the hallway and asked, "Has he called you?"

"No," Edith answered.

Sofia tried Jude's number once more, but his phone was still off. She raked her fingers through her hair, wanting to yank it all out from its roots in frustration. She shook her head and turned to Lily again. "What has happened to him, Lily?" She bit her lip. "Where on Earth is he?" She felt like breaking down and sobbing, but that would definitely not help.

"You are going to wear yourself out with worrying. It's not five o'clock yet, Sofia," Lily said, wrapping her arm around Sofia's waist. "Please calm down. I am sure nothing has happened. He will be here any moment now."

Sofia looked at her, annoyed. "How do you know that? And it is nearly five o'clock." She threw her hands up, emotionally weary. Even though she had only known him for a short time, this was not like Jude. If for some reason he was held up, he would have at least tried to contact her to let her know.

"Maybe he changed his mind and decided to go back to his ex," she said, fear gripping her at the thought that he might be with his ex-fiancée now. Another more fearful thought replaced that: *Or maybe he is lying dead somewhere.* She couldn't hold back her emotions or the fear that ran through her. Tears filled her eyes and ran down her cheeks. Lily and Edith thought she was overreacting, but she could feel it. Something was wrong.

Lily held her close and tried to comfort her. "Stop crying, Sofia." She wiped her tears away. "You will ruin your makeup." Lily smiled teasingly, clearly trying to ease her fears and sadness.

Sofia looked at Edith once more. "Please try his number again."

Edith stood up and went to her. "I just tried to call him. His phone is still not ringing." She put her hand on Sofia's shoulder. "I don't know why he isn't here or where he is, but I know that Jude loves you. He would never stand you up or jilt you."

Sofia's heart ached as though someone was squeezing it tightly. Edith's words were not helping much. "Then that means something bad has definitely happened to him," she said. "Edith, what could have happened to Jude? He would be here if…"

"Stop it!" Edith cut in. "Stop saying all these things. Nothing bad has happened to him. There has to be an explanation for his lateness. He will be here."

"When?" Sofia lamented. "When will he be here?" She walked toward the entrance of the courthouse. "I have to go and talk to his friend, Samuel. I can't just stay here doing nothing. Maybe Samuel knows where he is."

Edith shook her head. "No, Sofia. Don't go. It's your day. You shouldn't be running around the city. Besides, you might get locked out if you go. Let me go and talk to Samuel. I have his address."

Sofia pressed her lips together tightly and then sighed. "Fine. Go quickly, Edith. Hopefully, Samuel will be at his apartment."

Edith left, and Sofia sighed again. She resumed pacing the hallway.

Lily followed and rubbed her back soothingly. "Sofia, Edith has gone to find him. I'm sure she'll have more information for us when she gets back. Why don't you sit down over there and tell me about Jude? It might put your mind at ease and help you forget he isn't here yet."

"How is talking about him going to help me

forget?" Sofia asked. But she said, "I love him with all my heart, and he loves me, too. He had an opportunity to go back to his ex just days after we started dating, but he came back to me because he's that kind of guy. He honors his commitments." She bit her lips, worry flooding her again. "That is why it is really strange that he is not here."

She paused for a short moment and then went on. "He said that, above all else, he came back to me because he had begun to fall in love with me and knew he wanted to marry me. When I was with George, I couldn't stop thinking about him. I knew by letting him go, I had made the worst mistake of my life." She began to cry again. "He's my everything, Lily. What will I do if I lose him?"

Lily rubbed her back. "He's not your everything, Sofia. You have the Lord now." Lily looked up with a thoughtful expression on her face. "I'm sure there's an explanation for all this."

Sofia's heart began to pound even faster as a security officer starting shutting the doors of the courthouse. Sofia pleaded with him to leave the doors open for just a few minutes more, but he refused.

"We have to leave the courthouse now," Lily said.

Sofia sighed sadly and walked out the doors with Lily. She winced as they shut firmly behind her. There was no way she and Jude were getting married today. She followed Lily to the car Lily had rented specifically for the wedding. They both stood, leaning their backs against the car doors, and Sofia looked up as a feeling of helplessness settled over her. She covered her face with her hands and said, "It's all ruined, Lily. I'm not getting married to

Jude today. Maybe I'll never get to marry him."

"Stop saying that! You will get married to him, Sofia. Everything will turn out alright in the end. You'll see."

"If I haven't already pushed him away," Sofia said. "Maybe I did something really wrong without knowing it. Or maybe he developed cold feet and could not bring himself to tell me."

"I don't know this Jude, but from all you've told me about him, I don't think he would do that to you."

"Then why isn't he here?" Sofia wrung her hands. "Where could he possibly be, Lily? I don't understand."

Lily pulled her close again and Sofia wrapped her arms around her, trying hard to believe there was a good explanation for Jude's absence. "Lord, please let him be okay," she whispered.

About twenty minutes later, Edith returned and shook her head. "I saw Samuel leaving the house just as I was approaching. He was surprised when I told him Jude had not come to the courthouse. He said Jude had dressed up for the wedding and was very excited when he left the apartment.

Sofia felt sick with worry and dread. So something bad had definitely happened to Jude. Tears formed in her eyes again. "I told you two," she said. "It's not like him not to call if he's held up somewhere. Something has happened to my Jude."

Lily brushed back her hair. "You don't know that, Sofia."

"What other explanation is there?" Sofia pulled away from Lily. "I have to go look for him. He could be anywhere. Anything could have happened to him. Maybe ICE found him and had him arrested." Various thoughts raced through her mind, all of them distressing. "Oh my Lord, please help me. Please protect Jude, wherever he is." Without thinking she marched away from Edith and Lily. She had to look for Jude. She could not just stand around waiting for him to appear when it was clear he was in some sort of trouble.

"Where are you going?" Lily called out.

"I'm not sure… but I think I will go to Samuel's first and see if anyone else saw him leaving the apartment. And then I will go to the university campus and ask around. Someone has to have seen him." She began to walk away again.

"Sofia!" Lily called. "Wait!" She ran up to Sofia and held her hand. "Wait, Sofia. Aren't you forgetting something?"

Sofia turned around. "What?"

"The car. It will get us to Samuel's faster."

Sofia sighed loudly and walked back to the car with Edith and Lily. She got into the back seat with Lily, while Edith took the wheel. Edith drove fast, weaving through traffic, and Sofia alternated between gritting her teeth impatiently, and praying they would get to Samuel's apartment quickly. She also prayed that, through a miracle from God, Jude would be there with an explanation for why he had missed their wedding.

***

Jude felt like sobbing. Without a doubt he had missed his wedding. Sofia would be distraught. *What am I going to do?*

"Jude, have you made your decision?" Felix asked with an impatient look. "Whatever you want to do, you have to do it now." Felix brought the laptop closer to Jude. "Should I make the call to end your father's life, or will you come with us?"

Jude groaned.

"Five minutes more," Felix said, looking at his wristwatch.

Jude placed his hands on his head, his emotions in tatters.

Felix began a countdown that shredded Jude's nerves. He could not breathe. He felt as though any minute now he would pass out. Felix refused to take the laptop away, forcing Jude to look at it. He agonized over every second that passed. He had to make a decision, but what could that possibly be? Any decision he made would end in unimaginable heartbreak.

He watched his father on the computer screen, feeling an excruciating amount of pain in his heart that he had never thought was possible. He could not look away as Felix's men held him in place. Neither could he stop thinking about Sofia.

"Three minutes," Felix said coldly.

Jude almost screamed. He shut his eyes, trying to calm down and make a rational decision, but he could not think rationally. His mind seemed to be made only of dread. He sighed. He had thought his dad was dead for some time now. If he went to Sofia and his dad was shot, it might still be the same for him. But if he went back to Bakali and left Sofia without her knowing what had happened to him, who knew what she would do? And he would certainly never see her again. The thought was unbearable.

But so was the thought that he would let his father be killed.

"One minute more," Felix said, looking at his wristwatch again.

"Oh, Sofia!" Jude lamented. He shut his eyes for a brief moment and then winced in pain and opened them again when Felix's man slapped him hard. He had mourned his father, believing him dead. But now he had a chance to see his dad again after so long. He had a chance to save his father's life. How could he allow anyone to take that away? Sofia was alive and well. She had Edith and her other friends. She would not be alone.

But if he left without a word, she would be heartbroken. So would he. Would she ever forgive him?

You have twenty seconds," Felix said. He paused, his eyes fixed on his watch, and then began to count. "Ten, nine, eight..."

Jude squeezed his eyes shut and held his head in his hands, praying that Felix would stop counting, but he did not stop.

"Two...one..." Felix frowned and then took his phone out of his pocket and dialed a number.

Jude watched in horror as the gunman in the video answered his phone as Felix said, "Hello, Saul..."

He shuddered. It was real. There was no doubt about it now.

"Kill him," Felix said.

The man pointed the gun to his father's head.

"Stop!" Jude screamed. "I'll go with you! Please don't kill him!"

"Stand down!" Felix said on the phone. The gunman moved away from Jude's father, and Felix closed the laptop and smiled at Jude. "You've made the right decision." He called out to the pilot. "We are ready to go!"

Jude collapsed into one of the chairs. Waves of anger and anguish washed over him, and he shut his eyes and screamed. Everyone on the plane ignored him. The small plane taxied down the runway and an overwhelming despair settled over him. He felt a hand on his shoulder and looked up. Keziah was looking down at him.

"Cheer up, Jude! At least you'll get to see your father again."

He glowered at her. He knew he should rejoice. Some would say the silver lining in all this was that his dad was alive. But he couldn't stop thinking about how hurt and devastated Sofia would be. He felt terrified that she would hurt herself.

And yet, Keziah was right. The father he'd thought was dead was alive. He wasn't sure what Felix and his "organization" wanted him to do, but he would go along... until he could get his father released, and then he would fight to break free

He looked out the window as the plane soared higher and higher in the sky and once again thought about Sofia. He closed his eyes and prayed for her — that she would be safe and that she would forgive him for leaving so abruptly. A grim determination gradually entered his heart, and he vowed to himself that he would come back to America one day to find her, no matter what it took, even if it cost him his freedom... or his life.

***

Samuel was standing at the front door, making a call. He raised a finger as Sofia opened her mouth to ask if he had heard from Jude. Ending his phone call, he said, "I've been calling some of our friends. None of them has seen or heard from him." He placed his hands on his head, a look of despair on his face. "I saw him leave for the wedding, Sofia. I am trying to figure out where he could possibly be."

Edith said, "We will go to the police if he doesn't turn up in a few hours."

Sofia did not feel comfortable with that because of Jude's immigration status, but it was not like they had a choice. It was better that he was safely found, even if he had to leave the country, than for him to be left wounded somewhere. Her stomach hurt from thinking about the awful things that may have happened to him. The best scenario to her at this point was that he'd been apprehended by ICE and taken to be deported, which was bad. Very bad. She wrung her hands again and began to sob.

"Sofia, you need to calm down," Edith said. "Please."

But she could not calm down. She couldn't help thinking that she would never see him again.

"Sofia, Edith is right," Lily said. "You have to calm down. We will find him."

Sofia bit her lip and tried to gather herself together. But she could not stop the ache in her heart or the tears that welled up in her eyes. She ran her fingers through her hair, fear gripping her again. How could she be calm when everything in her screamed that Jude was in trouble? And she was certain of it. Nothing else would have kept him away from their wedding. She had considered briefly back at the courthouse that he'd gotten cold feet and left her, but that wasn't possible. He had proven to her again and again in the short time she'd known him that he loved her dearly. "Lord, I ask for a miracle," she prayed. "Please deliver him from whatever trouble he is in right now." The Lord had to, because she did not know if she could go on if Jude did not return safely to her.

She began to walk away from her friends again and called out to them, "I am going to the university campus to find out if anyone has seen him."

Lily, Edith, and Samuel hurried to her and fell into step. They reached the large university campus, and Sofia immediately began to ask everyone she saw if they had seen Jude. As she expected, many of them did not know who he was. She described his physical appearance as clearly and as best as she could, but no one she spoke to had seen him.

Samuel led them to the hostel where two of their friends stayed. One of them was not in his room or answering his phone, but the other one was there.

"I have not seen Jude for some time now," their friend said.

Sofia shut her eyes, panic taking hold of her again.

They all left the hostel minutes later and walked around the grounds trying to find anyone that might have seen Jude. It was a desperate attempt on their part. Sofia knew it was unlikely that they would find him in such a vast place. But they had very few options.

When they were all tired of searching and asking around for Jude, they left the campus "The only option left is to go to the police" Sofia said, sighing.

As they walked to Samuel's apartment, Sofia prayed silently again that God would keep Jude safe. For his sake as well as hers.

"Don't worry, Sofia. I am sure Jude is safe," Lily said, as though she'd read Sofia's mind and heard her exact prayer.

She gave Lily a sad smile. "Thanks," she said, trying to believe Lily's words were a sign from God that Jude was safe wherever he was.

A supernatural peace descended on her, and she heaved a sigh. She suddenly felt a deep certainty in her heart that Jude was safe and well and knew that the feeling was from God. Again she sighed, relieved. It did not stop the ache in her heart because, if he was alive and well, it meant he'd purposely decided he did not want to marry her anymore. But even though that thought felt excruciating, she could live with it as long as he was okay.

She wiped the tears from her eyes, but the pain in her heart remained. Whatever his reasons were for skipping their wedding, they had to be good, even though she could not possibly imagine what they were. Maybe she would see him one day and find out. Maybe not.

She winced as sorrow tore through her, and then she pressed the sadness away. Days ago, she would have gone over the edge, maybe even swallowed some pills as she had done when George broke up with her. But she had Jesus in her heart now. And with Him, she would weather any storm.

A LOOK AT:
FINDING DESTINY

INTRIGUE, ROMANCE AND THE LOVE OF GOD – AUTHOR OF THE SISTERS OF ROSEFIELD, EMMA EASTER, INTRODUCES A NEW SET OF FLAWED AND LOVEABLE CHARACTERS IN THE DESTINY SERIES.

After a horrific incident with her former husband Mike Cadwell, Davina Brooks is left a widow. She became free to pursue a relationship with her childhood sweetheart, the tall, brawny, and bearded town sheriff Daniel. Daniel, however, has a bit of a temper and struggles with intense jealousy, which makes Davina often question their relationship.

When Davina gets an offer to become an actress and move to Los Angeles she has to decide what is more important, her relationship with Daniel, or her new dream...

COMING AUGUST 2020

ABOUT THE AUTHOR

Like the characters in her stories, Emma Easter juggles a range of identities.

In the low-income community where she works, Easter is known as a family medicine physician who treats patients of all ages and backgrounds.

College friends see her as an accomplished musician, having studied and mastered five classical instruments—but behind closed doors, she's just as comfortable rocking an air guitar to Creed. And when she isn't giving her heart, soul, and sanity to her three young children she's indulging in her most secret identity of all: meeting new characters, crafting fresh plots, and exploring every corner of her imagination.

Across all these different roles, one cohesive thread has tied everything together: her faith and love of Jesus Christ.

Find more great titles by Emma Easter and Christian Kindle News at https://christiankindlenews.com/our-authors/emma-easter/